**"What I'm trying to say is that your daughter needs stability."**

Rachel continued. "She doesn't need someone like you coming into her life only to fall out of it because you've taken one risk too many or you want to be somewhere else."

Cole stared at Rachel for a moment without speaking. Then he leaned forward and asked, "Why are you so good for her when you've done the same thing–risking your life on some stunt?"

"That *stunt* saved the lives of a fire crew." A crew she'd been certain was Cole's.

"You know as well as I do how lucky you are to be alive." Cole leaned even closer. "Don't talk to me about stability, either. I can't imagine you make it home to cook dinner every night."

Dear Reader,

Have you ever had an unrequited high school crush? If so, you'll relate to Rachel Quinlan, who adored Cole Hudson in high school, even though he always treated her like a younger sister. Now that Cole is back in Eden, she has to learn to see him through the eyes of the woman she is today, not the starry-eyed gaze of a teenage girl.

Cole has a lot to learn himself. He's always been protective of others, and now he wants to enclose Rachel and her family in a bubble, despite the fact that doing so will keep all of them from achieving their dreams.

I love to hear from readers, either through my Web site–www.melindacurtis.com–or regular mail at P.O. Box 150, Denair, CA, 95316. To the many who've written about Victoria, yes, her story is coming!

Warm regards,

*Melinda Curtis*

# Back to Eden

*Melinda Curtis*

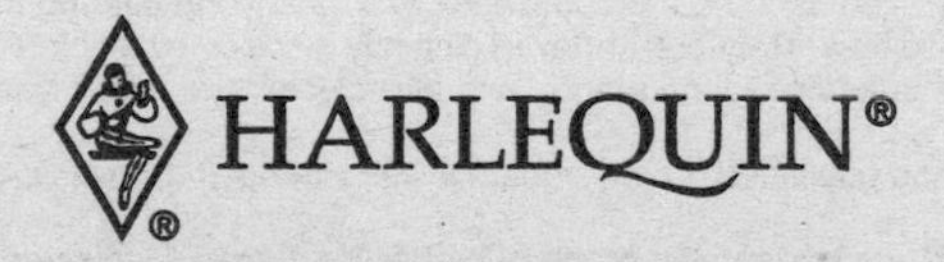


TORONTO • NEW YORK • LONDON
AMSTERDAM • PARIS • SYDNEY • HAMBURG
STOCKHOLM • ATHENS • TOKYO • MILAN • MADRID
PRAGUE • WARSAW • BUDAPEST • AUCKLAND

ISBN 0-373-71340-1

BACK TO EDEN



This edition published by arrangement with Harlequin Books S.A.



www.eHarlequin.com

**Printed in U.S.A.**

**Books by Melinda Curtis**

**HARLEQUIN SUPERROMANCE**

1109–MICHAEL'S FATHER
1187–GETTING MARRIED AGAIN
1241–THE FAMILY MAN
1301–EXPECTANT FATHER

As always, with much love to my family, who continue to
think of pepperoni pizza as fulfilling all major food groups

Special thanks to Susan Floyd and Anna Stewart
for providing inspiration and reality checks
when I needed them most

# *PROLOGUE*

COLE HUDSON WAS NEVER going to love her.

Rachel Quinlan stared at Cole's parked truck. The engine wasn't even pinging or popping because it had long since cooled, and the sick sensation caused by unyielding truth settled in her gut.

Oh, Cole liked her well enough and had even taken her out to dinner and to the movies a time or two. If pressed, he might even say he loved her. But it would be clear that he didn't "love her" love her, not in the happily-ever-after kind of way.

With tear-filled eyes, Rachel stared up at the blue sky blossoming above Eden, Wyoming—a sky that cruelly promised a beautiful October day fit for a wedding—someone else's wedding.

It wasn't just that Cole was four years older than Rachel and treated her as if she still hadn't reached puberty. Heck, she'd filled out a bra three years ago, and Cole hadn't seemed to notice.

And it wasn't for lack of bodily contact. He gave Rachel a hug every time he saw her, sweeping her up and twirling her around, his deep laughter rumbling through to her soul.

Rachel sighed. Nope. The problem was Cole Hudson didn't love her like a man loved a woman. He could never love her that way.

Because he'd lost his heart to Rachel's older sister, Missy.

Not that this was a news flash. But in that moment, staring at Cole's truck on Missy's wedding day, the reality of it all smacked into Rachel harder than it ever had before. She was a silly, daydreaming girl, just like Missy always told her, wasting time staring at the sky and weaving fantasies that would never come true.

Missy didn't understand Rachel's dreams, which tended to involve leaving home. Missy was a big homebody. Heck, Missy protested if she had to leave Sweetwater County. She'd refused to fly anywhere since their mother had gone away, claiming to want only to provide a good home for Rachel and their father. And Missy had. Because of her, Rachel could dream. She'd earned her pilot's license, reveling in the joy of soaring through the sky. Rachel had even helped her father rebuild the engine on his C119 warplane.

It did seem disloyal to have such strong feelings for someone Missy had once so dearly loved, but Missy had let Cole go, which left the door open for Rachel, didn't it?

Rachel fidgeted. Only if Missy and Cole didn't still love each other, which didn't seem to be the case. The impossibility of having Cole love her threatened to overwhelm Rachel as she stared at his truck parked in front of room twenty-two of the Shady Lady Motel on the outskirts of Eden.

The question was: Who was in the motel room with Cole?

Rachel shivered, crossing her arms against her suspicions and the early-morning chill.

In less than four hours, Missy was supposed to be marrying Lyle Whitehall in front of God and everyone at the Chapel in the Valley on Main Street. Lyle was the son of Eden's shyster mayor, who was also the bank president and holder of the note on the small Quinlan ranch and airstrip. Brian Quinlan ran an air freight business, but he wasn't very good at making money, and Lyle and his daddy knew it.

Not that Missy didn't seem to care for Lyle, but Lyle's affection for Missy was…not what Rachel would call love. Rachel shivered again. This time for a different reason.

If Missy…*when* Missy married Lyle later today, their worries were supposed to be over. Rachel had no clue as to what would happen to them if Missy didn't marry Lyle at eleven o'clock, but she'd bet it wouldn't be very good.

Rachel had known there'd be trouble when Missy had slipped out of her bachelorette party last night, running down the sidewalk to Cole's waiting truck, blond hair flying behind her. Rachel had been the only one to see her leave. She'd lied to cover Missy's absence—by that time most of the women were too tipsy to notice the bride had flown the coop anyway—and driven home in Missy's truck, hoping old Sheriff Tucker wouldn't catch her driving without a license. After spending a sleepless night waiting for Missy to come home, Rachel had climbed into Missy's truck again, her heart heavy, and driven back into town at daybreak only to discover what she'd dreaded to find—Cole's truck parked at the motel. Now she wondered—was there going to be a wedding?

What in the world was Cole doing messing things up like this? Rachel's dreams, her home, all would be lost. Suddenly filled with an anger demanding an outlet, Rachel ran up to the door and pounded on it.

Before her knuckles hit the warped wood a second time, Cole opened the motel room door and stalked past Rachel without so much as a glance. Missy huddled in the mussed bed, a sheet pulled up to her shoulders and tears streaming down her pale face.

Missy, who had always been Rachel's rock as well as sister, mother, friend and confidante, and who always looked model perfect, looked as if she was thirty-nine, not nineteen.

Rachel forgot all about her own shattered dreams as she ran across the worn, stained carpet to comfort her sister.

# CHAPTER ONE

COLE HUDSON FINISHED sweeping the razor across his chin, rinsed the last of the shaving cream from his face and paused to stare into the sliver of a mirror someone had hung above the outdoor sinks at the Flathead, Montana, base camp.

"We made it through a day without the fire getting the better of us," Jackson, the supervisor of the wildland firefighters known as the Silver Bend Hot Shots, announced beside him. "I think that calls for a beer, don't you?"

"And a thick, juicy steak," Logan seconded, shoving his shaving kit into his pack, pausing to look at the plastic-encased picture of his family dangling from the strap.

Cole hesitated. It had been a tough few weeks in the Flathead Mountains of Montana. The beast had toyed with the crews on a daily basis and finally overrun them with near deadly consequences two days ago. Cole's best friend, Aiden, better known as Spider in Hot Shot circles, had nearly lost his dad in the flash fire. Spider now sat vigil at a hospital in Missoula waiting for his father's recovery.

"I heard they were serving steak tonight, too."

Jackson dried his hands with a towel, lingering over his wedding band.

"But not beer," Logan lamented. Alcohol wasn't allowed in fire camps. "Let's get into the chow line before they run out of beef. If I lose any more weight this season, Thea will kill me."

Cole knew exactly what Logan meant. After six months away from home, the entire crew was pretty lean. Thanks to the demanding physical labor and the fight against dehydration, they didn't carry much fat.

"Just another day or so," Cole murmured. They'd served their time, and the Forest Service would have to decide if they would stay on with a day of rest, or if they'd be sent home.

Now that they had air support, this fire just might be brought under control. Although some teams would continue working for another few weeks, others would begin winding down from the long season and go home in time to take their kids trick-or-treating and make plans for the holidays. This year, for the first time in a long time, Cole would be the only one of his friends to go home alone.

Jackson had reunited with his wife. Logan had found someone who'd brought light to his dark side. And now Spider had reconciled with his dad and was about to become a husband and father himself. Spider, who Cole had been certain would never grow up, was eager for his new role.

Poor, lucky sap.

Cole stared into the mirror, noting the wrinkles and the laugh lines emphasized by so many fire seasons under the hot summer sun. It wasn't that he didn't have a pretty decent life. With a job he loved and a group of friends he'd trust with his life, Cole had nothing to complain about. He even had someone at home, or at least someone in his heart. A woman he loved.

A woman he'd let go.

"You're the only one for me," Missy had whispered to him.

Eleven years ago he'd walked out of Missy Quinlan's life, hoping she'd follow. Today, after battling a monster of a fire, and about to face three to four months of life alone in a small apartment, something unsettling crept into his thoughts.

It was time.

He was finished waiting for Missy. He had to know if she was happy without him. If so, he'd move on, no regrets. As soon as they were released from the fire, Cole would drive to Eden and find out if he'd been a fool all these years or an incredibly wise man.

"LOOKING FORWARD to the end?" Danny asked as he and Rachel walked through base camp on their way to dinner. He moved with a limp and shoulders stooped with age, but he was still one of the best air tanker pilots around.

"Hey, we're heading into October and I'm in the black this year. Why would I want it to end?" Rachel joked, even as she wished herself home with her family. It was weird how she absolutely loved to fly and absolutely hated the guilt her job created.

Rachel operated Fire Angels air tanker service. She'd picked up several good contracts from the Forest Service in states to the east of Wyoming over the past few years, purposefully avoiding Idaho and Montana. But at the end of a long season, federal parks were still burning in many of the western states, so all the firefighting resources and personnel were shifting west instead of hunkering down in their homes for the winter.

Danny removed his baseball cap and gestured at the firefighters in front of them with a laugh. "Yeah, these losers are probably more than ready to head home, and we're itching to get in the air again."

"We've got the promise of tomorrow. That's more than we'll have next week." Although Rachel wanted the fire to be out and the season to be over, she couldn't help but appreciate any reason to take to the skies. Nothing could compare to the feeling Rachel got from flying.

"Look at these ground pounders," Danny said, casting his gaze over the men around them. "I'm almost three times the age of most of them, and they're dragging their asses like little schoolgirls."

One of the men in front of them shot Danny a deadly look, so Rachel decided to let the conversation drop. The last thing she wanted was a fight drawing attention to herself, just in case she knew someone here.

Trying to appear like the professional she was, Rachel glanced around, but it was impossible to pick out anyone she knew beneath the yellow helmets and layers of grime. A few of the men looked her up and down, then flashed an interested grin Rachel ignored. With a body built for sin—or so Missy used to tell Rachel—and eyes that even Rachel had to admit slanted more provocatively than Missy's, it was often hard for Rachel to blend in. And she desperately wanted to blend in today.

Rachel knew Cole was, or had been, a Hot Shot in Idaho eleven years ago. It was with mixed feelings that she'd looked at the fire camp roster a few minutes earlier and seen two Idaho crews listed. Eleven years was forever in a Hot Shot lifetime. The work was tough on the body and the mind. Chances were slim that Cole was still on active duty. With his love of horses and his bent for the big thrill, Cole could have turned from the Hot Shots to the rodeo or NASCAR for his adrenaline rush.

Still, Rachel pulled her baseball cap low over her eyes as she fell into the dinner line with the other fliers and ground support teams. The pilots and their crews had been bussed over to base camp from the airstrip twenty miles away with the promise of hot showers and a steak dinner celebrating the containment of the fire.

"Let's not go looking for trouble." Out of the corner of her eye, Rachel caught a glimpse of someone with blond hair and broad shoulders. Controlling the flutter in her stomach, she turned away from the man. "Besides, Danny, you know you'll have cabin fever at first snowfall. Who wants to hurry home to that?" Back to the slow routine at the ranch, back to homework and laundry, back to the limited repertoire of meals she could cook. In the winter, she felt she was twenty-six going on forty—bound to Eden by love and a responsibility she hadn't asked for.

"That's why you and I get along, kid. We're too much alike." With a playful flick of a gnarled hand, Danny broke her reverie by flipping Rachel's baseball hat off. There wasn't much of a breeze, but it was enough to carry it several feet.

Rachel scrambled to pick it up, but someone beat her to it. As the man straightened, Rachel felt her knees go weak and the blood drain from her face. She half turned, as if to run.

"Rachel?"

It was sad, really, how Rachel recognized Cole Hudson's voice with its gentle Texas twang more than eleven years after she'd last heard him speak, sadder still that her heart raced at the sound. If she'd been frying in the Indian-summer heat of Montana before, she was broiling now. Rachel was suddenly grateful that she hadn't looked in the mirrors in the portable latrine, because she preferred to hold on to what little dignity she could muster and pretend she looked presentable. At least she could hide behind a pair of mirrored sunglasses.

*"You're such a tomboy, Rachel," Missy said, braiding Rachel's hair before she went to school. "Why don't you try out for cheerleading?"*

*"The only thing better than flying is fixing an engine," Rachel said. "Cheerleading is for sissies."*

*Missy shook her head. "Boys don't like tomboys."*

As Rachel turned back to face Cole, she caught a

whiff of herself—sweat and a combination of exhaust fumes, slurry and engine oil. Ugh. Cole had always liked girlie girls. Rachel plastered what she hoped resembled a smile on her face, hoping at least her manner would convey what a cool, polished woman she'd become, and not raise suspicion about the secrets she was hiding.

"Hey, Cole. Long time no see." Good. She sounded unfazed, not like a woman whose heart pounded crazily in her chest.

And then Cole was laughing as he scooped her up and spun her around in a crushing embrace.

The world slowed down, winding back, back, back, to a simpler time when anything was possible and happiness had seemed so easy to attain.

*Cole.*

Without thinking, Rachel clung tighter, pressed closer, until she heard the buzz of a small Cessna's engine overhead and reality came crashing back.

What was she doing? "Put me down!" Rachel struggled against Cole's rock-solid chest and her traitorous emotions. "Dammit, Cole. Put. Me. Down."

Unceremoniously, his arms released her and Rachel stumbled, but somehow managed to regain her balance.

"This guy buggin' you, Rachel?" Danny asked, a steadying presence at her side, even though his wiry physique was no match for Cole's.

"No. He's an old friend," Rachel admitted after a moment spent unable to avoid looking at Cole. "Why don't you get back in line, Danny. I'll catch up with you in a minute."

Danny moved slowly toward the chow line with a few dark looks for Cole.

Meanwhile, Cole didn't say a word. He just stood there watching her with bright blue eyes that she'd hardly dared stare into when she was fifteen, much less now. With a linebacker's build, a square jaw and short blond hair, he carried his age well, probably better than Rachel. He looked at peace, far different from the worried expression Rachel saw in her own reflection.

"You look like hell. I almost didn't recognize you," he said finally, handing her the baseball cap. "What are you doing out here?"

Rachel put the hat back on her head. His words shouldn't hurt, but his tone implied she had no business being at a wildland fire camp miles from civilization. Rachel looked beyond Cole to the smoke-filled horizon. Things were so much easier in the air than on the ground.

"I'm contracted with the Forest Service, working the fire just like you are." Making good money to tide her over through the lean winter months.

He frowned, taking in her appearance from head to toe. "Hot Shot?" She wasn't wearing the Hot Shot garb that Cole was—fire-resistant drab-green slacks and a yellow button-down.

Rachel flicked her thick ponytail over her shoulder with a laugh. "Fight fires on the ground with nothing more than a shovel or a chainsaw? I'm not that foolish. I'll leave that to you, thank you very much." And she should leave him standing there with the question she knew he was dying to ask—*How's Missy?* But Rachel's boots seemed to have taken root in the dirt.

The disapproving expression didn't leave his face. After a moment Cole said, "You're not flying air tankers, are you?"

"Yep." Rachel squared her shoulders. She was proud of the fact that she was one of the few female tanker pilots, prouder still that she was owner of her own tanker service. She flew a PB4Y2 Privateer, an airplane that had served in at least two wars. Dumping fire retardant on forty-foot-high flames on runs reminiscent of those barnstorming fighter pilots who'd come before her was Rachel's idea of heaven. Sometimes she couldn't believe they paid her to do it.

Cole cursed under his breath, taking Rachel by the arm. "Look, kid—"

Kid? Rachel bristled at the word. In the back of her mind, she'd always believed that Cole would approve of what she was doing, would jump at the chance to make a run with her. She'd never imagined he'd treat her as if she were still fifteen and waiting for her first kiss. Rachel shook off his touch, even though part of her trembled with the contact.

"This isn't a game out here. You've always been a risk taker, but..." Cole lowered his voice and leaned closer. "I'm sure you've noticed how air tankers have been dropping from the sky lately."

He was right. A lot of the old beauties weren't able to take the stress of diving into deep valleys and pulling up to avoid the trees on the opposite side of the basin. But Rachel had rebuilt the Privateer herself and knew that its engines could withstand tremendous stress.

"Maybe there have been a few older models that

haven't held up after fifty or more years of hard service, but my plane is different." Rachel resisted the inclination to tell him she was one of the most respected pilot mechanics in the business, something she could thank her father for. "I know what I'm doing, Cole. Why can't you just wish me well?" Instead of making her feel two inches high, which was how she felt anyway, because she wouldn't tell him about Jenna. And then there was Missy… Rachel had never liked hiding the truth. Yet, that seemed to be all she did nowadays. And Cole was, in part, to blame.

Rachel looked for Danny. She couldn't last much longer without spilling her guts or losing the facade that she was a fully functioning adult.

Unexpectedly, Cole reached out and removed her sunglasses. "What happened to your freckles?"

Rachel snatched them back and thrust them into place. "I grew out of them." If only she'd outgrown her feelings for Cole.

"And Missy?" Cole finally asked the question she'd been dreading. "How is Missy?"

Rachel's throat closed as she recognized the expression in Cole's blue eyes—hope. She'd thought she'd loved this man at one time. Later, she'd realized it had been a foolish teenager's crush. But it was clear that he was still in love with Missy, the woman he'd slept with just hours before her marriage to another man, and then left alone to face the consequences. And then there was what he'd done five years ago.

Rachel was such a sentimental fool.

"She's dead," Rachel managed to tell him, holding

her heart together by willpower alone as she waited for Cole to say he'd wondered why Missy hadn't shown up on his doorstep five years ago, waited for him to explain why he'd never called to see what had become of her.

Instead Cole swayed as if he might be felled by the heartbreaking news that Rachel had been living with for what seemed like an eternity.

Rachel frowned.

"I had no idea." His gaze wandered around, from the latrines to the chow line to the trucks rumbling out of camp. Then his attention swung back to her. "When?"

Rachel tried to hide her confusion. How could Cole have forgotten? He had to have known. "Five years ago." Although the vibrant spark that had once been Missy had been extinguished on her wedding day and none of Rachel's efforts had rekindled that flame. "Car accident. We lost her." Rachel's voice sounded distant, as if someone else was speaking, someone who hadn't known Missy and somehow failed her.

Rachel wouldn't fail Missy now. She wouldn't tell Cole the secrets pressing at the back of her throat, the most pressing of which was that he'd created a beautiful little girl on the eve of Missy's wedding to Lyle.

Rachel had made her sister a promise, and she was sticking to it.

*"IF YOU LOVED ME, you'd stay with me here in Eden. I can't leave Rachel."* Missy's voice had been filled with

an aching sadness, as if she'd known her fate was sealed if Cole left her.

What had Cole done?

"Chainsaw, you look like you've just seen a ghost," Jackson observed as he parked his booted feet near Cole's.

Cole squinted up into the sunset to find Jackson and Logan regarding him.

After hearing the devastating news, Cole had staggered over to the latrines where he'd tried to decide if he was going to puke or not. Minutes later, with his friends standing in front of him, Cole still wasn't sure.

Missy was dead.

He wiped a hand over his face. He'd always believed she was The One—the woman he was meant to be with. All she'd had to do was touch him and he'd combusted. She'd given him an ultimatum that last morning he'd seen her, either settle down in Eden or leave her be. There was nothing for him in Eden—no family since his had moved to Idaho, and there sure as hell weren't any jobs in the dying town. In the heat of anger, he'd told Missy he'd wait for her through her foolish marriage. He'd told Missy he'd wait until she grew up and realized they were destined to be together.

And he had waited, living as if he'd had a marriage vow to honor, knowing she'd come back to him someday.

Only to find out Missy was dead.

"I, uh…" Cole struggled to find the words to tell his friends what had blindsided him. "I just heard that…Missy is dead."

Without a word they sat on either side of him on the hard-packed Montana earth.

Jackson put a hand on his shoulder. "I'm sorry. How did you hear?"

"Her little sister told me a few minutes ago." Rachel had looked just the same as the picture he carried in his wallet—a stubborn lift to her chin, wisps of long black hair escaping from her ponytail, slender as a reed, wearing cowboy boots, scruffy blue jeans and a T-shirt. If it wasn't for the way she filled out her T-shirt, she'd have tomboy written all over her.

What Rachel didn't have written all over her was grief, because she'd had five years to come to terms with her sister's death. All Cole's dreams—

"Missy's sister?" Logan broke into Cole's thoughts, leaning forward and looking at Jackson, then at Cole. "The little girl who rebuilt your truck engine before she had a license to drive it? The one who beat you in a bareback horse race?"

"Logan." Jackson held up a hand in Logan's direction.

"Yeah. She's a tanker pilot. I should have known she'd end up doing something crazy, especially with Missy gone…." Cole stared down at his boots. Rachel was no longer a little girl. She was a woman who'd never outgrown the daredevil spirit that he'd been sure Missy would temper as they aged. Crap. He still couldn't believe Missy was long dead. "I don't want to talk about it."

"Maybe after we finish here, we can take a run over to Wyoming and pay our respects," Jackson suggested softly.

Cole shook his head slowly, in wonder. "You didn't even know her."

"No, but we know you, buddy, and even if you're not ready to talk about it, we'll be there for you when you are."

"LAST RUN OF THE DAY," Rachel said as Danny landed Fire Angel One. They'd done nothing more exciting than drop retardant around the fire all day long. The fire had died down, so that there were no flames raging out of control and no firefighters trapped and in need of rescue. Very ho-hum.

"Last run of the *season,*" Danny corrected wistfully as he taxied the Privateer to the retardant base.

Despite the shift in winds this afternoon, the dragon appeared to be contained, and they'd been ordered to drop one last load of slurry on the steep eastern slope near the road before refueling and heading home to Wyoming. A season of flying was over.

Rachel sighed. At least she wouldn't have to see Cole again.

In their passes over the fire, she'd caught glimpses of the crews below, bolstering the last of the fire lines before this beast burned itself out. She couldn't help but wonder if Cole was one of them, if he looked to the sky as she flew over. How was Cole handling the news about Missy? Rachel had dreaded meeting Cole again. She had so much to blame him for. Even though she'd idolized him all those years ago, Cole Hudson never looked before he leaped, and that had contributed to Missy's downward spiral and death. After so much time, Rachel had thought he'd shrug, offer his condolences and move on, but he'd appeared shaken.

Beside a shed on the edge of the runway, boots in puddles of red muck, the ground crew stood ready with hoses that would pump another twenty-five hundred gallons of fire-smothering slurry into the belly of the Privateer. Originally a long-range Navy patrol bomber built for World War II, Fire Angel One had been stripped clean to make room for the massive tank that had been riveted within the plane's belly.

Without waiting for Danny to cut the engines, the ground crew approached, each dragging a hose and looking like aliens from the red planet, because their clothing, hats, goggles, gloves and masks were covered with a sticky glaze of crimson slurry. It would take them only a few minutes to fill the tank to capacity.

"My turn to fly." Rachel faced the old bomber pilot, raising her voice over the whoosh and splash of slurry pouring into the Privateer. "How much do you want to bet this is the most boring run of the season?"

"I'll pass on that bet." Danny turned his cap backward and pushed his sunglasses firmly onto the bridge of his crooked nose. "It's back to the boob tube for me and engine rebuilds for you."

"At least I've got something to do this winter." Rachel had an engine to rebuild on an old C119 warplane for a collector in Nevada. Danny would have to wait until spring to pick up work.

Danny laughed, rising to switch seats. "Yeah. Better make this last run stellar, then, kid. Are you up for barnstorming the camp?" Danny was always suggesting risky deeds, probably because as a fighter pilot in Korea and Vietnam, he'd cheated death more than his share of times.

"Are you up for having your pilot's license revoked?" Rachel groused as she climbed behind the pilot's controls, wondering why she was so somber. Was it because she'd reawakened her grief over Missy's death through telling Cole? Or was it that Cole's shocked reaction wasn't at all what she'd expected?

The slurry hoses quieted. The tank was sealed back up. With a wave, the men in red retreated to wait for the next plane.

Unaware of Rachel's mood, Danny grinned, shoving his mirrored glasses on. "Where's your sense of adventure? Life is meant to be lived. Let's take to the air, kid!"

"WHO'S READY?" Jackson yelled at the other eighteen Silver Bend Hot Shots packing their gear in base camp.

Doc and O'Reilly, among the youngest of the crew, already had their iPod earphones on and were oblivious to Jackson's question.

The Silver Bend Hot Shots had been given marching orders. The fire was almost at the mop-up stage. That meant that less-skilled crews with lower hourly rates could be utilized. And since Silver Bend wasn't a Montana crew, they were among the first to be released and sent home. States took care of their own.

Their duffels were stuffed with dirty clothes and

reeked of smoke. They'd been fed and assured their paychecks were in the mail. All that was left to do was to pack up, load up, gas up and head for Idaho. Still, they weren't in their civvy gear yet. There was always a chance when you were on a fire that you'd be called back into the thick of things. And this fire had created its own weather almost every afternoon since they'd been here, wreaking havoc with predictions and putting lives in danger when the winds whipped flames to dangerous heights.

Even now Cole could feel the wind pick up and change direction.

At the roar of an airplane overhead, Cole looked up. It was one of those antique planes that the Forest Service kept threatening to ground because of performance issues, planes so old they had a high likelihood of crashing. Cole had no way of knowing if it was Rachel or not, but he couldn't take his eyes off the plane. In some weird way, she was the only thing he had left of Missy. The sisters hadn't looked alike, and they were as different as milk to wine, but it was a link Cole was reluctant to break now that he'd found Rachel again.

WITH A SIGH Rachel took out her camera and snapped a quick shot of the base camp as they flew overhead. She tucked the camera back into her utility vest pocket. When Rachel got home, she and Jenna would sit together in front of the computer and look at her pictures from the season. This year she'd got some spectacular shots from above of other tankers dumping their payloads on hot targets. Jenna always seemed to enjoy looking at her pictures.

Voices crackled urgently in her headset.

"Did you hear that?" Rachel shouted over the roar of the four prop engines.

"You heard right." Danny grinned. "Wind's shifted. There's a crew that might be trapped if they don't get help soon. This is no longer a milk run, kid."

Rachel banked and brought the plane into a new trajectory. They were minutes away from the location—a deep slope in a narrow part of the valley. As approaches went, it would be easy. They'd have to fly as low as they could over the canopy of trees. It was the climb out that was going to be tricky. Not impossible for Danny and Rachel, but it would by no means be a cake walk.

Rachel flew over the drop site once, taking in the fire racing after the fleeing men and women in yellow shirts before losing them in thick plumes of smoke, examining the seamless horizon broken only by a lone pine towering forty feet above the main tree line.

"Not much time," Rachel noted as she prayed that wasn't Cole down there running for his life. As Rachel angled around for a final approach, she rejected the feeling of guilt for keeping the truth about Jenna from Cole.

"Don't need much time if your aim's good," Danny said, always fearless.

"We've got to watch out for that granddaddy pine as we come out," Rachel observed, scanning the gauges for any sign of stress in the Privateer. Everything looked normal.

She spared a quick glance at her latest picture of Jenna and Matt. Jenna smiled with the unworried expression of a preteen who hadn't yet discovered boys. Matt's grin had been known to melt the hearts of ice-cream store clerks.

Coming out of the turn, Rachel leveled out the plane before pushing it into a steep dive through the thickening smoke. Down, down, down they plummeted toward the flaming treetops. Rachel flew as if she had no fear. Part of her reveled when her stomach dropped at their rapid descent. Part of her worried about Jenna and Matt, orphaned back at home if Rachel ever miscalculated.

She wouldn't disappoint her kids.

"Slow down. Don't lose them in the smoke." The voice of the attack boss, circling high overhead in a small Cessna, crackled through the airwaves. "You're coming in pretty damn fast."

"Don't listen to him. He's never flown a bird like this in his life," Danny yelled, leaning forward as if that would help him see better through the smoke. "We need speed. More speed."

Rachel agreed with Danny. They had to come in fast and slingshot out, even if they were breaking a few safety regulations by flying in near-blind conditions. She gave it more throttle.

The plane shuddered with anticipation. The air seemed thick with the heavy threat of danger, making it hard to breathe. Usually Rachel imagined a young Cole was there at her side on adrenaline-pumping runs like this, egging her on, past the fear and into a zone where she operated on instinct.

She couldn't find that Cole today, couldn't bring the image of the object of her teenage affections to mind. But Rachel didn't let the fear hold her back or keep her from diving into the shrouded air space over the retreating crew, who might be consumed by flame if she didn't slow the fire and create a path to safety.

Visibility dropped as smoke wrapped around them. Rachel craned her neck as she tried to see out. She had no time to acknowledge the fear that clenched her heart, no time for more than a fleeting thought of home.

Pockets appeared in the smoke, showing her the way, then disappeared and teased just at the edge of her vision. Common sense screamed for her to pull up, get out, but Rachel had a job to do.

She kept her hands steady. There'd be time to let the shakes and the what-ifs take over later.

"Almost there. Don't let up." Danny wouldn't back off either. "And…now!"

With economy of motion, Rachel punched the button on the steering yoke and felt the first three drop doors shudder open. At their rate and angle of descent, the red slurry would fall at a ninety-degree angle. She'd planned this run to catch the front flank of the fire with her first drop, hoping it would slow, if not halt completely, the raging head of the beast.

"Right on target, kid. Hit it again," Danny cried, peering down at the flaming forest.

Rachel released the final three doors, catching sight of some of the fleeing crew as she did so, hoping this drop would provide a safe escape route for them.

The Privateer was long gone by the time the slurry hit the ground.

The smoke ahead was dense and dark. Visibility dimmed as she entered the plume, then cleared, then dimmed again as Rachel threw the flaps to bank, forcing the plane into a blind move against their momentum, against gravity. The Privateer bucked and groaned in complaint. The cockpit was dim, the air ahead of them impenetrable to the eye.

The attack boss cursed over the airwaves. "Can't see a damn thing. Where are you, Fire Angel?"

"Hold together, baby," Rachel murmured, praying for a clear windshield, even if it was only a view of the smoke-filled sky.

"Steady," Danny cautioned. "You're doing great." He'd undoubtedly be crowing when they made it out of here. It was just the kind of adrenaline-pumping last run he'd wanted.

The smoke thinned as the plane climbed, shuddering from the effort.

Then they were bursting out of the smoke into a blinding dose of sunlight toward a thick spire of green. Too close. It was too close!

"The tree! The damn tree!" Danny shouted, as they raced toward the lone pine. It was fifty feet ahead of them and they were flying nearly one hundred miles an hour.

But it was too late to turn. Fire Angel One took the pine head-on about thirty feet from its top. The crack of the tree and the rip of metal was all Rachel heard as the windshield shattered into the cockpit, bringing a barrage of glass, branches, wood and pine cones onto them.

Rachel's face stung and the air whooshed out of her lungs as something struck her in the rib cage. Impossibly, the plane seemed to float there, as if deciding whether to continue or give up. And then it bucked forward.

"We're still flying!" Danny cried, as if that were the best news ever. "Three engines running. Hot damn!"

Danny didn't know how hard Rachel was fighting to keep the plane going or to keep her shit together. Or maybe Danny did know and was just trying to keep her spirits up.

Her ribs were on fire. Something must have hit her when the windshield shattered, because breathing had become agony. But she didn't dare spare a glance down at herself, because she could barely control the steering yoke, much less reach the other controls hidden beneath piles of green.

The Privateer bobbed and dipped dangerously above the canopy. Rachel didn't think they could stay in the air much longer. They'd lost an engine on the right side, possibly damaged by debris. The landing strip was too far away, and the only thing between them and the airport was miles and miles of trees.

Something sputtered to her left.

"More thrust!" Danny reached for the thrusters. "Crap," he yelled as he realized what Rachel already knew. Even if she could reach the control panel, it wouldn't matter. The thrusters and gauges were covered with chunks of tree, barricaded in as if the old pine, in death, wanted to make sure it didn't go down alone. Danny tugged at the wood, but a good portion of the trunk lay across the controls.

And pinned Rachel to her seat.

Double crap. Now that Rachel had looked, her hands started to shake.

The noise level decreased as one of the engines on the left died. Something an awful lot like doom swirled in Rachel's gut. She couldn't leave Jenna and Matt like this. The corner of their picture peeked out from behind pine needles.

"Fuel?" Rachel shouted as they shot out over the ridge and a new crop of trees waiting to shish kebab them.

Danny tugged frantically at the wood covering the thrusters. "Fuel's fine, but we need more power. I'll try restarting the engines."

"We're losing altitude," she said, unsure if Danny heard her.

Danny released a string of curses and dug for the controls Rachel was sure wouldn't work, her eye momentarily caught again by a corner of the photo still visible on the dash.

What had Rachel done?

Now Cole would never know the truth.

## *CHAPTER TWO*

"DID YOU HEAR THAT?" Cole craned his neck to look up into the smoke-strewn sky.

"It's just a plane," Logan answered, busy packing his bags.

Cole shook his head. "It was a crack or a boom or something."

A small two-seater plane was circling low over a point to the northeast.

"Look at that." Jackson pointed at the Incident Command tents pitched on the rise above them. "Something's happening."

Sure enough, members of the IC team were running out of their individual tents that served as mini-offices tracking fire behavior, weather, personnel and the like, and were heading for the main tent. Just as a pair were about to yank open the door to the IC tent, the camp helicopter pilot burst out and ran toward the makeshift chopper pad at the end of the parking lot.

Something cold and unpleasant gripped Cole, momentarily freezing him in place. He didn't need to possess Jackson's near-psychic abilities to guess what had happened. The observation plane, which coordinated air attacks, was circling, flying too low. A plane had gone down.

"Come on." With one hand, Cole dragged Doc to his feet. The kid had finished medical school in the spring and was about to start his internship. "You and I are getting on that chopper." They'd be asking for volunteers to go on the rescue, crew members with medical training or rappelling experience, not that Cole had a lot of either.

Hearing Doc's protests, Jackson moved closer. "Cole, what are you doing?"

"You'll need your medical kit, Doc." Cole swung the red bag emblazoned with a big white cross from the ground into Doc's chest and started towing the slighter man in the direction of the chopper.

"Cole?" Jackson trotted beside him. "Where are you going?"

"A plane went down." Cole didn't slow up. He was getting on that bird.

The helicopter pilot was hurrying around the chopper, checking out rotors or flaps or whatever pilots did before they took off. A younger man in coveralls ran to the helicopter. The two men exchanged words and then the younger man hopped into the cockpit. Cole assumed he was the copilot. They wouldn't allow the rescue team in the cockpit.

Jackson wasn't giving up. "You think the plane that went down was Missy's sister's?"

Cole didn't think; he knew. Yet it sounded stupid to say it out loud.

"Let me find out what's going on first." Jackson had

spent the past few days of the fire working with the IC team. "There may not have been a crash. It might not be Missy's sister."

"No. By the time you do that, this bird will be gone."

Jackson ran a few steps ahead and stopped in Cole's path. "Don't go running off based on a feeling."

"Why not? You do it all the time." Cole gave Jackson his fiercest glare.

Jackson shook his head.

"Look, I wasn't there for Missy when she died. I'll be damned if I'm not there for Rachel when she needs me," Cole said through gritted teeth. "Now, step aside. Me and Doc are getting on that chopper."

Jackson swore and did step aside. "Let me talk to the pilot. I know him."

"Just get me on that chopper."

"THERE!" Cole shouted above the whine of the helicopter rotors. The fuselage of the plane rested precariously on a canopy of trees fifty feet above the ground to their left.

"Holy crap. Will you look at that," Doc said beside him. "What lucky SOBs."

Cole could only hope Rachel had been lucky. The nose of the plane was smashed in and the windshield shattered. From this angle, he couldn't see inside the cockpit. Branches thrust through the windshield. No one flagged them down as they approached.

*Not dead.* Rachel couldn't be dead.

The copilot came back to the area where Cole and

Doc sat. He snapped a hook attached to his harness to a safety line, then opened the side door.

Wind and the smell of smoke—both wood and fuel—rushed into the cabin as the copilot began prepping the equipment needed to drop someone out of the airplane.

Cole unbuckled his seat belt and stood, grabbing a hand loop for balance and stepping toward the door.

"Sit down," the copilot commanded with a stern look, yelling over the din.

"I'm going down there." There was no way anybody was going to keep him from being a part of Rachel's rescue.

"Of course, you are," the copilot agreed, still shouting. "But you'll fall out if you aren't strapped in. The air up here is choppy. Ever see a man fall eighty feet to the ground?"

Doc looked up at Cole and swore.

"Now, sit back down so you'll get your chance at being a hero."

As if emphasizing his point, the helicopter pitched Cole in the direction of the open door.

"I think I'm gonna puke," Doc moaned as he yanked Cole back.

The copilot laughed. "I always knew you Hot Shots were a bunch of wusses."

Buckling in next to Doc, Cole glared at his friend. "Hang in there. I need you."

"You could have taken the camp medic." Doc closed his eyes. His skin had become a sickly shade of white.

"I chose a doctor instead. Now, quit your griping."

"Have you rappelled out of a helicopter before?" The copilot shouted at Cole. Who didn't even blink as he nodded.

Despite his nausea, Doc managed to raise his eyebrows at Cole.

Cole scowled back at him. So what if he'd only rappelled once? So what if he'd rappelled onto solid ground? Rachel was down there hurt, perhaps dying.

Cole recoiled at the thought, leaning back into his seat. The little girl he'd once rescued from a flash flood couldn't die. She was too stubborn, too full of life.

"Get into this." The copilot tossed a four-point body harness at Cole's feet.

When Cole had the harness strapped on tight around him, the copilot hooked a nylon rope to it, fit him with a helmet containing a built-in headset and positioned Cole near the door.

"I'm going to let you down slowly until you get to the wreck. Try not to put your weight on the plane because we don't know how stable it is. You will *not* be going inside, copy?"

Cole nodded.

"Once you're there, let us know if the pilots are salvageable or not."

"*Salvageable?*" Damn him. "There will be survivors," Cole growled.

The copilot looked down on the fuselage. "I hope so, although we'll have a hell of a time extracting them in anything more than a basic harness. We won't be able to get a cage down there."

Cole nodded. He knew what the copilot was saying.

If Rachel or her copilot had neck or spine injuries, it would be next to impossible to get them out without increasing their injuries or killing them.

Cole glanced down at the crumpled metal shell that had flown through the sky less than an hour ago. No matter what, he was getting Rachel out of there.

"Ready?" the copilot asked.

Cole gave a tight nod and went to rescue Rachel.

When Cole neared the plane, he found purchase on the roof as he sought to steady his descent. Mistake. The branches beneath the fuselage cracked in protest, the sound nearly stopping Cole's heart. The plane swayed in the trees, and Cole looked to the forest floor with a start.

It was a long way down. No one would survive that kind of fall.

Cole worked up enough saliva to swallow. He would not send the plane plummeting to the forest floor. He would not be the cause of Rachel's death.

"Don't put your weight on it until you absolutely have to," the copilot chastised him through the radio.

Sweating, Cole tucked his legs in and continued down. With the help of the helicopter, Cole pulled himself forward until he was straddling the nose of the plane, hating to look inside, knowing that he had to look inside. Bearing Cole's weight, the plane swayed as if it were a playground swing.

*Not dead. Not dead.* He couldn't lose both Rachel and Missy.

Cole stared past the debris and shattered remains of the windshield and saw Rachel's face, looking fragile and white as a sheet. Her sunglasses hung awkwardly off one ear. Blood oozed from her temple, and little cuts crisscrossed the rest of her face, probably from the windshield breaking.

"Rachel, wake up."

Her eyelids fluttered and she gasped as if in pain.

"She's alive." Cole extended one arm through the windshield, but he couldn't reach her. Too many branches were in the way, one of which—a thick, splintered shaft about eight inches in diameter—seemed to have pinned Rachel to her seat.

"There are supposed to be two," the helicopter copilot reminded him.

"Can't see anyone else. The cockpit is covered with branches." Maybe the other pilot had been thrown out the window. Damn. Not the most pleasant way to go.

"We're sending down a second harness."

Cole inched to the edge of the cockpit, but his lifeline prevented him from reaching Rachel. He couldn't unbuckle her safety restraints from outside the plane.

"Come on, honey. Help me out here. Can you release your harness and scoot forward?"

Rachel didn't move a muscle. In fact, she seemed to have stopped breathing. Hell! If she needed CPR, he needed to be in there. *Now!*

Cole unsnapped his lifeline and slid into the cockpit headfirst. The plane groaned as Cole struggled to get his feet beneath him through a thick mess of branches.

"What the hell are you doing? That plane could drop at any moment. Is he crazy?" The helicopter copilot was as shocked as Cole was.

Cole wouldn't be surprised if Doc did puke this time.

The plane continued to sway and something snapped beneath him. Crap, bad idea. His feet finally found something solid to stand on. He stood between the two seats, knee-high in branches.

"Rachel." Cole put his gloved hands on her cheeks. "Don't give up now. We've got to get out."

Her eyes opened a crack. Her lips moved. All Cole caught was, "Danny?"

"Your copilot? I don't see him." Cole glanced around again. The other side of the cockpit was covered in limbs. No one could be under there, could they? He recalled the slight, stooped old man he'd seen Rachel with in the chow line last night. A guy that size *could* be buried beneath all that nature. Cole swore and tried shifting the debris, which only made bad sounds happen as both trees and metal protested his movements.

And yet there was someone under there. Cole touched an arm, fought revulsion at its lifelessness, followed the arm to a wrist and searched for a pulse.

Nothing.

"He's dead, Rachel. I'm sorry."

Rachel moaned. "Did he get us back to the landing strip?"

"No. Do you feel the plane moving? We're sitting in a couple of trees." Something clattered on the plane. Another harness.

Her eyelids drifted closed again.

"No, no, no. I've got to move you." If only he could

be sure she hadn't injured her spine. "Can you move your neck or your toes?"

"I hurt everywhere."

Not good. He began yanking off the branches that pinned her to her seat.

"Are you checking in for the night or coming out?" The helicopter copilot snapped.

Pulling away as many branches from Rachel as he could, Cole confirmed, "We're coming out." Finally there was just the big branch wedging her in. No wonder she seemed to struggle for each breath.

With one hand on Rachel's shoulder and one on the branch, Cole pulled the shattered limb away from her ribs.

Whimpering, Rachel slumped forward and then shot back in her seat, her face white.

Shit. He'd practically killed her. And there was blood in her hair. Lots of blood. He released the catch on his harness and yanked it off. "Are you all right?"

"I can wiggle my toes," Rachel answered with her eyes closed as he unbuckled her seat restraints.

"Good." As gently as possible, Cole slipped Rachel's feet into his harness and tugged it up her body. She was in no shape to climb through the windshield. Cole hauled her to her feet, pulling the remaining straps over her arms and clicking the four-point clasp home. She was no help at all.

The plane dropped a foot, sending them sprawling onto the branches covering the copilot. Branches poked Cole everywhere, as he scrambled to get them both standing again.

With rolling eyes Rachel awakened. Then her gaze steadied, caught by something on the control panel.

"You'll need that," she gestured toward the debris-covered gauges where a bit of yellow peeked out…a picture.

Without looking at the photo, Cole plucked it from the panel and pocketed it. Anything to get Rachel to move faster.

The plane tilted sideways.

"Get the hell out of there!" the copilot shouted.

JENNA WOULD HAVE GOT to the phone before Pop if she hadn't been washing dishes.

Aunt Rachel called at the end of every day, and the sun was now setting. Aunt Rachel didn't fly after dark when she fought fires unless the fire was really bad. It had to be her.

"Hello." Pop winked at Jenna. He knew it was Aunt Rachel, too. Then his voice got real serious. "This is Mr. Quinlan."

Not Aunt Rachel. Jenna bit her lip in disappointment and handed Matt a plate to dry. Pop ran the house when Aunt Rachel was gone, which was all the time. Aunt Rachel was never home anymore.

Jenna frowned.

She wanted Aunt Rachel to give up flying her airplane and stay at home. She worried about her aunt. Every October, Aunt Rachel brought back scary pictures and told wild stories about flying that made Jenna want to hug her aunt so tight she'd never go up there again.

Still on the phone, Pop turned his back to Jenna and sank down in a chair really quickly.

*Bad news.*

Even though she was only ten, Jenna had seen enough bad news to recognize it when it was delivered.

"Where?" Pop stood on his shaky, toothpick legs and scribbled something on a piece of scrap paper on the counter. He couldn't see very well and wrote letters and numbers bigger than Matt did. Jenna sounded out the big word from where she stood.

*Hospital.*

Pop looked in the direction of the sink and then away. A big knot tied up Jenna's stomach.

Not Aunt Rachel.

Jenna's hands drifted down in the soapy water as she stared out the kitchen window at the blue-and-pink sky. Aunt Rachel meant everything to Jenna.

"Are we done with dishes?" Matt asked, standing on the stool next to her, totally clueless about what was going on.

First she'd lost her mom and now Aunt Rachel. Her family was cursed.

With a sob, Jenna ran out the back door, stopping only to pull on her boots. She was halfway to the hangar when she heard the screen door creak open behind her. Ignoring Pop calling to her, Jenna continued on to the hangar. Only then did she stop. And that was just to stick her soapy fingers in her mouth and whistle.

Once. Twice.

Tears spilled down her cheeks.

Not Aunt Rachel.

God had taken everyone Jenna cared about.

Her breath came in ragged gasps as she tried to whistle a third time, only nothing came out.

Jenna sank to the ground, hugging herself tight.

Even Shadow had left her.

Stupid, stupid horse.

She whistled again. This time, there was an answering whistle, clear and strong above the sound of thundering hooves.

A dark horse stopped nearly on top of Jenna. Jumping up, she grabbed a handful of thick mane, then swung herself onto Shadow's back and guided her one true friend out across the open prairie at a full gallop.

"YOU SHOULD GET some rest," Jackson advised Cole, having driven the Silver Bend's van and crew to the hospital to meet Cole and Doc. They were planning to leave as soon as they heard if Rachel was okay. "You don't know how long the exam will take."

"I'll wait until we see the doctor," Cole said, stretching his legs out in front of him as he slouched deeper into the waiting room seat.

Doc suspected Rachel had a couple of bruised or broken ribs, as well as a severe concussion. But she was alive, which was a much better fate than her copilot.

"I still can't believe you took off your harness and crawled into that wreck. I had no idea you were so crazy," Doc said, reclining across three waiting room chairs.

Jackson frowned, spinning his wedding band. "He's not *that* crazy."

Not anymore. Cole had been wild in his youth, but joining the Hot Shots had made him realize that crazy stunts like that led to early retirement...or death.

"He just lost his mind." Logan came in with four cups of coffee balanced in his hands. "Even my kids know Cole's as predictable as a rock."

"We didn't think you were coming out," Doc said almost cheerfully, sitting up and reaching for a coffee. "It was like some action movie watching you click your lifeline on her and grab the second rope just before the plane fell."

"Rachel was injured." And in a daze from her head wound. And then... "But she was alert enough to make me grab a picture from the instrument panel."

"A picture? Of what? Her boyfriend?" Doc perked up.

"It would have to be important," Logan agreed. "More than just a photo of her faithful dog, Shep."

"Maybe it was of her copilot, poor bastard," Jackson said.

His three friends looked at Cole expectantly. What would be so important to Rachel that she'd stop during their escape? He didn't know, and yet—

Cole pulled the crumpled photo out of his pocket. It was a snapshot of two kids—a little boy and an older girl. It was the image of the girl that sent Cole's heart pounding. She looked like his sister, Sally, in the fourth or fifth grade. He squinted at the face. No. Not his sister, but the same blue eyes, the same white-blond hair, the same dimpled smile.

Rachel's daughter? Not unless she'd had a high-school pregnancy with a boy having the same Nordic coloring as Cole's family. With her dark eyes and hair, Rachel had taken after her father, while Missy had been the spitting image of their blond bombshell mother.

Cole focused again on the glossy picture. The boy was younger, maybe five or six, with dark coloring and chubby cheeks. Cole's attention turned back to the girl. There was something about the slant of the child's eyes that was familiar.

Missy's eyes.

*"Someday, we'll have kids together and live happily ever after." With one bare toe, Missy sent the porch swing moving and snuggled deeper into Cole's arms, sliding a hand beneath his waistband.*

Cole tried to remember the face of the guy Missy had foolishly wanted to marry. Lyle had been tall with brown hair and eyes.

Something cold and unpleasant stole Cole's breath. At least part of Missy's promise had come true.

This was his daughter.

Doc snatched the picture from his fingers. "Hey, it's just a couple of kids." His voice was filled with disappointment.

Jackson and Logan crowded in to see for themselves. After a moment, Jackson gave Cole a knowing look.

"Are you waiting for Rachel Quinlan?" A doctor in green scrubs stood in the doorway.

"Is she awake?" Cole asked. Because he needed answers to questions he hadn't even thought of yet.

RACHEL FLEW LOW through the forest. Branches whipped past her face too quickly for her to fend off. The wind was cold and there was snow on the ground. She was freezing. And scared.

"There's nothing like soaring far above the earth." Danny's voice, distant yet nearby.

Only, they weren't soaring far above the earth.

A fleeting memory of smoke-filled sky, and then Rachel was plunging into a green darkness with no end. Plunging—

"Rachel." Cole's voice this time, stern but comforting in the darkness.

She forced open heavy lids only to squeeze them shut against the bright sunshine.

Someone walked by, shoes squeaking. And voices were everywhere—urgent, loud, whispering, commanding, fearful.

Not sunshine, then. She was inside. So, why was she so cold? Her toes. Her left hand. Her head hurt. A lot. Where was she?

She pried her eyes open, determined to keep them open this time.

"Rachel." Cole stood beside her looking grim.

She was in a hospital bed surrounded by machines. Scary machines. Tubes ran into her left hand. Curtained partitions surrounded her on three sides.

"Was there..." Her voice was rough. "Was I in an accident?" She tried not to panic, but this didn't look good. And Rachel couldn't remember, could barely draw breath herself.

Cole nodded.

"You're in the emergency room. Do you know this man?" a nurse asked, leaning closer to look deep into Rachel's eyes with a small flashlight, making Rachel dizzy.

The need to vomit was intense, then faded as the nurse drew back.

"He's my sister's boyfriend." *Missy.* Where was Missy? She couldn't see any of the other beds around her. But Cole wouldn't be with Rachel if Missy was hurt, unless…

Cole's frown was no help, filled as it was with worry and something like disapproval. Rachel shied away from the thought that Missy was gone. But if something had had happened, he'd look like that, wouldn't he? Like the time he'd caught her snitching a bag of M&M's from Marney's general store.

"Where's Missy?" Rachel had to gasp the words out. It felt as if someone were sitting on her right side.

The nurse looked at Cole, who stared down at a small picture in his hand.

"Was I driving to the wedding?" She didn't have her license yet, but she was a safe driver. Why couldn't she remember what had happened? What had she done this morning? And the wedding. Missy was getting married today.

Worry threatened to overwhelm her. "Please. Somebody say something."

Cole didn't look so good. That's when Rachel remembered that Missy wasn't marrying him today. She was marrying Lyle.

"You've been in an accident." The nurse stated the

obvious. "A little disorientation is normal. Just try to relax and I'll get the doctor." She patted Rachel's arm before moving away.

"Cole? Is Missy…" *Dead?* She couldn't say the word even though she knew with cold certainty that Missy was gone.

Cole's clothes were filthy. He cleared his throat and opened his mouth to say something, then glanced at the picture in his hand.

The nurse returned with a man wearing green scrubs, a white coat and a stethoscope around his neck. He came to stand on her right side with a friendly smile.

"Miss Quinlan, how are you feeling? I thought it might help to wake up with a familiar face after that crash, but I hear that bump on your head has you a bit disoriented. Concussions can sometimes do that. How long do you think she was out?" He directed the question to Cole.

*Crash.*

The sharp, staccato images of green branches whipping past returned. Cockpit. She'd been in a cockpit, but the wind had been brutal, and something pressed against her ribs, making it hard to breathe, hard to move, impossible to handle anything other than the stick.

*"Keep the nose up!" Danny yelled as they went down.*

He hadn't sounded afraid, even at the end when they'd plowed through the treetops, while Rachel had been certain they were going to die.

She wasn't fifteen. She hadn't been in a car accident. She was twenty-six and had been flying over a fire with Danny. People were trapped, and she'd made that pass through the smoke to save them.

"Danny?" she whispered in a half croak.

"He didn't make it," Cole said quietly. "He was gone when we got there."

Rachel didn't remember. But she knew that Danny would have wanted it that way. Quick. In the air. While saving others.

That didn't stop Rachel's eyes from tearing up, or her nose from stinging as she tried not to cry. Danny wouldn't want her to cry. He'd want her to remember his hair-raising tales about one of the wars he'd served in, or the way he could skim the Privateer mere feet above a lake without popping a drop of sweat. He probably wouldn't want her to remember how he loved to visit local parks to feed the ducks, or the way he could read Matt a bedtime story with an arsenal of funny voices. But Rachel would remember it all.

Rachel wiped a tear away with her right hand.

"We're back in the present. Good." The doctor pulled up a chair. "You've been here at St. Patrick's in Missoula for several hours. I don't know how much you know about concussions, but it's an injury that attacks your equilibrium and takes a long time to heal. When those bruised ribs of yours are better, you'll still have some residual effects from the head wound."

"So I'll live to fly again." Fear, not her aching ribs, kept her lungs from filling with air.

Rachel turned her face away from Cole as more images of the crash threatened to shatter what little calm she had left. She'd faced death. How would she ever enjoy the freedom and beauty of an airplane again?

She had to fly. That's how she made her living. Yet, for the first time in her life, she didn't want to take to the air.

Not fly? As quickly as it surfaced, Rachel buried the thought. She was simply having a reaction to being in a cold, sterile hospital. She'd go back home to Eden, to Jenna and Matt, and try to salvage Fire Angels.

Rachel blinked heavily, suddenly worn-out.

"Are you drowsy?" the doctor asked.

"Yes." She was incredibly sleepy. Now that she knew more about what had happened, it was hard to keep her eyes open.

The doctor patted her hand. "We'll be taking you to X-ray soon. And you'll have to bear with us if we wake you up a lot. We don't want to lose you after such a daring rescue. You have this gentleman to thank for that." He gestured to Cole.

Cole had rescued her?

*Her knight in shining armor.*

Rachel sucked in a shuddering breath. She'd thought that's who Cole was once. She'd since learned that knights in shining armor didn't exist.

"I need to call home," she said, blinking back the tears again. She didn't like hearing how badly she was hurt or how close she'd come to not making it. At least if she talked to Jenna and Matt, she'd be able to pretend everything was okay.

"I called the ranch and talked to your dad," Cole

said, his voice unaccountably cool. "And base camp would have notified the next of kin for your copilot by now."

Rachel mumbled her thanks, though she knew Danny had no next of kin.

She wanted to call home, wanted to talk to Pop and Matt, wanted to reassure Jenna. Rachel didn't like the idea of her niece worrying, but she couldn't press for the call now, not in front of Cole.

She gave in to the exhaustion and closed her eyes.

When she opened them again, Cole was gone.

# *CHAPTER THREE*

"THE DOCTOR SAYS you can go home tomorrow." Cole stood in the doorway of Rachel's hospital room looking tired. But at least he'd showered, shaved and changed into clean, comfortable clothes, while Rachel had been wrapped for days in the same paper-thin hospital gown, confined to a bed.

Rachel hadn't seen Cole since she'd woken up in the hospital three days ago. During those days, she'd had to deal with bandages and bedpans, bossy nurses, X-rays and MRIs. She'd even had to listen to the doctor tell her they might have to drill a hole in her skull to relieve the pressure from the swelling around her wound.

It hadn't come to that, thank God.

She was ready to go home, and a bit irritated that Cole had found out about her release before she had.

"I thought I'd make sure you got home all right," Cole announced.

No! He'd see right off that Jenna was his. He'd try to take her niece away from her. The pain and discomfort Rachel had been through in the past few days was nothing in comparison to the threat of Cole taking Jenna away.

"That's very kind of you, but I've made other plans." Like pestering the nurse until she called the bus station for the time of the next bus to Wyoming.

Cole lifted one eyebrow before coming into the room and settling his large frame in the small plastic chair next to her bed. "I went home to Silver Bend with my crew in the van and came back in my own truck just to get you." He'd always barged right into her life without asking or apologizing.

Frowning created a stab of pain in her head. "You didn't have to do that." He'd driven from Montana to Idaho and back just for her? The gesture pleased Rachel, and yet she didn't want him to do that. How could she turn him down, now?

Easy. Because she had to.

"Cole, I—"

"I insist. I haven't been back to Eden in years." He was looking at his hands as if he were uncomfortable with the memory of his last visit to Eden. And why wouldn't he be? That's when he'd broken Missy's heart.

And most likely his own, as well, Rachel realized, feeling an unwanted sympathy for him. On the day she'd died, Missy had left a note saying she was returning to Cole, and that she was leaving the kids in Rachel's care. Then, on her way to reunite with her lost love, Missy's truck had plunged into an icy river. And Cole had never even bothered to call. Many of Rachel's illusions had been shattered that night.

"It hasn't changed much," Rachel admitted. "Though most of your old friends have moved away."

Thank God for that. If they'd stayed around, it wouldn't only have been Missy's husband, Lyle, who'd realized that Jenna wasn't his child.

"Sounds like you're trying to change my mind about going." Cole gave her a probing glance. How quickly he'd turned from remorseful to suspicious.

Apprehension scurried around her belly. What did Cole have to be suspicious of except the secret Rachel had so ardently guarded all these years?

"Is there some reason you don't want me to come back to Eden, Rach?"

"No. Not at all." God, she sounded desperate. With effort she held his gaze. "I appreciate the offer. It's just that you probably have a million things to do at home, what with fire season over and all." She raised a hand weakly. "You go on. I'll be fine on my own."

"I do have a lot of loose ends to tie up." His gaze was almost intolerable with its directness. Rachel resisted the urge to squirm. "Starting in Eden."

Something chilled Rachel's blood. She couldn't speak. Her heart began to pound in her chest.

Cole pulled out a bent photograph from his pocket and stared down at it for several seconds of strained silence while Rachel agonized, feeling as if someone had strapped her down so that she couldn't escape the truth.

"I was wondering..." He turned the photo around so that it was facing her. Matt's cherubic cheeks and Jenna's bright smile couldn't keep Rachel's skin from feeling clammy or slow the beat of her heart. "...Whose daughter is this?"

Cole's hard gaze demanded she stop the lie. With silent intensity, he dared her to deny Jenna was his.

Her sister's words came back to Rachel in a rush: *"Don't tell Cole about Jenna. It's not as if he wants her. You know how he's always searching for the next big thrill. Settling down is the last thing on his mind. It would just create one more disappointment for Jenna."*

*Don't tell Cole.*

Easy enough to say when Cole wasn't staring at you as if he already knew the truth. But Missy had been right in one respect. Jenna certainly didn't need another disappointment. Cole was still a Hot Shot, involved in a profession requiring a nomadic life—the kind of life that tore families apart. His track record with Missy confirmed that.

Cornered, Rachel announced in a weak voice, "She's *my* daughter."

Cole's jaw dropped. But before he could say anything, the nurse came in to check the tubes and machines connected to Rachel and take her pulse. "You're upsetting her." She glared at Cole.

He glared right back. "She's upsetting me."

"If this continues, I'll have to ask you to leave." She made a note on a chart and then walked away on her squeaky shoes.

"I don't remember you being such a liar." Cole glared at Rachel. "The truth," he demanded. He'd never talked to her with such disdain.

Of course, she'd never lied to him before. When they were kids, she'd worshipped the ground Cole walked on because he was brave and daring and handsome. Only later had she figured out he wasn't all he seemed.

Rachel swallowed thickly, feeling vulnerable and alone. She'd always had her father and Missy to catch her when she stumbled. Her sockless feet stung with cold under the thin covers as she looked everywhere but at Cole. There was no one to ask for advice or to deflect Cole's demand.

*Don't tell Cole.*

The lie slithered through her thoughts, demanding more lies to keep it alive, souring her stomach until Rachel couldn't turn away from the facts.

"Let me tell you a bit about the little girl in that picture," she began, tugging at a snag in the blanket. "She's been through a lot in her short life. First, she had a father who didn't want her, or Missy for that matter. Then after Missy died, she only had Pop and me to rely on." Rachel raised her eyes to his.

"What's her name?" Cole's question hung harshly between them.

"Jenna," Rachel sighed. "What I'm trying to say is that Jenna needs stability. She doesn't need someone like you coming into her life only to fall out of it because you've taken one risk too many or you want to be somewhere else." Rachel fervently believed this was true. She'd given up her dream of leaving Eden when she'd become guardian of Matt and Jenna. She'd settled into a role she hadn't asked for with no complaints.

Cole stared at her without speaking. Then he leaned forward and asked, "And you? Why are you so good for her when you've done exactly the same thing? Risking your life on some stunt."

"That *stunt* saved the lives of a Hot Shot crew." A crew she'd been certain had been Cole's. That just went to show what a softhearted dolt Rachel was.

"You know as well as I do how lucky you are to be alive." Cole leaned even closer. "Don't talk to me about stability, either. I can't imagine you make it home to cook dinner every night."

"You don't know a thing about me or what my life is like." But part of her acknowledged the truth in his words. She *wasn't* home eight months of the year.

"Let's call a spade a spade, Rachel. You and I are a lot alike, only I don't have a family waiting at home for me, wondering if I'm coming home safe." Something had darkened his eyes, sending a tremor of fear into Rachel's heart.

She had too much responsibility to shoulder fear, as well. Rachel shook her head slowly, making the room waver.

"You could just as easily have crashed on top of the crew after that crazy dive-bombing run you made," Cole accused relentlessly.

"But I didn't. I would have been fine if not for the smoke and that one huge, aberration of a tree." Rachel reached blindly for the bed controls with one hand, having had enough of lying at a forty-five-degree angle while he towered over her. She needed to be fully upright for this fight.

"The incident commander is considering writing you up for a safety violation."

*Damn it.* A violation like that and she'd have one hell of a time getting back into the air-tanker business.

The bed beneath Rachel's head and back rose at an excruciatingly slow pace, but the dizziness was immediate. She clapped her right hand over her eyes and willed her stomach to settle. "That's bullshit and you know it. I did what I had to do to save that crew. If anyone's lost anything from the crash, it's me...and Danny." Rachel blinked back the tears. Stubborn old coot. She hadn't even been able to say goodbye.

"The incident commander mentioned agencies investigating the accident, like the TSB, FAA and NIFC." He pronounced the acronym for the National Interagency Fire Center as NIF-see. "But that's not the point. The point is that this little girl is mine and no one saw any need to tell me."

"Did you want her?" Ignoring her head, along with the stabs of pain in her ribs and her heart, Rachel snapped at him, hating that it had come to this—she and Cole pitted against each other. "You didn't even love Missy enough to stay in Eden. What would you have done with a child? What would you do with one now?"

Before Cole could answer, the nurse came squeaking into the room. "That's enough. I'm going to have to ask you to leave."

"Fine," he growled. "I'll be back tomorrow to pick her up when she's released."

Rachel's head throbbed and her body was covered in a cold sweat. Ignoring Cole's continued insistence that he was taking her back to Eden, Rachel drove her point home. "It's fine to be offended because you didn't know about Jenna, but remember this—Missy sacrificed everything because she loved you enough to make sure you lived the life you wanted, which didn't include her or the baby. Are you willing to make as big a sacrifice for a little girl who doesn't even know you exist?"

"JACKSON?" Having punched a number in his cell phone without much thought, Cole struggled to hold it together, hoping that the roar of his truck's air conditioner would cover the sound of his ragged breathing. On shaky legs, he'd somehow made it to the hospital parking lot after Rachel had confirmed that Cole was indeed a father.

"Chainsaw?" Jackson paused to tell his wife, "It's Cole. I'll be a minute." A door opened and closed. "What's up? Did you make it back to Missoula okay?"

"Yeah, I'm here."

"How is she?"

"She looks like hell." Her head was swollen. Her complexion was pale despite her tan, and the smooth skin over her face was marred with tiny cuts.

And she'd lied to him.

Jackson replied with something totally appropriate that Cole instantly forgot.

Instead, he blurted, "The kid is mine. The girl in the picture. She's my daughter. Mine and Missy's." Their child existed, yet Missy was no more. Cole put his head on the steering wheel. "What in the hell do I do now?"

A few days ago he'd been envious of what Jackson, Logan and Spider had—loving wives. But kids…kids needed attention, closets full of stuff…and millions of other things of which Cole was blissfully ignorant. He'd wanted a wife, someone to spoil him with long, slow, passionate kisses and home-cooked meals. What did he get? A kid.

And what was he going to do about his mom? By some cruel twist of fate, Jenna looked incredibly like his sister, Sally, and Cole knew meeting her would send his mother over the edge, because she'd never really recovered from Sally's death at age ten. Maybe it would have been easier on his mother if Jenna had been a boy. But she wasn't. All in all, Cole was starting to think he was better off not knowing he had a kid. Could he just not tell his parents?

He swore. *Wasn't that just what Rachel had said?*

"You'll be a good dad. Don't worry about it."

*A dad?* Is that what he wanted? The title implied involvement—nearly impossible from another state—and demanded he come clean with his parents. And that was something he wasn't sure he could do.

"Who has custody?"

Cole's careening thoughts screeched to a halt on Jackson's question. "Rachel seems to," Cole answered woodenly. At least with Rachel Cole knew his daughter was in good hands, especially if he could convince her to give up firefighting.

"That's good. You've always gotten along with her."

"Sure. A decade ago we were friends." That was before he realized everything about his time in Eden was a lie. "Why did she do this to me?" Cole wasn't sure if he meant Missy keeping Jenna a secret or Rachel telling him about Jenna.

"Why don't you ask Rachel?"

"I will. Tomorrow." And all during the drive back to Eden. Like it or not, Rachel was getting a ride home from Cole. Cole hoped that was enough time to get to know more about his daughter and what he should do, and crack the mystery that had been Missy. Somehow, Cole knew that if he didn't understand Missy better, his heart would never let her go. And the only person with answers was Rachel.

"ARE WE CLOSE?" Matt asked, walking with wobbly steps as he tried to balance the plastic-wrapped flowers Pop had purchased in the gift shop with one chubby hand. His other hand held Pop's.

Jenna wasn't sure what to be more worried about—her grandfather falling down and hurting himself or Matt tripping and crushing the flowers. She pressed the bunch of flowers back against Matt's chest before looking at the numbers on the wall. "The lady said 112. This is 104."

Jenna didn't like hospitals. Bad things happened there. She walked next to Pop and Matt with her head down, concentrating on pulling the small wheeled suitcase. Trying to be quiet. Only, it was hard to be quiet in cowboy boots. She wished they could walk faster, but Pop had been wobbly on his feet since his eyes had gotten worse.

"Is this it?" Matt peeked into the next room. He'd

just started kindergarten and wasn't good with numbers yet.

Jenna shook her head. "No, 106."

Matt ran to the next doorway, almost tripping over his own feet. "Is this it?"

"No." Sometimes Matt was annoying. Jenna bit her lip to keep from yelling at him.

Pop's gnarled hand rested on her shoulder with a gentle squeeze. "I'm real proud of you. We couldn't have made this trip without you, Jenna."

"I got us lost," Jenna mumbled, burning with embarrassment.

"Yes," Pop chuckled. "But then you found us again."

Matt was running ahead, dragging the flowers on the gray floor as he stuck his head in room after room, calling out, "Is this it, Jenna?"

"Matt, stop," Jenna hissed, seeing the nurse at the desk ahead of them frown, then stand up. "Wait for us."

"Can I help you?" The nurse didn't smile. Jenna could tell by her frown she didn't really want to help them. The last time Jenna had been in a hospital was when Matt was born. Her mom had been crying. The nurse had pushed her out of the room and warned her to stay put or else.

Matt had stopped in the middle of the hallway, moving the bunch of flowers up and down and around as if he held a toy airplane. Jenna shushed him before he started making engine noises. Any minute now the nurse was going to kick them out.

Pop squeezed Jenna's shoulder again. "We're here to see my daughter, Rachel Quinlan. She's in room 112."

Jenna held her breath. That nurse was going to open her mouth and…

"Ahh, I was worried you wouldn't get here in time." The nurse came around the desk to them.

"In time?" Pop said, frowning in the nurse's direction.

Jenna knew it. Aunt Rachel was dying.

"THERE SHE IS! Mommy!" Matt ran on stubby legs across the gray linoleum to Rachel's bed, flinging his arms and a bouquet of flowers over her waist before resting his head on the mattress.

He didn't land on her with much force, but Rachel's muscles contracted around her bruised ribs, momentarily sending waves of pain through her chest.

When Rachel could breathe again, she ran a hand over Matt's dark, silky hair and smiled as best she could through sudden tears at the sight of her father hobbling through the door with one hand on Jenna's shoulder. She was glad to see them, yet she worried that if Cole came before they left he'd say something Jenna wasn't ready to hear.

"There's my girl," Pop said, without looking at her directly. Since macular degeneration had decreased the clarity in the middle of Pop's vision, he'd taken to looking at things sideways. "We're here to take you home."

"And bring you clean clothes," Matt added, plucking at her hospital gown. "Looks like someone stole yours."

"This is what you wear in a hospital. How was your trip?" Rachel lowered her voice to a whisper meant only for Matt. "Did you have any accidents?" He was having a bit of trouble remembering to go to the bathroom in school.

"Nope." The little guy gave her a thumbs-up sign.

Jenna's face was pale. She looked thinner than normal and remained rooted in the doorway, gripping the suitcase handle. Unlike Matt, who had the appctite of a teenager, Jenna didn't think much about food.

Rachel wanted to gather them all close, but knew if she sat up too fast, she'd keel over, scaring the daylights out of them all. She settled for reaching out to Pop. "How did you get here?"

Her dad wasn't allowed to drive long distances or at night, but he'd figured out how to get their family to Montana from Wyoming. Rachel wished they hadn't surprised her. She would have preferred to get some of the tubes out of her arms so that she didn't look like such an invalid.

"We took the bus," Pop said in a gruff voice, taking Rachel's hand and holding on tight, his bony fingers still strong despite his age and failing health. "Couldn't stomach you being here alone. We hoped to be here yesterday."

With an impish smile, Matt said, "It took Pop forever to find the bus place. Then Jenna read the thing wrong, and we ended up on the wrong bus." He rolled his eyes.

Ignoring Matt, Jenna moved forward with slow steps, asking in a strained voice, "What happened to your head?"

"I've got a big bruise." With effort, Rachel held her smile in place. She knew she looked scary. She could barely stand to look at herself in the mirror.

"I've never had a bruise like that." Matt peered at her hair.

Rachel prayed he never would.

"It looks like you're wearing a beanie on your head." Blue eyes wide, Jenna made a circular motion with her hand around her crown. "Are you going to be like that forever?"

The noise Rachel hoped was a laugh sounded more like a donkey braying. "Of course not." She wasn't particularly vain, but she'd asked two nurses and the doctor the same thing.

"What's the word on the Privateer?" Pop asked. "Can we salvage it?"

Hating to disappoint him, Rachel avoided his gaze. "There's nothing left to salvage."

"Did you wreck your plane?" Matt stuck out his lower lip. "Couldn't you save her?"

"You did save the most important thing on board," Pop said, squeezing Rachel's hand. A veteran of many wars and a few crashes, her dad was probably fully aware of what she was going through—the doubts, the fear, the guilt over Danny's death, the anger that she hadn't been good enough to avert disaster.

And she still had Missy's secrets to worry about.

"We'll find an even better plane. I'll call a couple of people when we get home." Pop's smile and words were meant to reassure.

But Rachel's throat closed. She'd come close to

cutting her life short, to letting them all down. How was she going to find the will to get in the air again?

Jenna stood at the foot of the bed, arms wrapped tightly around her torso. Missy's daughter understood how close she'd come to losing Rachel. She was an old soul who'd seen too much sorrow for a ten-year-old.

Rachel flicked a finger over Matt's nose, which elicited another smile from him. "I'm afraid we've lost her, Matt, but you've still got me."

Oblivious to the emotions of those around him, Matt bounced against the mattress a couple of times. "I hope we get a really fast plane next time, because Pop says I can start flying when I'm ten." His dark eyes sparkled with excitement.

*Next time.* Would there be a next plane? A next flight? There had to be. Flying was the only way Rachel knew to pay the bills and keep her family together. Flying was the only place where Rachel felt free.

If only Rachel's heart didn't pound a fearful beat at the thought of taking to the air.

"I NEED TO GIVE YOU instructions before you all leave."

Lost in thoughts of Missy and what might have been if he'd just stayed in Eden or if someone had told him the truth earlier, Cole almost didn't stop at the nurse's station. "Instructions?"

"Yes." The nurse eyed him as one would a misbehaving child. "Until the swelling in Miss Quinlan's head goes down, she'll be very unsteady on her feet. Don't let her walk on her own."

He was to be Rachel's nursemaid? Rachel wasn't going to be too happy about that. If only he could reclaim the easy relationship they'd had when they were younger. Then she'd let him help her. And maybe he could get her talking about Missy, which would help *him* understand what had happened. He knew that was the only way he'd be able to let go. It might also give him the answer as to what to do about Jenna and his parents.

Given the tragedy of his sister's death and how that had sent his mother into a tailspin that she had yet to fully come out of… Well, showing up on his parents' doorstep with someone who looked so much like Sally wasn't an idea he'd even remotely consider. Custody, which he hadn't even thought about until Jackson had brought it up, was not something Cole was looking for. So what *did* he want from this?

He wanted Missy. He wanted to go back to Eden, to a time when Missy had loved him and he'd felt as if he'd belonged to someone, to a family.

Too late. He'd blown his chance.

The nurse tapped the tip of a pen on the counter to reclaim his attention. "No unassisted walking. Not even to the bathroom. Every time her head rises above her feet, she'll feel as if she's just gotten off a roller coaster. That means even sitting can be a problem."

"Yes, ma'am. I'll have a hand on her every time she so much as sits up." Since Rachel needed such delicate care, she wouldn't be able to send him away the moment they arrived back in Eden. In light of that, playing nursemaid was bearable.

"Be careful of her ribs when you help her up and down. Bruised ribs are no fun."

Nodding, Cole rubbed his chest. He'd cracked a couple of ribs his first year as a Hot Shot when a tree he'd been trying to take down had nearly crushed him. He'd learned a lot about falling trees since then, and adopted a more conservative approach to life.

The nurse interrupted his meandering thoughts. "If you can't wake her up, take her directly to the emergency room."

That got his attention. Cole had never been around anyone recovering from a concussion before. He'd noticed Rachel's head was swollen, but hadn't realized the consequences of the injury lasted so long.

Poor thing.

Poor lying thing. He had to remember that she'd kept so much a secret from him all this time. Missy had been gone five years. Five years! The realization that he'd never see Missy again still turned his stomach, and yet, the fact that Missy had had so little faith in his love stung. Rachel hadn't been the only lying Quinlan.

The nurse shifted into his line of vision. "When she gets home, she'll need constant assistance and lots of sleep. Dressing will be a challenge, and things requiring a good bit of standing, like cooking, are out for at least a few weeks."

As it became clear just what an invalid Rachel was, Cole felt a bit overwhelmed by the responsibility of it all. Wasn't the nurse going to write any of this down?

"Nod if you understand," the nurse said with a steely gaze.

Cole nodded slowly.

"It seems as if I can trust you, although after that episode yesterday, I'm not so sure." She looked him up and down. "You won't upset her, will you?"

Cole scratched the back of his neck. "You've seen what kind of patient she is. She doesn't like sitting still or taking orders. Do you honestly think anyone caring for her won't upset her?"

The nurse grinned. "All right, you'll do. Let's go get our patient." She pushed the wheelchair briskly down the hall to Rachel's room.

Cole hesitated. The time had come to face Rachel after the bluntness of her parting words. What would he have done if Missy had called him up and told him she was pregnant all those years ago?

Cole frowned. The past eleven years would have been different if he'd known about Jenna. A part of him felt guilty to have had such a good life, free of the responsibility and financial burden a child brought. Cole didn't want to acknowledge that Rachel and Missy might have been right. He'd been itching to do things, to go out and tackle the world. A child, hell, even a wife, would have fenced him in.

He'd like to think he would have found a way to make things work with Missy, to create a home for her and the baby, to make peace with his mother, but the truth was Cole would have resented going back to Eden and taking up some mundane job at a gas station or grocery store. And Missy had made it clear she wasn't leaving Eden. Cole lived for the outdoors and had come to love the risk and adrenaline rush of being a Hot Shot. If he'd known about Jenna their relationship would have been doomed.

"THIS IS ALL UNNECESSARY," Rachel said as she eyed the wheelchair her nurse pushed into the room. She wasn't that helpless.

Cole appeared in the doorway, glancing from Rachel to the wheelchair. Rachel tugged self-consciously at the wrinkled T-shirt her family had brought her and wondered if she could get rid of Cole before the others got back from the cafeteria. "I can walk out of here on my own."

"Uh-huh." Ignoring her protests, the nurse swung Rachel's booted feet slowly around until they hung off the side of the bed.

Rachel stared at the dark splotches on her boots and tried to swallow back the fear the bloodstains awakened. Fear of flying. Fear of dying. Fear of failure. Inexplicably, Rachel's gaze was drawn to Cole's in the hope that he would dispel her anxiety the way he'd done when they were younger.

But Cole wore the same disapproving frown as her nurse. That made Rachel wish things were different between them, wish that she could smile at Cole and he'd grin back, as if they shared a private joke the punch line of which only they knew. But she was on her own. The only one who was going to handle the burdens Rachel carried was Rachel.

Disappointed, Rachel looked away. "Just call me a

cab, and I'll get myself to the bus station." She would not allow herself to be hurt further by Cole, or let him hurt Jenna.

"Sure, sure. I'd do that. But it's hospital policy that we give you a ride out of here." The nurse gave Cole a significant look and nodded toward the end of the bed.

Cole moved closer. Clearly he was going to help the nurse move Rachel into the wheelchair. Rachel frowned until her head throbbed in protest. She winced and cleared her expression.

"I don't like being babied," Rachel announced, squinting intently at the floor because judging the distance to it was somehow difficult. Doubt surfaced. Maybe she really did need help.

"I don't baby my patients," the nurse answered stiffly, flipping the wheelchair footrests to either side, then locking the wheels in place. She returned to Rachel's side, near enough to catch her if she fell, and then pushed the button to lower Rachel's bed.

It was now or never.

Wrapping one hand around her rib cage Rachel slid slowly off the bed, hoping to land on her feet. It didn't work out like that. Even though Cole and the nurse grabbed for Rachel's arms, she still ended up on the floor.

"Could you not have waited two seconds more?" Cole asked.

"I wanted to see if I could do it." Rachel struggled to breathe as the world came back into focus. Unfortunately, clear vision made it possible to see that Jenna had arrived.

"Are you all right?" the girl asked, looking as if she was about to cry. Between Rachel's appearance and nonexistent balance, her niece had every right to be shaken. It would have been better if Pop had kept her little family at home.

"I'm fine, sweetie," Rachel said as the adults helped her stand, her cheeks heating. She was reminded of one of her father's sayings, "There's a difference between taking a risk and gambling on a whim." She'd just gambled and lost.

Once on her feet, Rachel listed slightly to her injured right side. Neither the nurse nor Cole let go, but Cole could barely take his eyes off Jenna, who blinked back tears, fidgeting from one foot to the other, as if wanting to help but unsure of what to do.

Under Cole's unyielding stare, Jenna slumped, wrapped her arms around herself and drifted to the far side of the room.

"Are you going to introduce me to your visitor?" Cole asked, holding on to Rachel's elbows as she moved into the wheelchair. He spared Jenna a smile, but his little girl only had eyes for Rachel.

"Jenna, Cole. Cole, Jenna," Rachel said through clenched teeth.

"Who's he?" Jenna asked with a tentative gaze that bounced off everything in the room except Cole.

Frustration surged, increasing the trembling in Rachel's limbs. Lyle's abuse had made Jenna wary around men and downright panicky in new or stressful situations. Counseling, horse therapy and Rachel's love couldn't seem to help Jenna get over that. It made

Rachel ache to realize she couldn't do more. She had been too young to be a parent, yet what choice had she had?

"Cole rescued me. He's a friend." Rachel spoke with great care, somehow managing to control the conversation even if she couldn't control her body. "Jenna, do you see my utility vest? I was wearing it when...I came here." The vest had Rachel's camera in it.

"It's on the table by the bathroom. Do you want me to take your picture?" The sarcasm in Cole's tone wasn't helping.

Jenna stared at the vest, and Rachel realized her mistake. Her vest was splattered with blood.

"I'm not asking for a glamour shot, Cole. I just want to make sure that I don't leave the camera here."

Matt shouted something unintelligible out in the hallway. "Jenna, why don't you see what's going on out there?" Rachel suggested, uncomfortable about showing her weakness to Jenna.

"Okay," Jenna mumbled. She hurried out the door.

"Have you thought about what would have happened to Jenna if you'd died in that plane instead of your copilot? You're responsible for the welfare of my daughter," Cole reminded Rachel in a low voice. "And she's scared to death she's going to lose you."

"She's not so much scared as lacking confidence." Rejecting his opinion, Rachel closed her eyes, feeling as if she was going to fall, even though she was sitting down. "Lay off. You told me once that it's easy to pick on someone you think is weaker than you."

"When did I say that?"

"After you rescued me from the Baker brothers. Remember that time they wouldn't let me out of the alley behind Marney's store?"

"That was years ago."

Twelve-year-old Rachel had been fighting back tears caused by the frustration of not being strong enough to kick some butts. Back then, Rachel had hated being pushed around, and never backed down from a fight. Heck, if she was honest with herself, she was much the same today.

"Whatever happened to the Bakers?" Cole asked as the nurse left with a comment about paperwork. They'd been the town bullies and often Cole's adversaries.

"David got sent to the state pen on a rape charge, and Darden was found in the woods during hunting season with a bullet in his chest."

"And you wonder why I left." Cole knelt at Rachel's feet and flipped the footrests back down.

Rachel placed her feet carefully on the metal plates and sighed. "Oh, I never wondered why you left. I wondered a lot why we *didn't* leave."

He looked up at Rachel in surprise. "Missy loved Eden."

*"When I turn eighteen and graduate, I'm outta here," Rachel said, trying hard not to cry because their mother had left, although she wasn't sure if she was happy or sad.*

*"You'd leave Pop?" Missy demanded. "He chose us, not her. Face it, Rachel. You can't leave him. You and I aren't going anywhere."*

Rachel drew a heavy breath. "Missy hated Eden just as much as you did."

"How do you know that?"

Rachel gave a minute shrug. She didn't want to expand upon Missy's feelings at the moment. "She was my sister."

"And I loved her," Cole said bitterly, then fell silent as if dwelling on something painful. "What else was I wrong about all these years?"

Rachel was saved from answering by the return of her family.

"Is it time to go back on the bus, Mommy?" Matt half ran, half stumbled into the room. He stopped in between Rachel's legs, cupped his hands on her knees and grinned up at her.

"Yep, it's time to go, sweet cheeks," Rachel said before Cole could ask about Matt. She cradled the boy's chubby cheeks in her palms.

"I want to ride, too!" Matt climbed up into Rachel's lap.

Pop stared at Cole with a sideways glance and then squinted at a spot over his shoulder. "Is that Cole Hudson?"

"Yes, sir." Cole offered his hand. "When I saw the kids, I wondered if you were here." When it became clear no handshake was forthcoming, Cole stepped back, trying to hide his chagrin.

"We arrived this morning." Pop's words were anything but welcoming. Like Rachel, he still held Cole responsible for Missy's troubles. "What are you doing here?"

"We came by bus-s-s-s." Matt wriggled happily in Rachel's lap, unaware of the tension around him.

"And that's how we're going home, Matt," Rachel stated firmly, without looking at Cole.

"I've got enough room for everyone," Cole argued. "You'll be more comfortable with me than on a bus."

As if they all disapproved of Cole's motives, four pairs of eyes blasted their discontent.

"I want to go on the bus." Matt pushed out his lip.

Rachel couldn't agree more.

Before Cole could say another word, the nurse returned with a sheaf of papers in one hand. "Here's all your paperwork, including what you'll need to take to your doctor when you get home, my dear." She turned to Cole. "You'll see that she gets to her doctor within three days?"

"Yes, ma'am. I'm going to stay with her until she can move around on her own." He ignored Rachel's slight frown and Mr. Quinlan's definite one. Fishing for an ally, he added, "Rachel thought she might go home on the bus instead of in my truck."

Rachel started making noises of protest, until the nurse shut her up with a stern look and a shake of her finger. "If you fall, you will be right back in the hospital, possibly permanently."

Apprehension shot through Rachel, and Jenna gasped.

"You should be independently mobile in about two weeks," the nurse continued. "Until then, you'll need all the help you can get. Forget the bus."

## *CHAPTER FOUR*

"I WANT AN ICE CREAM," Matt said from his seat behind the big man.

Jenna had made sure that she was sitting as far away from him as she could. Big men made her nervous. And this man kept looking at her funny.

"Everyone just fell asleep," Cole said. Jenna could tell he was trying to keep his voice low.

"Not everyone, just the adults," Matt argued, kicking his feet against the back of the driver's seat.

"Hey, you ate lunch a half hour ago. I need to wake your mom up in thirty minutes. We'll ask her then." Even though he answered Matt, Cole looked over at Jenna sitting behind Rachel and smiled as if he'd just eaten something that tasted bad.

"But I'm hungry now," Matt whined.

"Matt, be quiet," Jenna said before Cole lost his temper. Big men had big tempers. She'd learned that when she used to live with her dad. He and his friends would drink, get loud and then—

Matt made a huffy noise and stuck out his lower lip. "Okay," he mumbled, rolling his eyes at Jenna while Pop slept between them.

Cole did the cheesy smile thing to Jenna. She wished he wouldn't. Jenna didn't trust him, and he was coming to stay at their house until Aunt Rachel got well. Jenna hoped Aunt Rachel got better really quick.

But what if she never got well? What if her head always looked like a balloon? What if she had to be in a wheelchair forever?

Jenna wanted to throw up. But not here. Not in the stranger's truck, because he might get mad.

Clasping her hands in her lap, Jenna looked out the window. When that didn't work, she closed her eyes and thought about home and about riding Shadow. She thought about anything but the big stranger and Aunt Rachel's crash.

"WHY IS IT SO BRIGHT outside? What time is it?" Rachel grumbled when she woke up as they traveled south on Interstate 15. It was scary how she fell asleep so easily and slept so deeply, scarier still to bounce back to awareness fully alert, as if she'd never napped.

With the setting sun on her face, Rachel couldn't open her eyes beyond mere slits, and the world spun with nauseous speed when she tried to lift her lids farther. What she wouldn't give for her aviator glasses.

"It's seven o'clock at night. Is the sun bothering you?" With half a smile that seemed to tease, Cole handed her a piece of plastic cut in the shape of sunglasses. "You can always use the sunglasses the nurse gave you."

Rachel had originally rejected the plastic because it was incredibly ugly, but with a sigh of defeat, she put the dorky things on. Immediately she felt better. The nausea receded, but did leave the dull ache in her head. Slowly Rachel turned her head to the left, which—surprise, surprise—gave her a perfect view of Cole.

Turning her head a bit farther, she could see her dad snoring softly in the back seat with one kid tucked against each side of him.

Cole changed lanes smoothly to pass a cattle truck. "You keep going out like a light. How are you feeling?"

"Like I've been in a bar fight and can't shake the hangover." Her eyes wanted desperately to close, but she wasn't ready to stop studying Cole while he was occupied and couldn't notice her staring at him. Despite her worries about Jenna and how Cole might break up Rachel's small family, now that Cole was in touching distance, her infatuation with him stubbornly remained.

Cole gave her a disbelieving glance, so familiar that it made her ache. "I take it you've been in a lot of bar fights."

"No."

"You were starting to worry me. I've heard stories about you badass pilots." His attention was back on the road, but he was smiling.

Rachel hadn't seen Cole smile like he'd meant it since he'd spotted her in the dinner line in base camp. Her reaction was depressingly predictable. Warmth blossomed in her chest, as familiar now as when she'd been deep in puppy love with him eleven years ago. "We're not nearly as badass as you Hot Shots."

"Yeah, you probably only go to classy bars."

She laughed at that, something she regretted as a sharp stab of pain from her injured ribs stole her breath.

They passed a road sign—Idaho Falls, Idaho, Sixty-Five Miles.

"We're not at Idaho Falls yet? Are you driving the speed limit? We won't get home until…until…" She should know when they'd arrive in Eden. She just couldn't seem to grasp the number. "Until the middle of the night," she finished lamely, attributing her muddled state to her head wound and the pain medication.

"We didn't leave the hospital until almost one. We had to stop at the pharmacy for those pills. We ate a late lunch before getting on the freeway. Plus, I've pulled over every hour to wake you up. Yeah, progress has been slow." Irritation laced his tone.

Rachel ignored him. After four days in the hospital, she wanted to be home. "You don't need to stop for me. The nurses quit waking me up every hour days ago." Wasn't that a scary thought? That they'd been checking her to make sure she wasn't slipping into a coma. The second day in the hospital, she'd been terrified to close her eyes, yet unable not to. Rachel had been incredibly relieved when that part of her care was over.

"I need to make sure you're cognizant. That's not something I want to risk while driving seventy miles an hour down the highway." He gripped the steering wheel tighter.

"I'm fine," she protested. "If I was going to die of my injuries, I would have done so by now."

"Don't even joke about that. We're going to have to

stop sometime for dinner and ice cream. I promised your boy that he could have some, but then he fell asleep."

*Your boy.* What would Cole say when he found out the truth about Matt? Rachel sighed. She knew letting Cole drive them home was a bad idea. "Look, I just want to get home as quickly as possible." She wanted to sleep in her own bed without tubes or monitors attached. "Drive on. We'll eat when we get home."

His laughter was harsh. "How about a reality check? The nurse said to go slow. You're not at full strength yet. You nearly died. I pulled you out of that plane wreck, remember?"

Although she didn't remember Cole pulling her out, Rachel didn't want her strobelike memories of the crash to return. She closed her eyes, hoping she'd go back to sleep, only to be deluged by images of branches battering the plane and the scream of metal against wood. With memories like these, how was she ever going to fly again?

"If you've got so much energy, when we stop for dinner you can fill me in on Missy's life after I left Eden, and how she died."

"No." Rachel's eyes snapped open.

"What?" He spared her a quick glance.

"Promise me you won't ask about Missy in front of the kids." Rachel fought to keep her voice down, wanting the kids to go on sleeping behind her.

"Why?"

Because Rachel had promised Pop that she wouldn't tarnish Missy's memory. Because Rachel had promised to lie for the sake of Jenna and Matt, so they wouldn't realize their mom had made some terrible mistakes—like sleeping with an old love before her wedding and leaving her kids for that same man. Rachel was finding her promises meant she had to lie to everyone.

Someone stirred in the back seat, yawning softly.

Rachel would protect those kids at any cost. "We can talk about this later. Could you just set aside your stubborn streak for a minute and promise me to wait?" Rachel whispered, reaching over and touching his arm. "Please."

"I'll wait," he said. "But I won't wait long."

"I HATE THIS," Rachel said as Cole walked up the front walk in the dark, hip touching hers and his large hands wrapped around her elbows.

The lack of intimacy in Cole's touch—a touch she'd longed for yet knew was forbidden—was sobering, as was the way he wouldn't give her an inch of breathing room. It had been the same in the restaurant where they'd eaten dinner. Rachel couldn't move without Cole directing her every step. She'd rather lie in a hospital bed than be unable to move without someone helping her.

"You'll get your legs back, soon," Cole said, misreading how awkward she felt.

Rachel was so incapacitated that even Pop had ambled up the porch stairs before her. She hated being so exhausted and too unsteady to stand by herself. Her limbs thrummed with the need to move on their own. And this was only her first day out of the hospital.

She'd been strong and independent five days ago, able to shoulder the responsibilities she carried. Now she felt as weak and hemmed in as a toddler in one of those wheeled walkers. Worse, it also reminded her of how powerless she'd felt as a little girl.

As if that wasn't enough, when Cole had excused himself to go to the restroom during dinner, Pop had reminded Rachel that this was one man who didn't need to know everything. Rachel would have found it easier to keep things from him if Cole wasn't practically connected to her at the hip.

"Easy, now." Cole moved at Rachel's pace—slowly—and with a maddening patience she'd never seen in him before. He'd had no tolerance for anything that wasn't fast as a teenager. Today, he'd put up with her crankiness, doled out her medicine and walked at the speed of a ninety-year-old. If he had his way, it would take weeks before she walked under her own power.

Weeks of Cole's hands on her body. Rachel sighed. Nirvana.

Weeks of Cole's questions. Of half-truths. Rachel gnawed on her lip. Purgatory.

In the blackness of a moonless night, something moved around the corner of the house. Rachel flinched in fear, and pain coursed through her rib cage.

*"Momma, don't leave me out here. I'll be good, I promise." Instead of the door opening wider, the bolt shot home.*

Rachel kept moving even though it was hard to breathe. She gritted her teeth as she made her way at top snail-speed through the front door.

Something snorted, and Rachel almost collapsed with relief.

"Is that a cat or a dog out there?" Cole asked, leaning out of the doorway to peer into the night.

"It's just Shadow." Rachel continued inching forward until Cole had no choice but to let her fall or follow her. "Shut the door, would you?" Trying to sound calm, Rachel couldn't stop herself from stabbing at the switch for the floodlights, turning them on and bathing the yard in light.

"I'll put Matt to bed," Pop called from the hallway.

Matt was already nowhere to be seen, having been half awake when he walked into the house and now most likely sprawled across his small bed.

Jenna sat on the couch, her arms folded over her chest. She tossed her head. "Where's *he* sleeping?"

"On the couch," Rachel said, at the same time that Cole said, "On the floor of Rachel's room."

Rachel's jaw dropped. Pop turned in the hallway, a disapproving frown on his face.

There was a time when sharing a room with Cole had topped Rachel's teen dream list, but not anymore. There was a reason she slept on the far side of the house, and she didn't want Cole or anyone else to know about it.

Cole returned their regard with equal disbelief. "Rach, you can't get up in the night and walk to the bathroom by yourself. Somebody needs to be near you at all times."

"Pop and I can help her." Jenna stuck her chin out. "We'll sleep in her room."

"I've never allowed a young pup to sleep with my

girls under my roof and I'm not about to start now." Pop staggered back into the living room, looking as unsteady on his feet as Rachel was on hers.

Cole urged Rachel forward, but she didn't budge. "I sleep alone," Rachel said. No way was he sleeping in the same room with her.

Instead of arguing with Rachel, Cole focused on Jenna and Pop. "Look, guys, neither one of you can support Rachel's weight. You don't want her to fall and hit her head again. Do you?"

Jenna tightened her arms about herself. "I won't let her fall." Noble, but not probable given her small frame.

The expression on Pop's face shifted, his allegiance transferring to Cole as he realized the truth in Cole's words.

Okay. Intellectually, Rachel understood that she had a mobility challenge. Emotionally, she rejected everything Cole suggested. She was a woman used to taking care of herself. And she valued her independence and privacy, particularly at night when her childhood fears returned.

"You two go on to bed. I'll be fine until morning," Rachel said. She'd figure out a way to convince Cole he wasn't sleeping within earshot once she was safely in bed.

"I'm glad you're finally seeing reason." Cole's breath brushed her ear, sending shafts of unwelcome heat through her body.

Despite her best intentions, Rachel swayed, bringing her closer to Cole. She was hard-pressed not to let out a yowl of frustration. Her body was letting her down after years of rigid control. Her veins fairly hummed with wanting, which was pointless, because Cole still saw her as his greatest love's little sister. "Can we argue about this after I sit down?"

"Fine. Are you still in the bedroom down at the end of the hall?"

"That's *my* room," Jenna said righteously.

"How do you know which room used to be Rachel's?" Pop demanded.

"Jenna. Pop," Rachel said, trying to calm her family. "It's all right. Go on to bed. I'm in the bedroom off the kitchen, now," Rachel said to Cole.

Jenna stalked off down the hallway. After a moment more of glaring at Cole, Pop did the same. Apparently, even if he thought Cole was making sense, he wasn't happy with it, or the sudden knowledge that Cole may indeed have spent time in his daughters' bedrooms all those years ago.

As one, Cole and Rachel stepped together, shuffling across the worn brown carpet and across the scuffed black-and-white linoleum. Rachel wished his touch didn't ignite images that were strictly forbidden. She had to remember Missy and all her mistakes where Cole was concerned.

"When did you move into this room?" he asked.

"When Missy moved back in." She'd thought it was best to give Missy a room close to Jenna.

Rachel groped for the light switch in her room, regretting that she'd splurged on a black sateen bedspread with a rich paisley pattern that seemed to say, *Take me now.* Thankfully, Cole made no comment.

When Rachel was settled on her bed, propped against the headboard on four pillows, Cole tilted his head as he regarded her. "Are you comfortable?"

"Yes," she lied, as irritable as a wet cat. She was aroused and there wasn't a damn thing she was going to do about it.

Cole turned on the television and handed her the remote. "Will you be all right if I bring in my things?"

"Of course." Good. He'd finally tuned in to her broadcast that she didn't want him here. The sooner he left her alone, the better. "If you put them in the hall closet, they'll be within easy reach of the couch."

He raised an eyebrow before turning on his heel and giving her some much-needed space. Shamelessly Rachel watched Cole as he left the room, noting the play of muscles beneath his T-shirt. Cole may have left Texas for Idaho and traded his saddle for a chainsaw and shovel, but he was a cowboy through and through, from his slightly bowed legs to his worn jeans and cowboy boots.

Rachel closed her eyes and shifted on the bed, trying to get more comfortable, trying to cool off. But she only slid down a bit on the satiny comforter, which did nothing for her too-optimistic libido. Rachel was not going to touch Cole anymore. She would move around on her own if she had to crawl.

"I'm going to take a shower. Do you need anything? Bathroom break? Water? Pain pill?" Cole's voice cut into her consciousness.

"I'm fine." She didn't have to touch Cole for her body to react to him. At least he'd be showering on the other side of the house. The last thing she needed was to hear water sluicing over Cole's body.

A door shut close by. Rachel's eyes flew open. He'd gone into her bathroom!

Egads, he was going to be naked with only a thin door separating them?

Rachel groaned. She squeezed her eyes shut. *Get a grip.* He was so clearly not the person she'd adored all those years ago. Sometimes she felt as if she barely knew him. And other times…

Other times, Rachel yearned for Cole more than the boy she'd had such a crush on.

It was only when the shower had been running for a few minutes that Rachel realized Cole had put his bag on the floor by her closet. The only way she was going to sleep in something other than the clothes she was wearing was if she changed now while Cole was busy elsewhere.

Besides, her mind kept drifting to thoughts of Cole in the shower.

How depraved was that?

Rachel inched herself to an upright position. More like deprived. It had been years since she'd been with a man. Relationships were too complicated when she had so many responsibilities. Matt, Jenna and Pop always had to come first.

Rachel's dresser was a few feet from the end of the bed. Not that far to traverse. Doable, she was sure.

Easing her feet off the edge of the bed, Rachel held her breath until the worst of the dizziness subsided. She was going to prove she could do something on her own.

She pushed her torso away from the pillows and tried to scoot her bottom toward the foot of the bed. But her head lolled heavily to one side and the room started to spin.

Rachel willed herself to hold it together, digging her fingers into the paisley-print coverlet, letting her eyes be captured by the blending of patterns. The paisley went round and round with no end.

Mistake. That made her even dizzier.

Somehow, she managed to scoot to the end of the bed without falling off, but she was exhausted. Unfortunately, her goal was still a few feet away and out of reach.

The shower fell silent. Cole would be out soon, telling her that she shouldn't be trying to move on her own, telling her exactly what to do and when.

The memory of Rachel's mother's commanding voice clawed its way to the edge of her consciousness, as chilling as it was vivid.

*"Move from that spot and you'll regret it." Rachel was eight, standing as she had been for hours, soiled and exhausted, but afraid to move as the bedroom door closed, leaving her in darkness.*

Defenseless. Rachel moaned. She would not be defenseless. It was now or never.

Rachel took a deep breath and tried to stand. But when she set her foot down, it didn't meet the ground. And then the pain was so intense that Rachel couldn't see anything but black.

"WHAT THE HELL?" Cole scooped Rachel up off the floor, rousing her out of the darkness. If only his solid embrace could soothe her humiliation. Instead it increased, especially when he added, "I leave you for ten minutes, and what do you do? Try to get up. Do you want to explain that to me?"

"I wanted my pajamas." Rachel couldn't keep the defeat out of her voice as he gently placed her back on the bed. Her life had never been easy, but to be so helpless…

"You can barely lift a glass of water by yourself. What made you think you could walk?"

Rachel blinked back tears.

His voice softened. "I would have brought you your pj's."

"Yes, but I can't get into them myself," Rachel said miserably. "How am I going to slip out of my pants and unhook my bra? There's no nurse here to help me this time. Do you see a nurse? Or another woman? Anywhere?" Her voice had risen to a hysterical crescendo. Unshed tears made it hard to see. It had been years since anything or anyone had made her feel so weak and helpless.

When she dared to look at Cole, who stood silently above her, wearing a pair of worn, baggy sweats and a wrinkled T-shirt, a tear did fall over her cheek. She wiped it away, not wanting his pity, and that was all she saw in his expression.

"We'll get your damn pajamas on," he said gruffly, moving to the dresser and opening drawers until he found the one with her underthings.

Rachel could feel her cheeks burning as he touched panties and bras, finally pulling out a silky leopard-print shift that she'd won at someone's bachelorette shower. Rachel dressed in jeans and boots every day and slept in boxers and a T-shirt—never anything as provocative as that. She should have told him what to look for. She should have stopped him, but she didn't realize that having him touch her things would feel so intimate.

"Somehow we'll—" As the nightgown slipped between his fingers and dropped to the floor, Cole gave up on whatever he'd been about to say. He frowned at the wall behind Rachel, then his gaze dropped to her, taking inventory in a detached manner.

Rachel held her breath. Was he really going to undress her?

"Let me see if Jenna's still awake."

No. He wasn't. Rachel sank back into the pillows, filled with both relief and disappointment.

But when Cole returned, Rachel knew her niece was asleep. "How about a compromise? We'll turn off the lights—"

*"Off?"* she said in a strangled voice, heart pounding.

"—and I'll tug off those track pants and unhook…if you need anything…you know…undone. You can sleep in your T-shirt and—" Cole couldn't say panties. "Can't you? If the lights are off?"

"I…I… The bathroom light will have to be on." Rachel was still more unnerved by the possibility of total darkness than by the fact that he'd be undressing her.

Cole regarded Rachel as if she were crazy. At times like these she thought she might be.

"I insist on the light being on. You can close the bathroom door almost all the way." Just a sliver of light. That was all she was asking for.

LYING ON TOP of his sleeping bag, hands propped behind his head, Cole stared up at the faux stars in the speckled ceiling above him. It was after midnight, yet the glow from the bathroom was keeping him awake. Cole had to tell himself the light was keeping him awake or he'd go back to thinking about undressing Rachel. And thinking about touching her warm bare skin made him hard. He hadn't bargained on his caregiver role being so intimate or him responding to Rachel as if she was only a desirable woman. Being turned on by Rachel felt wrong when he considered how many nights he'd dreamt about her sister.

With effort, Cole pulled out a memory of Missy on the Quinlan porch one sultry summer evening after high-school graduation. She'd worn cutoffs and a white lacy blouse with thin straps that showed an enticing bit of cleavage. Her blond hair flowed over her shoulders, and he couldn't wait to touch her.

*"Come out with me," he'd said, smiling as he reached for Missy. She'd been distant since he'd told her he was going to train to be a Hot Shot, although she'd kept telling Cole that nothing was wrong.*

*"I can't. Pop's not home yet." Missy stepped back. "You know Rachel gets scared when she's alone."*

*"We can take the little hellion. You know she'll behave for me." He liked Rachel. A couple of quarters for the video games at the pizza parlor and he and*

*Missy would have a dark booth to themselves for a while. Long enough for Cole to steal a kiss or two, perhaps slide his hand over that smooth skin. They never fought when they touched or kissed or had sex. Although they hadn't really fought at all until the past few months.*

*"Sometimes I think you like Rachel more than me." Missy was backed against the door now, no longer smiling. "It doesn't matter, though. I don't have permission to go anywhere."*

*"Neither do I, but I came over anyway." He rarely asked his parents for permission. Cole doubted they cared where he was most of the time. Just this morning, they'd told him they were selling the house and moving to Idaho. One more place where no one would know of their heartache over losing Sally.*

Staring at Rachel's ceiling, Cole frowned. Why couldn't he have recalled one of their more tender moments? It was as if his best memories of Missy were fading.

Rachel thrashed her legs, the sound of bare skin against silken sheets out-of-bounds erotic. Then she moaned in her sleep, as she'd been doing the past twenty minutes or so, her sounds solidifying his problem.

Cole clamped his eyes tightly together. He should have gone on that blind date Spider had wanted him to go on months ago. A sure thing, his friend had said. Holy moly. He was feeling his abstinence now.

If Rachel would just settle down, he'd be able to sleep.

But then Rachel whimpered as if in pain, sending Cole bolt upright. "Are you okay, Rach?"

She stilled. Cole assumed she'd had a bad dream, probably about the crash. His words seemed to calm her. Cole sank back onto the floor. Maybe now he'd get some sleep.

"Don't," Rachel yelped, then she made a small mewling sound, like a weak kitten. If this was a nightmare, she must want it to end.

"Rachel, wake up." Cole sat up again.

"Don't leave me here, Momma," she wailed in a fear-filled voice.

"Rachel, wake up." Cole held her hand. It was clammy. "Rach."

Her eyes snapped open on a gasp, searching the room, particularly the shadows. "What happened? Where are we?"

"You're home." Cole moved his thumb over her wrist, feeling her pounding pulse. "You were having a bad dream. You called for your mom to help you."

With a wavering hand, Rachel wiped at her forehead. "I wasn't calling for her to help me. I was begging her to stop." Rachel looked at him with wide eyes as if realizing she'd said too much.

And then she said nothing at all.

"Rach?" Cole had moved to Eden in the eighth grade. Missy and Rachel's mother hadn't been around. There were rumors that she'd run off or that she'd been taken to a mental hospital. Missy had explained they didn't see their mother, and Cole, who knew about disappointing families, had left things there. Now Cole seemed to remember the Baker brothers teasing Rachel about her mom behind Marney's store.

"What happened to your mother, Rachel?"

She pressed the heels of her hands into her eyes. "I don't want to talk about her."

"Did she do something to you? Did she do something to Missy? Is that why Missy never left home?" When Rachel didn't answer, Cole gripped her shoulders. "Rachel, whatever happened was a long time ago." He was seeing these deep scars for the first time. If Rachel was so wounded, what had he overlooked in Missy?

"I don't want to talk about her," Rachel repeated in a louder voice.

Cole lowered his. "Not even with me?"

"Especially not with you." Rachel made a small movement with her shoulders, probably as much as she could do without getting dizzy.

He slid his palms down her arms, coming to rest with a soft touch on her hands. Rachel shivered, but didn't yank her hands back. She wanted to tell him, he was sure of it. Otherwise, she would have pulled away.

Cole turned on the bedside lamp, then held her hands again. "See? There's nothing here. No ghosts. Just you and me." Cole looked at her steadily, certain that learning the truth about Mrs. Quinlan would show him all he needed to know about Missy. "What was your mother like?"

Frowning slightly, Rachel retreated into silence, staring past Cole at nothing, yet revealing her pain. Her eyelids dipped slowly, as if she were fighting exhaustion.

Seeing that, Cole forgot about his own questions, only wanting to make Rachel feel safe. "It's okay, Rachel. I'm here. No one can hurt you."

Rachel's eyes drifted shut and her breathing slowed.

A few minutes later he cradled Rachel in his arms with every light on in the room. Rachel snuggled against him, as if they had no secrets between them, as if she needed his strength to keep the nightmares at bay.

As if they were lovers.

Cole stared up at the ceiling again, trying to bury the thought.

What had Mrs. Quinlan done to Rachel? Why hadn't he known about it before? Why hadn't Rachel or Missy told him? And how was he going to uncover the truth about their past, now?

As a kid Rachel had freaked out if she had to stay in the ranch house alone. So, he and Missy had never left her when Mr. Quinlan was gone. In his senior year in high school, Rachel had come to Cole's house after school every day. Once away from the ranch, Rachel was up for anything, sometimes gutsier—all right, he was old enough to admit it now, more foolish—than Cole or his friends.

With a sigh Cole acknowledged he wouldn't get much sleep that night. Not with the enigma that was Rachel resting peacefully in his arms.

## *CHAPTER FIVE*

WHILE RACHEL REGAINED her strength and slept more peacefully, and with the sunlight streaming through a crack between the curtains, Cole stretched out the kinks he'd acquired from dozing upright with Rachel using him as a pillow.

Jenna poked her head into the room, noticed Rachel was still asleep and backed away without a glance at Cole. Unlike Sally, Jenna seemed painfully shy, which was okay considering it hurt Cole to look at Jenna for long.

"That stretching stuff is for city-boy sissies." Mr. Quinlan shuffled through the door, forcing Jenna in front of him. He wore wrinkled blue jeans and a well-worn checked shirt. "How's my girl?"

"Sleeping." Cole lowered his voice, somehow succeeding in keeping the irritation out of it. He didn't want to come across as a superhero to his daughter, but he didn't want to be labeled a sissy, either. "She had a rough night with a lot of nightmares." Cole made sure he met Mr. Quinlan's odd, sideways gaze.

"That'll happen after accidents." Mr. Quinlan seemed unconcerned, although he gripped the door frame as if he needed the balance. "Where did you sleep?"

The old man's cavalier attitude about Rachel's nightmares rankled. But Cole wouldn't confront him with an audience.

"On the floor." Cole gestured to the rolled sleeping bag in the corner. No sense admitting he'd spent many sleepless hours in Rachel's bed holding her. The old guy already thought he was pond scum.

Stumbling because his eyes were still half closed, Rachel's little boy staggered into the room and climbed into the bed next to Rachel. "Mommy, what's for breakfast?" he mumbled, snuggling up to Rachel. With his face so near Rachel's, Cole could easily see the resemblance of son to mother—the same slanted eyes and dark coloring.

Cole hadn't yet had a chance to ask Rachel about Matt's father, but he could admit to himself that he was relieved Matt was Rachel's. Sure, he'd been the one to leave Missy, but that didn't mean he hadn't felt regret at the thought of Missy creating a family with someone else.

Everyone in the room had fallen silent while Cole's mind wandered. It was as if they were all expecting something. Cole knew there was no way Rachel was going to make breakfast. But he wasn't sure it was his place to tell them that.

"It's cereal again," Rachel's father said, as if disappointed. Mr. Quinlan turned around in the tight space, holding on to the wall for support.

"Don't want cereal," Matt whined with his eyes still closed.

"Me, neither." Jenna stared at a soundly sleeping Rachel, and sighed wistfully, as if a hearty meal was a luxury, not a necessity. With Jenna's skinny arms and legs, she looked as if she could use a big breakfast.

His kid deserved as much food as she wanted, damn it.

Surprised at the strength of his reaction, Cole couldn't help but scowl. He was here to resolve his past with Missy and take care of Rachel, not play nanny to the rest of the family.

Still, Cole couldn't resist making an offer. "I'll make you guys a deal. You two kids watch Rachel and I'll cook breakfast."

Matt didn't open his eyes, but he smiled, which was more than Jenna did.

"Sure." Without looking at Cole, Jenna climbed onto the opposite side of the bed from Matt and snagged the remote from the bedside table.

"You makin' coffee, too?" Mr. Quinlan asked when Cole entered the kitchen. Rachel's dad was slumped over the kitchen table, looking too worn-out for first thing in the morning, which would have hooked Cole's sympathy, except that the old man frowned at him and added, "That is, if you know how to make coffee."

Cole's steps slowed. Nursemaid. Chauffeur. Cook. What was next? Housekeeper? Swallowing his pride—because after all, it seemed his daughter needed a good meal or two—Cole ignored the old man's jibe. Instead, he started taking stock of the pantry, ignoring the worn and cracked linoleum and the cobweb-draped kitchen windows. Rachel meant well. Cole knew she did, but from the state of the house, she must be gone as much as Cole was.

The refrigerator held outdated milk, a variety of condiments, chocolate syrup, shriveled grapes, some block cheese and little else. Those kids couldn't have had cereal if they'd wanted to, although there was vanilla ice cream in the fridge.

Cole discovered a can of SPAM, instant mashed potatoes and condensed soup in a cupboard. Coffee beans that had lost their aroma sat in another, along with a grinder and an electric coffeepot. The sugar in the sugar bowl was hard as a rock, as was the powdered creamer.

Grim, but not a total loss. Given the rundown condition of the old ranch house and the frailty of the old man left in charge while Rachel worked, Cole had expected worse.

"Is this your summer home?" Cole attempted to joke with Mr. Quinlan. "Because there's next to nothing in this kitchen."

"I haven't been to the store in a few days," the old man grumbled. He must have known Cole had guessed the truth—that there was nothing fit to be eaten in the house—because he added, "It's tough raising kids alone. But you wouldn't know anything about that, would you?"

"No." Cole shot Mr. Quinlan a dirty look over his shoulder. "But someone chose to do it alone, didn't she?"

"WHAT'S THIS?" Matt turned up his nose at the plate Cole put in front of him.

The big man didn't look happy to have the food he'd

made questioned. Ready for anger, Jenna sank into her seat at the kitchen table, trying to make sure Cole wouldn't notice her.

"Cheesy potato pancakes and fried SPAM." Cole didn't yell, but his voice was loud.

Surprised that Cole didn't blow up, Jenna poked her pancakes with a fork. At first, she'd thought they were regular pancakes. They looked like regular pancakes, but they had little bits of cheese in them the size of chocolate chips.

*Yuck.* She didn't want to eat these things. Jenna didn't trust strangers, especially big men who made her feel too small. For all she knew, Cole could have poisoned them. "Do we have to eat it, Pop?"

Pop had been looking into his coffee cup and may not have heard Jenna. "Why's my coffee such a funny color?"

"It's mocha latte. People pay a lot of money for flavored coffee like that. Why not give it a try?" Cole tried to smile, but he didn't look like he wanted to. "I made the kids hot chocolate."

Jenna liked hot chocolate. She peeked into her mug, but it wasn't the hot chocolate Aunt Rachel made. There was a big lump of something white on top and it wasn't whipped cream.

When no one ate or drank, Cole shrugged and said, "Look, I spent last winter working as a short order cook in Silver Bend. I know how to make do with what I have. Usually people like it."

Matt stared at Jenna. Jenna stared at Pop. Pop made a funny face. No one touched anything.

But Cole didn't give up. "You like potatoes, don't you? And cheese?"

Jenna did like those things. And she was tired of there being nothing to eat around here. She was hungry. Her stomach growled just loudly enough that everyone could hear it. Jenna snuck a quick look at Cole.

Cole wrinkled his nose and looked at the wall behind Jenna as if he didn't like her but didn't want to say so. "And you like hot chocolate, don't you, Jenna? That's what's in the mug with the ice cream."

"Ice cream for breakfast?" Matt grabbed his mug greedily and took a sip, leaving a brown mustache on his upper lip. "Good."

The good news was, Matt didn't drop dead. He picked up a pancake like it was a cookie and took a bite. "Mmmm."

Pop drank a little of his coffee, looked at Aunt Rachel's closed bedroom door, then set down the cup. "It'll do."

"The next time we sit down at the table to eat, everyone needs to wash their hands and brush their hair," Cole said, looking at Matt's spiky bed head and then at Jenna's hair.

Why was he picking on her? Jenna wanted to cry. She should just get up from the table and go riding.

Only, Jenna's stomach didn't want to. It growled again.

Knowing Cole was watching her, Jenna used her fork and her finger to tear off a small bite of the pancake, then put it on the tip of her tongue, ready to spit it out if it tasted yucky.

But it didn't taste yucky. It tasted pretty good. Like crusty mashed potatoes and cheese.

Making sure not to look at Cole, Jenna began eating. Already she had a plan. She would avoid the big man and show up for meals. Aunt Rachel would get better, he'd leave, and she'd never see him again.

DRIVING DOWN Main Street later that Saturday morning, Cole was assaulted by memories. The narrow street was still lined with diagonal parking spaces filled with beat-up trucks like Cole used to drive. His bare-bones, two-year-old Chevy truck was high class by comparison. The lumberyard was at the end of the street by the railroad tracks, just down from the Shady Lady Motel, which was looking a lot shadier than when he'd last stayed there with Missy.

Cole drove past two kids out in front of the ice cream place laughing and eating cones. In the summer, he and Rachel had done the same thing while waiting for Missy to have her hair cut at the beauty parlor next door. Cole wondered if Rachel could afford to treat Jenna to the ice cream parlor. It certainly didn't seem like it.

Cole pulled into Marney's small parking lot. He selected a cart and began shopping the produce section. The old store still seemed to be part grocery store, part drugstore and part hardware store. He'd spent more than one summer stocking shelves and bagging purchases at Marney's. It had been one of the few places in town where he'd felt welcome, since the small town hadn't exactly opened its arms and said come, be one of us, a gesture Cole would have spurned back then, anyway.

"Hudson?" A man with a receding hairline and a gut from too many beers leaned against a huge display of beer cases. "Ain't this a kick in the head."

An image of a younger face bearing the same slick smile clicked in Cole's head. Missy's husband hadn't aged well. "Lyle Whitehall?"

"Yeah." Lyle snorted the way others laughed. "When did you get back in town?"

"Last night. I gave Rachel Quinlan's family a ride home from Montana."

"Yeah? I heard she was in a crash. She survived, huh?" Lyle showed no concern for his former sister-in-law, making Cole wonder if Lyle had grieved for Missy.

"Things look pretty good." At least Rachel had slept most of the morning without nightmares. The fact that she wasn't in bed alone—flanked by either Cole or the kids—seemed to help her rest more peacefully.

"Things always look good with Rachel. She's hot. Those long, thin legs topped with that great rack..." Shaking his head, Lyle seemed to retreat into his imagination.

Cole kept silent. It was coming back to him now. Lyle Whitehall was, and had always been, an asshole. Setting fire to other kids' gym lockers. Slipping a hand under cheerleaders' skirts. Spinning doughnuts on the school lawn. And his daddy had always bailed him out. Only, now Lyle didn't look like the wealthy mayor's son. Dressed in a torn T-shirt and faded blue jeans, he looked as if he'd fallen on hard times.

"We expected you back for Missy's funeral." Lyle's expression narrowed as he waited for Cole's response, as if gauging his reaction would tell him something.

Like the fact that Cole knew Jenna was his.

Cole wouldn't give him the satisfaction. With effort, he kept his expression neutral. "I guess the Quinlans couldn't find me." More likely, the Quinlans hadn't wanted to try. They didn't seem to recognize the fact they'd had a moral obligation to tell Cole he was a father.

Cole pushed the cart forward. He'd had enough of Lyle Whitehall for one day.

But Lyle hadn't had enough of Cole. "Lot of changes in Eden since you left." He picked up a twelve-pack and followed Cole. "People *married,* had *kids.* Some even had the misfortune to get divorced."

That made Cole wonder if Lyle and Missy had divorced before she'd died, but he sure as hell wasn't going to ask Lyle. He felt uncomfortable enough to say, "Yeah, I hadn't realized Rachel had been married or had had a kid." Poor Rachel. Briefly, Cole wondered why her marriage had failed. "That Matt is a pistol."

"Rachel never married. Is that what she told you? That some other guy's the kid's father?" Lyle's smirk just begged to be wiped off with a fist. "Well, that's plain wrong. Matt's my boy."

"WE DON'T EAT THIS green stuff," Matt said later as he helped Cole carry in the groceries. The little boy had come out on his own with a sunny smile when he heard the truck pull up. If Matt was Lyle's kid, he was nothing like his father.

Jenna was inside with Rachel, and Mr. Quinlan wasn't in any shape to carry much more than a loaf of bread. Cole didn't really want Matt's help, not after the bomb Lyle had dropped on him, not after realizing he'd been duped again by the Quinlans.

"Is that corn? We never eat that." Matt slowed as he peered into the bags. "I don't know what this is, but we don't eat that, either."

"Just get the groceries into the kitchen," Cole urged, juggling too many bags.

Why had Rachel let him think Matt was hers? Cole felt betrayed. Especially since she let the boy call her Mommy. With his dark coloring, so like Rachel's, Cole had made assumptions. He'd forgotten that Missy's eyes, though blue, had slanted, too.

"Did you buy potato chips? Or Ding Dongs?"

"I bought food to help your aunt Rachel get better." He was irritable because of his encounter with Lyle and the feeling that Rachel had duped him.

"She's not my aunt. She's my mom," Matt corrected easily, as if he was used to doing so.

That left Cole speechless. Lyle and Rachel? No. It couldn't be.

"Why are you lookin' at me, mister?" Matt regarded Cole with an unblinking stare.

Not sure what to say, or what the real story was, Cole mumbled an apology and began putting groceries away.

"I'm gonna call Marney and have her deliver some chips next time, okay?" Matt reached for the kitchen phone.

"Deliver? Marney delivers?" That would explain how Mr. Quinlan, who could barely see, kept some food in the house, and how Matt kept himself stocked with unhealthy snacks.

"She only delivers to people who don't drive so good, like Pop." Matt started to punch phone buttons.

Cole plucked the cordless phone out of Matt's hand. "Let's hold off on that order. The last thing you need is more junk food."

In a heartbeat, Matt was blinking back huge tears. "But…but…I'm hungry," he whined loudly.

The kid looked and sounded so pitiful that he almost had Cole dialing for the grocery store himself just to make sure Matt wouldn't starve…until Cole saw the boy start to smile.

Matt was a first-class manipulator. If Rachel wasn't careful, Matt would turn out just as spoiled and sour as Lyle was. Just as he opened his mouth to put Matt in his place, Rachel beat him to the punch.

"Matt, don't try to put one over on Cole," Rachel called from her bedroom in a weak voice that still managed to convey her amusement. "He's too smart to fall for that."

"But, Mommy," Matt began. "I wasn't doing anything. He was just gonna—"

"I said, stop it," Rachel called, weaker this time.

Cole shouldn't have worried about Matt. Even with her injuries, Rachel knew what her nephew needed.

Matt wasn't giving up. "But—"

"Hey, I'll make you a deal." There was no way Cole was letting that kid upset Rachel. "You clean up that room of yours and we'll make cookies together." Oatmeal and raisin. Those had to be healthier than store-bought ones.

The tears disappeared. Matt grinned. "Deal!" Then he ran into Rachel's room in that funny gait of his, causing Cole to smile. "Guess what? We're making cookies, Mommy."

*Mommy.* Was Rachel Matt's mother? Or was she just bighearted and brave enough to take on her sister's children?

"Someday, Matt, that grin of yours is going to get you in trouble," Rachel said.

She didn't know how true her words were. Despite his disappointment in Rachel's lies, Cole was smiling as he finished putting away the groceries. Rachel was something else. She was the only parent these kids had and was doing the best she could, always giving them attention, despite how she felt.

Was that what a good parent did? Could he do it? He'd barely spoken to Jenna. But then again, he'd been trying to observe his daughter rather than talk to her or do something with her.

CUPBOARD DOORS OPENED and closed with just enough care to tickle Rachel's parenting radar.

Someone was in the kitchen searching for something to eat.

With effort, Rachel pried her eyes open and squinted at her bedside clock. Late afternoon. Not the best time for a meal-spoiling snack.

Another cupboard door closed.

Despite what seemed like G-forces pulling her eyelids down, Rachel filled her lungs with air to challenge whoever was out there.

"What are you doing?" Cole's voice was tinged with just the right amount of annoyance to bring the sneaking snacker in line.

No one answered, which told Rachel that someone shrugged—the universal sign for guilt. No telling whether it was Jenna or Matt out there.

"I'm going to start dinner. No more snacks." Cole was firm. "What is this potato doing on the counter?"

Cole had parent potential. Now, there was an unpleasant surprise. What if he used his charm to win over Jenna and then left for another eleven years? Despite her worry, the pressure of the G-forces numbed Rachel's brain and drew down her eyelids like a window shade.

"I was going to microwave one for dinner," Jenna said, sounding startled and meek.

Rachel's eyelids snapped open so quickly that her ears rang. Damn Lyle for breaking Jenna's confidence.

"Only one? Didn't you think the rest of the family would be hungry?" Cole teased.

"Sorry." Jenna's apology was filled with hurt at what should have been taken as simple banter.

Instinct kicked in and Rachel was able to force her eyes open. Something similar to a growl rumbled up her throat as she readied to defend Jenna, simply because her niece wouldn't defend herself.

"Look, I'm making lasagna for dinner and I could use some help. We'll have potatoes tomorrow," Cole offered.

Silence.

*Come on, sweetheart. Say yes.* Don't let five years of living with Lyle rule the rest of your life.

Rachel had struggled to rebuild Jenna's confidence. Jenna's horse, Shadow, was a big part of Rachel's plan, but even after five years, Jenna cowered when any man other than Pop spoke to her.

"Maybe tomorrow," Jenna finally said in a soft voice. "I don't know how to make lasagna."

Rachel swore under her breath. With the door nearly closed, Rachel couldn't see Jenna, but she could imagine her niece slouching in an attempt to appear as small as she could as she backed away from Cole.

"Are you sure? It's one of the first meals I learned to make. You get to grate cheese and boil noodles and get really messy," Cole said, and Rachel wanted to kiss him for trying. "Cooking is ten times more fun than Play-Doh, and you get to eat it when you're done."

Jenna giggled, giving in to Cole's charm. "What do you want me to do?"

"Well, first we have to lay out all our ingredients on the counter…"

Tears pressed at the back of Rachel's eyes, blurring her vision and making her want to hug someone tight—maybe Cole, maybe Jenna, maybe both. The Cole in her kitchen had the same big heart as the boy she'd ridden horses with as a girl. Where had the hard man she'd encountered at the hospital gone? Rachel didn't hear much else Cole said, as the G-forces reasserted control and pressed her back into a deep sleep.

"DON'T LEAN YOUR face over the pot like that, Jenna. If it's boiling, you'll burn your face." Cole didn't look up from cutting tomatoes.

Jenna stepped away from the stove. "How am I supposed to know when the water is ready if I don't look?"

"You can see the bubbles burst on top of the water." Cole cut the tomatoes into small squares. "Can you slice these while I brown the hamburger meat?"

"Sure." Jenna shrugged and stepped over to the cutting board. Cooking was kind of fun.

"The oven doesn't seem to be getting hot." Cole leaned over and opened up the oven door, stuck his hand inside, then stood and turned the knobs on the top of the oven around and back as if he was angry. "What the…?"

"The oven doesn't work," Jenna said. She hadn't even started cutting. She couldn't, not when she knew Cole was upset. Her dad used to throw things and punch walls when he got mad, and it had scared her.

"How do you cook anything?" His voice had gone from regular to louder.

"Pop fries it or microwaves it." Jenna's voice got very quiet.

"How am I supposed to feed you? This is great. Just great." Cole reached into the oven and grabbed something long and skinny beneath the lowest rack.

Something sparked, and Cole fell to the floor with a loud thud. Then he jumped up, shook his hand and starting saying bad words.

Dropping the knife, Jenna inched toward the mudroom and escape.

"What's wrong?" He stopped cussing and looked at her strangely.

But Jenna didn't answer. She was headed out the back door.

COLE WAS STILL in a bad mood thirty minutes later when he wove his way through a maze of refrigerators displayed in Eden's small-appliance repair shop. He carried the faulty heating element that had shocked the hell out of him. His hand still tingled.

"Got to be quick. I'm about to close." A paunchy, graying man wiped his hands on a blue rag as he came out of the back room.

"I need one of these." Cole handed the oven's heating element to him.

The repairman read the numbers off the end aloud. "Not a problem. I have a couple of these in the back."

While he went to get the part, Cole leaned against the counter. He really had to watch himself in front of Jenna. He must have startled her with that string of curses. But why had she run?

The bell over the front door clanged. "Hey, Benny, I need some cash. I've got a stove and a refrigerator in the back of my truck. Are you buying?"

Cole recognized the voice just as Lyle walked into view. He stopped when he saw Cole.

"You found gold at some yard sales, huh?" Benny called from the back. "All right. I'll take a look."

"And here I thought you'd go into the banking business," Cole couldn't resist saying. Instead, the man Missy had chosen to marry seemed to be a scavenger.

The scowl on Lyle's face was meant to intimidate, but even though Lyle was a couple of inches taller than Cole, Cole's muscle could take Lyle's flab any day.

While Cole paid for the heating element, Lyle slouched near an old dishwasher.

"Do you think you're better than me because you got out of here?" Lyle finally found his voice, and it was dripping venom.

"I never thought I was better than you, Lyle." He'd always considered Lyle the luckier of the two of them. Cole walked past the bitter man, pausing at the door to add, "Until today."

"HAVE A GOOD DAY at school." Cole waved to the kids as they walked to the bus stop in the crisp October morning air. He closed the front door, feeling inanely like an underappreciated house frau.

This was day three of his stay at the Quinlan ranch. The third day of puttering around a house that hadn't changed in fifteen years. Except to get worse. Rachel's bedroom looked more like a cheap motel than a woman's sanctuary. There were no knickknacks or vases or lace. The only thing in the room that expressed Rachel's style was the sexy bedspread and a few simple, forgettable framed photos of flowers. But even that could be packed up with her clothes and moved out in a matter of minutes. Did Rachel want to leave home or had she spent more time in her airplane and hotels than here?

Three days, and he didn't know much more about Rachel, Missy or his daughter than the day he'd arrived, because Rachel had been hibernating, and Jenna had avoided him since he'd asked her to help make dinner Saturday night. From what Cole could tell, Jenna was nothing like Sally. Jenna was timid and shy, often disappearing for hours at a time, making Cole wonder what she was doing and if she was safe.

Sally had been outgoing and had never met anyone who wasn't a friend. And she'd been impossible to get rid of on Saturday afternoons.

Over the past few days, Cole had tried to come up with a way to tell his mom that she was a grandmother. He'd almost tricked himself into believing her reaction would be positive. But no matter how hard he tried, he couldn't get past the sorrow he expected to resurrect in his parents, and the disappointment Nan Hudson would continue to have in her remaining child. So he wondered…did he have to tell her? They'd lost their home in Texas and sweet little Sally in a fire nearly twenty years ago, and the Hudson family had yet to rebuild. In truth, Cole had spoken more to his daughter in the past few days than he had to his mother in the past few years.

Circumstances had dictated he do so. The Quinlan family was a mess—unkempt house and kids. Heck, even Mr. Quinlan needed a little extra care.

Stepping into Rachel's role as guardian, Cole had demanded the kids find something clean to wear to school, something that didn't have wrinkles, and that Jenna's hair be brushed. From what he could tell it was a perpetual rat's nest. How on earth the girl got to be ten without the need for girlie frou-frous was beyond

Cole. If he could braid hair, he would have braided Jenna's. As it was, he'd settled for a ponytail at the base of her neck when he'd gotten all the tangles out, which he'd done only moments before the bus had arrived.

Now that the kids were off to school, his morning wasn't free. Cole had dishes to do, a roast to prepare for dinner and laundry to sort.

Except he didn't want to do any of it. He wanted to sit down at Rachel's side and will her out of her deep sleep. He wanted her to open her eyes and sit up and talk to him.

Once Rachel was able to stay awake for more than a few minutes, Cole wanted answers.

Out of habit, Cole went to check on Rachel, hopeful that she might have woken up. But she was still drifting in dreamland. And to further add to his bad mood, Mr. Quinlan, who seemed intent on making Cole feel as unwelcome as possible, was pouring himself a cup of coffee in the kitchen when Cole came out of Rachel's bedroom.

"Morning." Cole poured himself a cup, too, added the requisite dose of sugar and milk, then wiped down the counter. He didn't expect a response from the older man, and he wasn't disappointed. It was clear the two men weren't going to be best buddies.

When Cole turned around, he was surprised to see Mr. Quinlan hadn't retreated to his room. Instead, he'd sat down at the table with a couple of prescription bottles and a weekly pill organizer. Mr. Quinlan spilled out an odd assortment of colors, sizes and textures of pills on the table, cocked his head to one side and leaned down to peer at them, his nose inches away from the tabletop.

Cole had visions of Mr. Quinlan taking the wrong pills in the wrong combination and overdosing. Wouldn't *that* just complete the happy mood in the Quinlan household? The place was already so like his own had been years ago that it was hard for Cole to stay.

With a sigh, Cole offered, "Do you need some help?"

"Of course not." Mr. Quinlan was nothing if not predictable. Cole had met a lot of old-school men just like him. Their motto? I don't need help. I'm a man. That must be where Rachel got her independent streak, too.

Leaning against the counter and drinking his coffee, Cole watched the old guy roll the pills around the table, study them and basically look lost. He closed his eyes for a moment, reminding himself that however the old guy wanted to take care of himself was none of Cole's business. But when he opened his eyes and Mr. Quinlan had yet to figure out his pill assortment, Cole caved.

"It looks like you could use a good pair of eyes to sort those suckers out." Cole set his coffee cup out of the way on the far side of the table as he sat down next to Mr. Quinlan.

"I told you I don't need your help." But Mr. Quinlan wiped at his mouth the way some people did when they were trying to take a stab at a decision.

"I've got nothing better to do." Except the man's laundry and any other chores the old man had been unable to do while Rachel had been away. "I'm just going to sort these by size and color." Without waiting for permission, Cole quietly set about his task.

When he was done, Cole asked, "Which ones are you supposed to take in the morning?"

Mr. Quinlan rattled off the names of three different medicines. Cole found two that were stamped with the name. It took them a bit of debate to find the third.

"Did you get these filled at the drugstore in town?"

"Yes. There's a pretty young pharmacist who smiles every time she sees me coming, because she knows I'll be emptying my wallet." Mr. Quinlan actually laughed.

"Do you have a heart condition?" Cole guessed, eyeing the man's sickly skin color and wondering if Mr. Quinlan needed to go see his doctor.

"My heart. My blood pressure. Macular degeneration is stealing my eyesight. You name it and it's in need of something."

Cole glanced at his watch. "Why don't we give the pharmacy a call a bit later and ask them to identify all the pills you're taking?"

Mr. Quinlan drew back. "I know which pills are which."

"I'm sure you do," Cole agreed. "But I don't. You wouldn't want me to make a mistake with these and give you a heart attack or something, would you?"

The skin on the old man's face paled even further. "Thank you," he finally managed to mumble. Nothing like the possibility of death to bring out manners in a man.

"I'd hate to see your grandkids go through any more upset than they've already had. I need you to be healthy." Cole pushed back his chair. "Can I get you some breakfast?"

"As long as it's not those potato pancake things you made the other day."

Cole kept up the easy banter as he pulled the egg carton out of the refrigerator. "I told you that I make do."

The old man was quiet while Cole prepared the pan and scrambled some eggs. Finally, Mr. Quinlan said, "You're not the same as before."

"I like to think I've matured some since I lived in Eden. I was just a kid, then."

"You didn't do right by my girl."

Turning, Cole met Mr. Quinlan's lopsided gaze. "I tried, you know. I swear to God, I tried. I guess I just wasn't good enough for her."

"That's the truth." Mr. Quinlan said it with more gusto than Cole felt was necessary.

What had he expected? Kumbaya and a big hug for helping the man with his meds? Cole's temper showed itself. "Would anyone have been good enough for her after what she went through as a child?"

"I don't know what you're talking about." Then Mr. Quinlan got all huffy. "And if I did, it wouldn't be any of your business, anyway."

"You better rethink that tight-lipped policy of yours. Remember when I mentioned Rachel has nightmares? She's not dreaming of the crash. She's having nightmares about her mother and the way she was treated by her." With that, Cole finished cooking Mr. Quinlan's eggs, slid them on a plate, set the plate on the table and then headed to Rachel's room.

"Not so fast, you," Mr. Quinlan said. "Come back here…to the table." He swallowed thickly, then added a low, "Please."

It was this last word that made Cole hesitate.

"Please." The old man repeated.

Cole found himself sinking into a chair across from him.

Angling his head in the general direction of the kitchen window, Mr. Quinlan seemed disinclined to speak. Or maybe Cole *had* mixed up his medication.

"Mr. Quinlan? Are you all right?"

The old man gripped his coffee cup and began speaking without looking at Cole. "I couldn't believe how lucky I was on my wedding day. Darla was beautiful. She looked like an angel. We started out with nothing but love." He sighed. "But love isn't always enough."

Cole didn't know where the old man was going with this, but he didn't dare speak and break his thoughts, not if he could shed light on what happened to Missy and Rachel.

"We were blessed with two girls as lovely as my Darla, and my air freight business did well, only I had to leave for long periods of time, and Darla… I hadn't realized she wasn't strong." He fiddled with his pillbox. "Taking care of the girls wore her down. I had the doctor prescribe something, but she didn't like how she gained weight when she took the pills. She was a bit vain about her appearance. She didn't realize I'd love her no matter what dress size she wore."

And then he fell silent.

"What did she do to the girls?" Cole prompted, unable to bear the silence.

Mr. Quinlan stared over Cole's shoulder in that odd way of his, although Cole knew that because of his macular degeneration he could only see Cole by putting him in his peripheral vision. "I don't know."

"Why not?"

"Because I always thought it was just Missy's burden." He wiped at his nose. "And now…now I'm not so sure."

## *CHAPTER SIX*

JENNA PEEKED OUTSIDE the hangar to see if Cole was around, shushing Shadow, who pawed the ground behind her. He didn't like standing around and doing nothing.

But the big man wasn't on the porch.

They'd been home from Montana four days. During that time Cole had become the house police. If it wasn't for school, he'd probably have Matt and Jenna cleaning house from sunup to sundown—ironing clothes, brushing their hair and teeth. Jenna was used to taking care of herself. She wasn't sure she liked being bossed around.

Every evening before dinner, Cole came out on the porch and called for her. A couple of times he sat there for a bit before calling. Jenna was sure he was looking for her. But why? She had no one to ask. Pop didn't like Cole and avoided him as much as Jenna did. Matt? Clueless. And Aunt Rachel slept through most of the day. Even when she was awake, it wasn't for long. Sometimes she drank some water with her medicine before she fell asleep again. Sometimes she'd fall asleep mid-sentence.

Shadow nudged Jenna's shoulder with his nose, pushing her out into the open where Cole could see her if he was standing at the kitchen window.

Jenna jumped back. "Shadow, don't."

The horse tossed his head, then plodded around the corner.

"Shadow! Come back here." Great, he'd given her away for sure. Her plan was to stay out of Cole's way as much as possible until she could ask Aunt Rachel about him. That had been easy the past two days because she didn't get off the school bus until after four.

Shadow continued walking to the water trough. Inside the pasture, Taffy, Matt's pony, came to the other side of the tank. After several big, slurpy drinks, Shadow clomped back to the hangar and walked past Jenna, probably headed for the shade trees down by the creek.

Jenna should have hopped on his back and left, but she was hungry, it was close to dinner and—

The screen door creaked open and Cole stepped onto the porch. Jenna hid behind the hangar again.

"Jenna? I need some help making dinner." Cole spoke in a loud voice. He didn't yell. He wasn't angry. He used a different voice than her dad, a different voice than he had when the oven shocked him. It was...nicer.

And Cole was teaching her how to cook. He made meals she'd only dreamed about—steaks, roasts, baked chicken, mashed potatoes, cornbread and biscuits. They'd never eaten so well, because Aunt Rachel only cooked things like grilled cheese and bacon, lettuce and tomato sandwiches.

Oh, man. Jenna's stomach rumbled at the thought of food even as she felt disloyal to Aunt Rachel. Jenna hadn't eaten anything since the awful spaghetti in the school cafeteria. Should she follow Shadow or go to Cole? He was supposed to have been friends with her mom. Jenna didn't remember much about her mom. Only how warm her lap had been and how bright her yellow hair was. Maybe Cole could tell her something about her mom. That would be cool.

"Coming." Jenna stepped around the corner of the hangar and headed to the porch.

"What have you been doing all afternoon?" Cole held open the screen door for her.

Shrugging, Jenna wiped the dirt off her boots before heading into the kitchen to wash her hands. "Nothing." She wasn't going to admit she'd been waiting for him to call her in.

"SATURDAY WOULD BE perfect." Mr. Quinlan ended his call and came to sit at the dinner table. He hadn't said more than two words at a time to Cole since their discussion yesterday morning, seemingly embarrassed that he'd told Cole something of his past. Not that he'd been able—or willing—to tell Cole what he wanted to know. The old man hadn't been sure what horrors Rachel had suffered under his wife's care, and Cole wondered…had Missy done the same thing to Jenna? Or had Lyle? That would explain why Jenna was suspicious of Cole, why she ran away and hid.

"Who was that, Pop?" Matt asked. The kid was like the Energizer Bunny. Once he woke up in the morning, he was a nonstop talker until he passed out at night. Since Jenna seemed to live outside, Mr. Quinlan rarely ventured out of his room and Rachel was still sleeping the hours away, Matt was the only person Cole had to talk to. Twice he'd fallen asleep in the living room and Cole had to carry him to bed.

"That, my boy, was an airplane salesman. He's bringing an air tanker by on Saturday for us to look at." Mr. Quinlan dove into his mashed potatoes with gusto.

"Saturday?" Cole set his forkful of green beans to rest on his plate. "Why would he bring it on Saturday?"

Mr. Quinlan spoke as if Cole were too young to understand. "Because deals like this don't last. If we want the plane, we have to act on it now."

Cole had a bad feeling about this. "Don't you have to fly a plane before you buy it? Like a test drive?"

"Of course." Mr. Quinlan scowled.

"Who's going to fly that plane?" Surely the old man didn't think Rachel was up to the task.

Mr. Quinlan's thin chest puffed out. "I am."

Cole bit back a curse. Jenna's eyes widened and filled with tears. At least the ten-year-old realized that her grandfather had a snowball's chance in hell of flying something as large as an air tanker.

"Cool!" Matt said. "Pop's gonna fly! Can I go, too?"

"No." Predictably, Matt's eyes got all watery when Cole squelched that idea. Crocodile tears weren't going to help the boy anymore. Cole was onto him. He leaned across the table toward Mr. Quinlan. "You can't be serious."

"In my day, I was quite the pilot."

"In your day you could probably see a field mouse on the ground while flying a mile above him." Cole couldn't stop his voice from increasing in volume. Surely the old man realized—

"I can still—"

"You can't." Cole stood, picking up his plate and Jenna's. Tears spilled onto her cheeks, further fueling Cole's anger. Why didn't Rachel or Mr. Quinlan realize how scared Jenna was of losing them? Was it because she suffered in silence? "And if you think somebody who's trying to sell a plane for tens of thousands of dollars would let you try, then you haven't been taking the right medications. Look at your grandkids." Cole set the plates down in the sink and pointed to them. "They know you can't do it." Well, at least Jenna did. Matt was oblivious to the real conflict around him, but he did look upset.

Mr. Quinlan's face contorted in a layer of angry, red wrinkles. "I can always have Rachel fly."

Cole couldn't stop the loud, sharp bark of laughter at the absurdity of the old man's solution.

Jenna cringed and cried harder, albeit silently.

With effort, Cole fought to explain himself calmly to Mr. Quinlan. "Rachel can't stay awake for more than a few minutes and you want her to operate heavy machinery? Call up the salesman and push this test flight back a week. Or better yet, two."

"This is my house and my business. You have no right to butt in." Mr. Quinlan held a knife and fork. Both shook with what Cole assumed was anger.

"I have every right." Cole glanced significantly at

Jenna, pushing to put the flying issue to rest and stop upsetting his daughter, even if it meant threatening to take Jenna away, even if he was sure his life would be a struggle if he had to stand behind the threat. "And if you don't act more responsibly, I'll have more rights than you do."

RACHEL WOKE UP with a jolt and a tremendous sense of disorientation as two small bodies bounced onto the bed on either side of her. Her entire body tensed, sending the muscles around her bruised ribs spasming and stealing her breath. Jenna and Matt snuggled up against her without even reaching for the remote.

Uh-oh. They were in trouble.

Since they'd been home, Rachel had been out. Literally. She'd given in to the exhaustion she felt. Had a day passed? Two? She'd lost track. And not just of time, but of her family. What had upset them?

Less than a minute later, looking ready to explode, Cole barged into the room, studied Rachel, his irritation oozing from every pore, then pointed at the kids. "You two, out. Rachel, I need to talk to you...*alone*."

Rachel raised her eyebrows at him, amazed when the gesture didn't hurt. She must be getting better.

Cole didn't have to suggest leaving to Jenna more than once. She jumped off the bed and was out the door in a snap. Rachel barely got a glimpse of her face, but Jenna's nose looked red. Had she been crying?

What had the kids done?

Matt moved a little slower, grinning tentatively at

Cole. His little nose looked red, too. "You won't forget we're making cookies later?"

"Do your homework, first," Cole countered, barely looking at Matt, who raced off in that wobbly, endearing gait of his, looking happy.

Amazement seemed to freeze time. Rachel hadn't expected Cole to step into a fatherly role, particularly with Matt. Had Missy been wrong to keep Jenna from Cole? If so, then Rachel had been wrong, too.

Since she was feeling so alert, Rachel pushed herself into a sitting position. The world only tilted a little and her ribs only protested with one stabbing jolt. Progress. If only her days of rest had obliterated her longing for Cole.

She risked a glance at him, sliding a bit to her right as she did so. He still looked to-die-for handsome. Her heart beat double time in response. Pavlov's dog had never been as predictable as her libido.

Rachel sighed.

"Do you know what your father did?" Cole blurted out, reaching out to steady her.

"No." Rachel's breath tasted days old, and her teeth wore a winter coat. She hoped Cole wouldn't come much closer. It was one thing to believe she wanted to cure herself of the lust-for-Cole habit, another to actually do something about it and let him smell her bad breath.

"He's talked to a salesman about an airplane for you. They're bringing it by on Saturday."

Fear clenched Rachel's empty belly. They'd expect her to give the plane a test run, put it through its paces. Flickering images of the crash burst through her mind's eye. The sour taste of fear added itself to her mouth. "What day is it?"

"It's Tuesday evening." Pop stood in the doorway, looking as belligerent as a man way past his prime could, with his hands fisted on his bony hips and a scowl on his face. "Don't you worry about it. I'll fly the plane on Saturday."

"You?" Her father hadn't flown in over three years. "You can't fly."

"Yeah, I told him that, too." Cole had a smug look, clearly pleased with Rachel's reaction.

In a way, Rachel was grateful that Cole was watching out for her family. Unfortunately, she suspected Cole lacked the tact necessary to make her father see reason. More than likely the two men had embarked on a pissing contest of who could yell louder, which would explain why Jenna seemed upset. Her niece had witnessed too many shouting matches in her short life.

But Pop was adamant. "Who says I can't fly? I've still got my license."

"Pop, I can't let you do that. It's too dangerous." Missy's voice echoed in Rachel's head. *"It's too dangerous for Rachel, Cole." He was about to take Rachel on the back of his motorcycle. "Besides, I don't think I want my little sister to see them drag a dead body out of the river, or to know where Moe's Curve is. Too many kids and drunks die on that cliff."* Rachel had been heartbroken that she'd been left behind. But the lesson she'd learned was not to ask for Missy's permission.

Cole crossed his arms over his chest and cocked an eyebrow. Rachel half expected him to tell her father, *I told you so.*

"Rachel, this S2 Tracker comes at a rock-bottom price. We can't afford to let someone else get it." Pop named a figure that was too good to be true.

The S2 Tracker was a Navy plane, most likely built in the late 1950s. It wasn't on the air tanker retirement list and probably wouldn't be for ten years. But it also offered less than half the gallon capacity of her beloved Privateer. However, if it hadn't been fitted with slurry tanks, it would be a collector's dream.

If truth be told, Rachel didn't want to fly the S2—or any plane. She wasn't ready, and had no idea when she would be. But Pop's money was tied up in Fire Angels, too. She had an obligation. Rachel symbolically stepped up to meet it. "Pop, the price is too low. What's wrong with it?"

Pop shrugged. "It's the end of the season. Someone can't meet the payments. The owners are getting a divorce. How would I know the specifics? We'll see come Saturday."

At such a low price, Rachel could understand why they needed to look at it quickly. Even if she didn't want to fly, she needed a plane to earn a living. But her dad was in no condition to take out a Big Wheel much less something as large and powerful as this. "You won't take it for a test flight." Rachel hoped she sounded firm but not hurtful.

"I'll leave that to you." Pop smiled triumphantly at Cole before making his exit.

"Like hell," Cole muttered. "Neither of you is flying on Saturday."

Rachel hugged a pillow to her chest. Could she really fly again so soon? Less than two weeks after the accident? Her head seemed clearer than it had in days, but she hadn't tried to walk. And flying these old planes could be more physically demanding than driving a car that didn't have power steering. Was she up to it?

She had to be.

"Don't even think about it, Rachel. You can call this sales guy and put him off a week or so. That's what I'd do."

"I can't. The price is too good to pass up. If we don't take it, someone else will." Rachel shook her head slowly. The world remained in focus and her stomach growled. But her mind couldn't shake the fear.

Cole leaned within smelling distance of her breath. "This is déjà vu. I'm telling you not to go up, and you're being totally irresponsible."

"It's not exactly déjà vu. I've got four days to prepare." Her smile felt weak. She wished she could do as he wanted, but they needed a plane if they were going to eat next year.

Cole put his fists on the mattress and leaned closer, pushing buttons that had nothing to do with her desire to fly, and everything to do with her desire for him. "Then I've got four days to talk you out of it."

"AW, COME ON." Rachel eyed the tray that Cole put in front of her a half hour later. "I can eat more than soup and crackers. Supersize me, please."

"You haven't eaten anything solid for days. Let's start slowly." Although there was color in her cheeks, Cole knew Rachel still wasn't able to walk to the bathroom on her own. She'd been slender before the accident. Now, other than her swollen head, she was starting to appear gaunt.

He stood while she tested a spoonful of soup, waited until she started eating with gusto.

"You are such a taskmaster." Rachel's smile between bites invited him to lighten up, yet there was too much on his mind. "I should be grateful you didn't give me Jell-O, right?"

He couldn't seem to summon so much as a smile for her. He had questions he'd kept bottled inside him for days—about Matt, about Mrs. Quinlan, about the past. In a house filled with people, Cole felt out of place and alone. With heavy steps, he moved to the end of Rachel's bed and sat down.

"Why did you let me think Matt was your son?" His question caused Rachel to freeze, her hand hung suspended in midair. "He's Missy's, isn't he?"

After a moment Rachel placed the spoon carefully on the tray and folded her hands in her lap. There was a resignation in her demeanor, as if she'd been waiting for this moment. "I didn't want you to get hurt. And you didn't ask about Matt, so I figured you didn't want to know."

"Hurt? You thought I'd be hurt?" Cole's entire body tensed, demanding he stand or run or punch a wall. He resisted, but whatever instincts had held his temper in check before vaporized. "Or was it easier not to tell me the truth? You're the one who didn't want me to talk about Missy in front of the kids."

Rachel hesitated. "You are hurt."

Cole ignored her observation and tried to contain the anger that had been banked for days. He failed. "Don't ask, don't tell. Is that it? Matt calls you Mommy. Why would you think I'd have to ask? I assumed he was yours."

"You didn't ask me who his father was. I think that says a lot about your interest in him."

*And me.* Cole could almost hear Rachel add the two words and wanted to kick himself for his insensitivity. Rachel's indignation was apparent in the ramrod set of her shoulders—as if his disinterest in her personal life hurt. She didn't realize he'd been lost in grief over Missy and his confusion over learning he was a father. "You didn't give me a chance to ask."

Rachel's gaze slid away as if his answer wasn't good enough.

"Missy died the week Matt was born." Rachel's clasped fingers seemed to clench. Her gaze came back to his. "Matt's never known any other mom."

"I called you his aunt Rachel the other day. He corrected me as if he'd had to correct others."

Rachel raised her shoulders in a weak shrug. "Some people in town don't think he should call me that or that I should have changed his and Jenna's name to Quinlan. I told him he's lucky to have two mommies. And we've practiced what he should say so he doesn't get hurt."

"You've been good to both of them. Missy would be proud." Cole was certainly proud of Rachel. No one would have said she had to take Missy's kids, but Cole was grateful she'd done it.

"I hope so. Missy wondered about your involvement with Jenna...and how you'd tell your mom." Rachel looked directly into Cole's eyes. "You do plan to tell your mom, don't you?"

Cole chose to overlook Rachel's question. "Missy knew about Sally? How? When? I don't understand." He hadn't told Missy or Rachel.

Rachel's smile was gentle. "Missy's radiator overheated at the bottom of your driveway one day. We walked up to the house and knocked on the door, but the music was so loud, we didn't think you heard us. So Missy opened the door, and we went inside."

"I don't remember—"

"You weren't there." Rachel interrupted him. "It was just your mom." Rachel shifted in bed, as if uncomfortable admitting, "She had the stereo up full blast—AC/DC 'Back in Black'—and all of Sally's pictures out, and she was wailing something awful."

"She was crying?" Cole couldn't believe it. "But she never cries."

"Maybe not in front of you. She probably knows how much it upset you. So she locked her grief away for the times when she was alone."

"And you know this after just one meeting with my mom?" Cole couldn't believe it.

"Cole, I used to get off the bus at your house to make sure your mom was okay." Rachel's smile was still gentle. "Why do you think I was there when you got home every day?"

"Missy said you didn't like to be home alone." Cole cast his gaze around the room, searching for the truth. But there was nothing in the spartan room to answer the questions he had, so he blew out a breath and demanded, "Is there anything else you didn't tell me? About Missy? My mom? Or Sally? Or your mom? Are there other secrets you're keeping from me?"

RACHEL COULDN'T BUY a break when she really needed one.

Cornered between lying and fessing up, Rachel hesitated too long before denying it.

Cole swore. "Every time I think I know you or Missy, you throw a curve at me." He stared at the ceiling. "Sometimes I wish I'd never bumped into you at base camp."

"Cole, it's not what you think." Rachel shut her eyes, hoping that when she opened them Cole would quit prying. She did not want to dissect her life with him, of all people. He couldn't possibly understand. "Okay, maybe we didn't have the all-American family."

"Like I did?" Anger still hung from his words. "I just found out you were closer to my mom than I was. Why is that?"

"I wasn't closer to her." Rachel sat back far enough that she almost bumped her head on the headboard. She leaned forward, aware she'd barely avoided hurting herself. "I just saw the pills she was taking and I worried that maybe...that she might—"

"Might be taking medicine like your mom? That she might be like your mom? That she might abuse me?"

"Yes." Rachel breathed a sigh of relief. He did understand.

"So you were trying to protect me? I was a senior in high school, years older than you." Cole stared at her in disbelief. "Weren't you scared of what would happen if she did go off her meds?"

Rachel had been terrified, but more concerned for Cole's safety than her own.

"Of course you were. Rachel," Cole said softly, gazing down on her. "It's just me. I don't want anything more than the truth. When I think of what you went through because I didn't tell you…I'm sorry. But don't you see? That's why we should be honest with each other now. We were friends once, even if you don't trust me anymore."

Rachel did trust him. That was the problem. She trusted him enough to lay her heart in his hands, but he wasn't the kind of man who would cherish the gift, so her heart would only end up broken like Missy's. "Why do you need to know any more?"

"I thought I knew you and Missy," Cole said slowly. "I'd like to understand why you'd risk yourself like that, and why you have these fears in the first place."

"Fears?" Her heart pounded. How did he know she was terrified by the thought of flying again?

"Fear of the dark? Fear of my mom?" he clarified.

Relief replaced the apprehension that she'd given herself away. But what could Rachel say? Talking about her mother and the darkness, about what she'd done to Rachel, might make Cole feel better, but it would make Rachel feel worse. As for his mom, she'd wanted to protect Cole because she loved him, but she couldn't tell him that. It was better not to speak.

"Start at the beginning, Rachel. Start at the middle or the end. It's probably not as bad as you think. Your father already told me a little about your mother, about how she was bipolar, but wasn't so good about taking her medicine."

How had Pop known that? She'd never told her father. Neither had Missy. Rachel pushed the tray toward her feet, giving her room to draw her knees up to her chest. Rachel's head swam only slightly, not enough to make her topple over, although passing out to avoid this conversation wasn't looking so bad right now.

Cole placed one hand on her foot. "Why do you have bad dreams about your mother?"

Knowing she'd never reach the door, let alone outside, Rachel realized she couldn't escape, couldn't walk away. She didn't want to talk about her mother and said as much.

"Why not?"

"Because..." Rachel couldn't choose just one reason. Mostly, she didn't want Cole's pity.

"Because she hit you?" Cole fished.

"No. My mother's form of punishment was worse than mere physical abuse." Rachel covered her eyes with her hands. "Can't you let it go?

"No."

"Why not?" Rachel demanded, letting her fingers slip away so that she could see him.

His expression was unyielding. "Because you haven't let it go."

"You're making me feel weak." She hadn't meant to say that. "I'm not saying any more."

"Why not? Did your dad swear you to secrecy? Did Missy?" Cole's grip on her foot tightened. "Did they know what she did to you?" Then tightened again. "Or how it would haunt you years later?"

"You're hurting me." Probing at scars. Her breath hitched in her throat as Rachel recalled her mother locking her in the bedroom after taking all the lightbulbs out.

Immediately, Cole released her, nearly leaping off the bed, pacing the small room.

Rachel was confused. "You're upset." She couldn't imagine why. She was the one who'd lived through it.

"Your silence raises questions." Cole stopped pacing. "Was Jenna abused, too?" His voice rose. "Did Missy treat Jenna right? Did Lyle? Do you? Damn it, tell me!"

His words soaked into her like a dousing in icy river water. She felt so cold she couldn't breathe. "How could you—" Rachel drew a ragged breath. She'd believed Cole was asking because he cared for her, but he was more concerned about Jenna. "How could you even think such things? Missy loved Jenna. I love Jenna. Neither one of us could ever hurt her." Rachel hadn't been able to bring herself to spank her niece when she was five, much less inflict the kind of suffering her own mother had on Rachel and Missy. "Do you honestly think I could abuse Jenna?" That he thought so little of her hurt. That he might use her mother's episodes to get custody of Jenna was frightening.

Fists at his side, Cole stood with his back to her. "I don't do well with silences. I had enough of those growing up after Sally died." He clenched and unclenched his fists, then turned, his voice dropping. "I don't want to believe a lot of things—that I didn't know the real Missy, or the real you. You're raising my daughter. I deserve an answer." He took out his wallet and tossed a photo at her. It landed on her lap. "I've been carrying around this picture of the two of you all this time, hoping that someday Missy would call and say she'd changed her mind, ignoring the fact that she'd made her choice and moved on. I've been living in limbo for more than a decade, fooling myself into believing that I loved Missy and should wait. I thought I had left that naive boy from South Texas behind, but I didn't. And perhaps I never will." He put on his running shoes, jerking the laces tight. "I'm going out for a jog."

Cole closed the door decisively, shutting Rachel in just as her mother had done. Only, this time the lights were on and no one heard Rachel whisper, "But she did call."

COLE HAD LET the situation get the better of him and lashed out at Rachel. It wasn't her fault that he hadn't known every aspect of her life back then. They'd been kids. Cole ran in the gray twilight, feet pounding the gravel drive, then the asphalt, as he made the turn onto the main road.

Rachel could never abuse Jenna. She cared too much for his daughter.

What was wrong with him? It was as if all the hang-ups he'd been avoiding were finally demanding to be heard. There were his feelings for Missy and the void where his relationship with his mother should have been, and his longing to be a part of a family.

Maybe he could make one of his own—with Jenna.

A family for a Hot Shot? Impossible. Hadn't he recently told Aiden that it took a special woman to make a man into a good father? Cole couldn't remember his exact words, but the gist was the same. It wasn't possible for a Hot Shot on his own to be a good father.

Cole pushed himself up a hill. He had to remember why he was here—to move past his dead relationship with Missy, to get to know Jenna and to help Rachel heal. At least his feelings for Missy were beginning to fade.

Reaching the top of the hill, Cole paused, taking in the final pink light of day. He wouldn't press Rachel—nothing would be gained by losing his temper—but he'd get his answers, all the same.

"RACHEL." Cole's voice cut through the darkness later that night, chasing away images of the past.

"Don't!" Rachel woke up in a cold sweat. She had trouble separating the demons from reality, had trouble recognizing her room, even though the light in the bathroom shone through a crack in the doorway.

"You were having a nightmare." Cole had his arm around her shoulders and his body pressed next to hers. She was tangled under the covers. He lay on top of them. “Shh, it’s going to be okay.” In his arms, Rachel could almost believe it would be, could almost believe that this Cole was the same Cole she’d fallen for as a teenager, not the man who’d let Missy down.

“I didn’t wake anyone else, did I?” Her heart pounded.

“No.”

Relief flooded Rachel’s trembling limbs. She didn’t want to scare the kids or alarm Pop. Then she realized something else—she didn’t want Cole to let her go. There had to be a rule about the recommended time allotment for comfort from a forbidden love. Rachel was probably pretty darn close to the limit.

Yep, pretty darn close. Doing the right thing really sucked.

Rachel sighed. “You can go back to the couch, now.” Rachel put as much bravado in her voice as she could, given she couldn’t see what was in the shadowy corner of her room. “Just open the bathroom door a bit more when you go.”

“I’m not going anywhere.” Cole moved away, no more than an inch. Just enough that he could see her face. “I’ve been sleeping in here every night.”

“Every night?” Rachel hoped she didn’t talk in her sleep. He’d probably already developed suspicions about her being the best choice to raise his daughter. “You can sleep on the living room couch. That’s halfway between here and the guest room. I don’t need a babysitter anymore.”

“Rach, this bed doesn’t have rails like a hospital bed. I usually start out on the floor but end up on the bed when the nightmares come and you thrash around. You seem to sleep better after that." His breath brushed over her ear, raising goose bumps. "The couch is too far away."

"You didn't think so a couple of hours ago. You couldn't wait to get away."

"I'm sorry. I-it's not easy being drawn back to Eden, especially when everything I know, or thought I knew, has been proven false. I want to help you, Rachel, and I want to help Jenna, too. I can't do either if I don't understand what's going on."

"Or what went on in the past." Rachel was distracted enough by the strength of his arms around her to say, "Jenna hasn't been abused by Missy or me. I think Lyle may have scared her, though. She gets timid around big, loud men."

Cole swore. "That explains why she ran when I cussed up a storm the other day over the broken oven." He rubbed her arm. "I'll try to tone it down around her. She's a sweet kid."

Warmed by his sentiment, Rachel wished she'd been cognizant of his nightly visits, but… "Do I say anything in my sleep?"

"Other than 'no' and 'don't'—which are tough on a man's ego when he's in bed with you—no."

Rachel elbowed Cole in the gut, a movement that sent a shaft of pain through her own rib cage. Then something wild and dangerous blossomed in her mind: He was flirting. "You're not sleeping in the same bed as I am." But he had been, and despite her vow not to ever share a bed with him, she had. Missy would not have been happy, but then again, nothing Rachel had done had made her happy.

"Don't be so hasty." Cole eased away and stood next to the bed. "I'm just trying to help. It's not all night." He picked up three couch pillows from the floor and put them on the bed next to her, fencing her in with chintz.

"Locked back in, am I?" Hemmed in by the wall on one side and pillows on the other. "And if I need to visit the bathroom?"

Cole stretched out on his sleeping bag. "Just ask. I'll be sleeping right here on the floor."

"Not on my floor." She'd never fall asleep. Not while she was imagining that he'd climb into bed with her at the first sign of distress.

"Honey, until you can walk on your own, you and I will be close friends."

She should ask him about Missy's last day but she didn't want to ruin such a wonderful moment, like old times and yet not. If Missy hadn't called, if the note she'd left had been a lie, then Cole really was as he seemed—a kind, caring man who Missy had rejected for Lyle. Which meant Rachel's heart was in trouble. She moved her feet slowly back and forth beneath the covers. For the first time since the crash, she felt as if her legs were getting back their strength. And that she needed a shave.

"Tomorrow," she whispered. She'd get her act together tomorrow.

"What did you say?" Cole asked.

"I'm going to try walking tomorrow." She had three days left before the plane got here.

"Let me at least dig out a crash helmet for you to wear before you try anything foolish. I'm sure you've got one in that disaster zone you call a garage."

He'd seen the garage? That was embarrassing. She'd been meaning to clean it for years. "A helmet will never fit over my head."

"Good. Then maybe you'll stay in bed."

She could stay in bed. She could stay in bed and fantasize about Cole all night long. But those thoughts would just make her more restless. She had to think of something else.

Rachel stared at the wall, willing herself to go to sleep, but she couldn't get past how much better than she'd imagined it had been to be wrapped in Cole's arms.

"And, Rachel?"

"Yes."

"Tomorrow, when I ask you about the past, can you keep in mind that I'm not trying to pry? I'm asking because I need to know so that I can move forward."

Cole was lucky. He seemed to think knowing the truth would help him move on. But Rachel knew that knowing the truth had no power other than to leave regret in its wake.

## *CHAPTER SEVEN*

COLE SLEPT ON HIS BACK in the middle of the floor, dressed only in his sweats. It took Rachel a few moments to realize she wasn't dreaming.

What a way to wake up.

There didn't seem to be an ounce of fat on him. He was all sculpted muscle, no doubt honed by months of wielding that chainsaw he'd told her he used. Cole's chest rose and fell with relaxed, deep breaths. Rachel found herself falling into the rhythm. Her eyes drifted closed.

"Are you hungry?" Cole's question startled Rachel, causing her to jump.

"I didn't mean to scare you." Head propped on his hand Cole stared at her with an unreadable expression. He rose and closed the distance between them until he stood next to the bed. His gaze skimmed her body from head to toe. Then he reached for her—one large hand heading toward her chest.

Rachel stopped breathing. She was sure her eyes had widened to the size of saucers. She didn't know whether to ask him what in the world he was doing or wait to see how his hand felt on her breast.

*Wait.*

Cole's hand missed her breast by what seemed like a mile. He snagged the covers and pulled them up over her. "I thought you might be cold."

He thought...

Rachel's cheeks burned as she realized she'd been lying on the bed in her skimpy panties and a T-shirt that had risen inches above her belly button. Her nipples ached with wanting him and were probably like pebbles poking through her T-shirt. He wanted to cover her up and she had assumed...hoped...he was making a pass.

How pathetic.

Rachel wanted to pull the covers up over her head. Her one defense against her foolish infatuation with Cole was that he didn't know about it. But that could change if she wasn't careful.

"I don't think I need a night nurse anymore," she managed to croak.

"Let me be the judge of that. This is the first morning you've woken up with focused eyes. You've barely eaten enough to keep a bird alive these past few days. I'll bring you something to eat." Cole grabbed a T-shirt from on top of his duffel and pulled it on. "But first, could you tell me how Missy died? Expand on the condensed version you told me in Montana."

Needles of shock stiffened her limbs. She gripped the covers and pulled them up higher. "Now?" But she knew it was time. She needed to discover whether Cole was who he seemed or who Missy made him out to be.

"Missy died driving to be with you. She called you, right?" Rachel watched Cole's reaction very carefully.

His eyebrows bunched together as if he was perplexed. "Missy hasn't called me in eleven years. I swear. Did she tell you that?"

Rachel nodded. "She left a note."

"Do you still have it?"

"It's in that small dresser drawer on the top right. I had to use it when I went to court to secure custody." Rachel reread it sometimes when she felt overburdened by her responsibilities.

Cole dug through her things and withdrew a faded envelope. "This one?"

Rachel nodded, but Cole was already opening the letter. And then he began to read it out loud.

"'Dearest Rachel, I can't do this anymore. It's your turn. Watch the kids and Pop for me. I can't live without Cole. Love always, Missy.'" Cole stared at the lined paper as if he could learn more from the few lines that Missy wrote than her actual words. "This says nothing about calling me."

"Let me see." Rachel held out her hand, but she knew Cole was right. "I just assumed…" Rachel read Missy's meticulously printed note.

"That she'd called me." He stared at Rachel so intently she had to look away. "You thought I was expecting Missy. What did you think when I didn't call to find out why she never showed up?"

Ugh. Guilty as charged. "Well, I—"

He swore and snatched the letter from her hands.

"What was I supposed to think, given your track record? I didn't think she'd just leave without knowing where you were or if you were home or if you still wanted…" Rachel's attempt to defend herself faltered as a darker reason for Missy's leaving came to her. Missy hadn't left for a vacation. She hadn't wanted to come home.

"She says she can't do this anymore, but she also says it's your turn. So, she can't be talking about Lyle. What did she mean?" He paced the length of the bed, ignoring Rachel.

"Missy took care of everyone after Mom left. I think she even married Lyle so that his dad wouldn't foreclose on our mortgage," Rachel explained with a miserable feeling in her belly. Missy couldn't have abandoned her kids, Pop or Rachel. She'd loved them too much to leave and never look back, hadn't she?

"Where did the accident happen?" Cole asked, not wanting to look at Rachel. He was still reeling from the revelation that Rachel considered him an uncaring bastard, someone who would encourage a woman to leave her kids to be with him and then not call when she didn't show up.

"She lost control of her truck on Moe's Curve the night she left."

It took Cole a moment to process Rachel's information. Moe's Curve? "Was she drunk?"

"Lyle was the drinker in the family, not Missy." Rachel looked miserable, but it was little consolation. "She sacrificed a lot, but we all knew it and loved her for it."

"What was she doing on that road in the first place?" An unpleasant suspicion formed in his head. Cole read the note again. No. It couldn't be. He sank down on the bed. "If she was coming to Idaho, she would have been on 191."

"Maybe she was lost." Rachel's eyes widened and she started shaking her head slowly. "She couldn't. She wouldn't."

"She didn't call me, Rachel." Cole felt sick to his stomach. He reread a line to himself, then said aloud what he was sure they were both thinking. "I wonder if 'I can't live without Cole' means she didn't want to live."

Rachel's gasp was followed by one last word of denial. "No."

"Tell me more about Missy," Cole said, not wanting to believe Missy had killed herself, either, but what else could have happened?

A full minute must have passed before Rachel spoke. "It won't make sense unless I start when you left, because after that, Missy changed." Rachel sighed. "We used to do everything together when you were here. But after she married Lyle, she wanted nothing to do with me."

"Missy was married, building a relationship, growing up, finally getting what she wanted. It makes sense that she'd spend less time with you." He held himself stiffly and wouldn't look at Rachel, not because they were talking about Missy and Lyle but because he didn't want to see the heartbreak on her pale features. The knowledge that Missy had taken her life was just as devastating as when Rachel had first told him Missy was gone. Rachel must be feeling that she'd lost Missy all over again.

"Missy wouldn't even talk to me. Before Jenna was born, I could be in the same room as Missy and it was as if she couldn't hear me." Rachel's voice was filled with anguish. "To go from such a close relationship with Missy to being shut out hurt. And Pop wasn't much help because he was flying a lot."

"What did you do?" The desire to comfort her was almost overwhelming.

"I kept busy by taking apart anything with an engine and putting it back together again. Well, back then I wasn't always able to get them going again, but I tried."

"We used to do that together." Cole wanted to smile but couldn't. Those were the days. Peanut butter sandwiches, a cold Pepsi, the radio and the two of them tinkering on some engine.

"Your Ford's engine was easier than some of my other projects." Rachel managed to smile, albeit weakly. "Things went downhill after Jenna was born. Not just with Missy, but with Missy and Lyle's marriage. Lyle got fired from the bank, and his dad washed his hands of him. Money got tight." She hesitated. "I began to see bruises on Missy—"

"Lyle knew Jenna was mine." Cole's mouth set in a grim line and he stood again, unable to justify Lyle's violent behavior.

"I think so." Rachel nodded. "I heard rumors around town, stories about Lyle humiliating Missy in public. And by that time Pop's health had gotten worse and I'd graduated from high school. I started flying more and discovered air tankers." Rachel's eyes sparkled. "I made enough to invest in one of my own with a hefty loan and Pop's cosignature. I was thrilled." And then the excitement seemed to drain right out of her. Poor Rachel had lost Missy long before she'd died. But she seemed to want to grieve alone, so Cole stayed where he was. "At the same time, it was tough because I was gone a lot more, and I knew Missy wasn't happy. But what could I do? She wouldn't let me help her. In fact, sometimes she even blamed me for the way her life turned out." Rachel wrapped her arms around her legs, letting her forehead sink to her knees.

"She didn't mean it, Rachel. She loved you," Cole said quietly, wanting to hold Rachel and reassure her that no one would ever hurt her again, but the taut way she held herself again sent the message to keep away.

With a sigh, Rachel continued her story. "A couple of years later our air tanker business was doing pretty well. Pop and I came home at the end of the season to find a very pregnant Missy had moved back into the house with Jenna. She still wasn't talking much to us, but she'd stopped talking to Lyle altogether and had filed divorce papers." Rachel's hand moved restlessly over the sheet.

Cole imagined Missy, withdrawn and beaten, hadn't been thrilled to come back home, but he was glad she'd done so.

He could tell that Rachel chose her next words carefully by how long it took her to speak. "Missy didn't seem very excited about anything—not the new baby or Jenna. And she seemed to resent me more than ever. With a history of mental illness in the family, we were worried about her, so Pop started staying home." She hesitated. "I feel so guilty about what happened next. I hired copilots and kept flying for NIFC and the Department of Forestry. Growing up, Missy had done more than her share for me. I should have hunkered down and been tougher when she lashed out at me. I should have stayed. Instead, I was relieved to let Pop deal with her."

"She would have come around, but she might not have wanted you to leave."

Rachel plowed on as if she couldn't believe it. "Pop called while I was away to tell me that Missy was having the baby. I got to the hospital right when Missy was delivering. Missy held Matt for a few minutes, but Matt wouldn't stop crying. Then Missy wouldn't stop crying, so I took Matt and he stopped crying right away."

"He knew you'd always be there to comfort him," Cole surmised.

"That's sweet. Thank you." Rachel blinked back tears. "It got ugly after that. Missy accused me of causing all her troubles. She said she'd never been happy in Eden, and the day after she came home from the hospital, she was gone."

"I wish I had known. I'd have come back." To help Rachel. To encourage Missy to do the right thing, to seek out happiness. But Cole was certain that her happiness would not have been with him.

"You couldn't have gotten through to her, Cole. No one could." She wiped away a tear. "Do you really think she drove off Moe's Curve on purpose?"

"Yes." Cole sank back onto the bed, close enough

to touch her. "How many times did someone fly off that corner when we were kids?"

"They were usually teenagers feeling invincible from booze. Not mothers who pined after a lost love. Pop must have known. That's why he doesn't want me to talk about it."

"But what about a woman who had sacrificed so much for others? Someone who lost hope in her own dreams?" Cole rubbed a hand over his face, feeling like crying himself. "I thought I meant everything to her once, yet when it came down to it, she wouldn't leave her family for me. You said she only wanted me to be happy. And when things soured with Lyle, she stayed for Jenna. You can only sacrifice yourself so much before you break."

Rachel no longer held back tears, and Cole no longer resisted putting his arms around her. As he held her, he couldn't help but wonder how much Rachel had sacrificed now that Missy was gone, and how much longer she could hold up on her own.

"FOOD'S ALMOST READY." Cole returned to Rachel's doorway a while later, after having cooked breakfast. Although, after the heartrending discovery that Missy had killed herself, Cole wasn't hungry.

But Rachel's bed was empty.

Cole rushed into the room, checking the far side of the bed to see if she'd fallen off again. That's when he heard the water running in the shower.

"How in the hell—" He pushed open the bathroom door and stepped into the steamy room "—did you get in here?" Through the thin shower curtain, Cole could see Rachel sitting in the tub.

"I crawled in," she admitted. "After discovering...you know...about Missy, I needed to."

"You're going to give me a coronary. I came in and I thought..." He didn't want to verbalize what he'd thought—that he'd lost her. Cole sank onto the toilet. "You are bound and determined to kill yourself."

"Did you think I'd gone out flying? No plane, remember?" There was something in her voice that Cole didn't want to hear.

"You're proud of this." Cole inhaled a careful breath. "You could have fallen like you did the first night we were home." Cole should have followed his first inclination upon leaving the house for his run last night and kept going. He wasn't nursemaid material.

"But I didn't."

The frustration over Missy's senseless death returned, blazing through his blood like a runaway fire. "Damn it, Rachel, those kids need you. I can't be responsible for you if you're going to act like this."

"I never asked you to be my keeper. You appointed yourself." Stubborn, as usual.

"What would make you act like an adult with common sense? Would you like to be permanently strapped to a wheelchair? Because that could easily happen." Cole was breathing as heavily as he did at the end of a run.

It took Rachel a moment to answer. "You never used to talk to me like this."

"If you mean I've grown up, hell, yes. I'm not the

angry, hurt kid you knew. I'm no longer tempting fate on a daily basis." Stop, he told himself. Take a breath. This was about Rachel, not him. "Every step you take endangers your life right now. Do not follow in Missy's footsteps."

"My getting out of bed is not about Missy. You're a Hot Shot and you take a few risks of your own," she countered.

"Calculated risks." Rachel had to be the most maddening person he knew.

"It's hard to calculate the risks with fire or with life. You take the hand you're dealt and play it as best you can." Rachel ran a hand up her face and over her hair, but with the shower curtain separating them he couldn't tell if she was crying or just wiping the water out of her eyes.

"That's what you've done. You've decided you've recuperated enough, so you're playing your hand." Too soon. If anything, she was bluffing about her strength.

"If you'll give me some privacy, I'll get out of the shower," Rachel bargained, as if she were capable of climbing out of a slippery tub on her own.

When Cole didn't answer, Rachel couldn't stem her frustration. "That's your cue to leave a towel on the floor for me."

Cole stood slowly, torn between giving Rachel the privacy she asked for and yanking the curtain back, gathering her up in a towel and carrying her back to bed.

Carrying her wet body back to bed.

He'd spent enough nights on the floor next to

Rachel to know she disliked sleeping under the covers. Cole wasn't a saint. So he would cover her up at every opportunity. Despite that, Cole looked forward to holding her every night, and yet touching Rachel felt like a betrayal to Missy.

Which was a laugh, considering Missy apparently hadn't wanted Cole's love.

Cole swallowed, frozen with indecision.

"I'll be fine on my own."

Rachel clearly did not want his help. Cole thrust a hand past the shower curtain and turned the water off. "I'll wait on the other side of the door in case you need me."

"READY FOR BREAKFAST?" Cole asked, his voice lacking warmth as he pushed Rachel's bedroom door open.

Rachel finished fumbling with the buttons on her worn flannel shirt, having somehow managed to look down and fasten them without vomiting on herself. She waited to answer until she was sitting upright against the mattress and her eyes had uncrossed. "I hope you didn't go to much trouble. If you're hungry, I make a mean omelet. Maybe you can prop me up on a kitchen stool so I can cook."

Cole narrowed his eyes. "You'd like that, wouldn't you?"

"Joke. That was a joke." She was in sore need of a joke right now or some good news. *Missy had killed herself.* It all made sense, yet Rachel hadn't wanted to see it. Grief threatened to overwhelm her, but Rachel refused to succumb.

But Cole continued to stare at her. "There's no one here but me and your family, Rach. No one cares if you're a tough guy." He turned and went back into the kitchen.

That's when the smell of bacon hit Rachel, along with a wave of hunger. She'd hardly eaten in the hospital, or the past few sleep-filled days at home. But now she was famished, which made it easy to ignore Cole's comment. She'd managed to crawl out of the bathtub, and into her clothes, but she really didn't want to creep across the cracked linoleum floor to the kitchen, and she doubted she'd manage to walk without Cole's steadying strength. He had to realize she needed a bit of help, didn't he?

The back door slammed. Rachel waited but didn't hear his footsteps.

Cole had left her without food. What a jerk!

Rachel pinched the bridge of her nose. Cole's treatment of her was no more than she'd pushed for.

Carefully Rachel rolled to her knees, biting her lip when the room spun, but she was already moving forward on all fours when the door opened again.

"You have the patience of a five-year-old," Cole said upon entering.

Rachel stared at his scuffed black cowboy boots because she couldn't look up at him without getting vertigo. She did not want to talk about Missy anymore, or be serious. "Clearly, you have the self-centered manners of a bachelor."

Cole's boots didn't move. Rachel wished she could look up into his eyes and decipher, without keeling over, what she'd said wrong.

"I don't plan on being a bachelor all my life."

Rachel pushed herself into a sitting position, her back against the bed, her head resting on the mattress as she looked up the length of him until her gaze finally landed on his face. His features could have been chiseled out of granite, not flesh.

"You don't?" *Be still, my heart. Remember that he thinks of you as Missy's sister.*

"I don't." Cole's jaw worked as if he debated how much else to admit. He helped her up. "I'm envious of my friends and what they have—a partner, a soul mate, a house filled with chaos."

Rachel let herself be led out to the kitchen. "I'm sure you'll find someone someday," she managed to mumble as he guided her into a chair, forgetting for a moment that he was treating her like she was helpless again.

"Thanks."

Rachel wanted to ask if Cole had anyone in mind, but her heart couldn't stand to know if he did. Propped against the kitchen wall, she waited as Cole walked over to the stove and poured pancake batter on the griddle. Rachel gripped the wooden seat to keep herself from falling off, and still Cole said nothing. Finally Rachel couldn't stand his silence anymore, so she asked about the subject furthest from matters of the heart. "Why don't you talk about Sally?"

Cole shot Rachel a dark look, a clear warning to back off. He leaned into the hallway and called Matt and Jenna to breakfast.

"You spent four years in Eden and you never even told Missy about your sister?" Not to mention Rachel.

Even as Rachel tried to tell herself that she'd only been the little sister of his girlfriend back then, she was hurt.

"She found out anyway, as did you." He looked out the window over the sink. The morning sky was a soft blue, promising a perfect day for flying.

"How's your mother?" Rachel asked, the now-familiar knot of fear forming in her stomach at the thought of taking to the air again.

With a sigh, Cole flipped a pancake, then another, effectively ignoring her. Cole mumbled, "You always were a stubborn pain in the ass."

"And you were an untamed force of nature," Rachel shot back, feeling sorry for his mom.

There was a pounding outside that increased in volume, then slowed to a stop near the house. A few moments later Jenna's inquisitive face appeared in the kitchen window.

"What the—?" Cole leaned toward the window. He seemed unable to take his eyes off Jenna. When he spoke, he spoke softly, but his words had an edge. "She's standing on a horse and it has no saddle, no bridle and no halter."

Rachel managed a weak wave to Jenna before leaning back into the seat with a smile. Sometimes her niece was one fearless girl. "Relax. No one knows Jenna the way that horse does, and vice versa. She's been riding him since she was five. And using Shadow as a ladder to peek in windows since she was seven."

"Without a saddle? Without a bridle?" His pancakes were smoking.

"Yeah. I used to ride bareback all the time."

"But you had a bridle and were damn near unstoppable. Jenna seems..." Cole craned his head. "Wait a minute. Those markings... I know that mustang. My dad and I picked him out my senior year, but I was too busy to break him right. Dad sold him when we moved to Idaho because he was too wild."

"Missy picked him up at an auction real cheap after she moved back home. I'm not surprised you couldn't break him. Shadow doesn't like men...or adults much." Neither did Jenna.

Jenna finally saw Cole, her expression turning to surprise. Then she disappeared and the sound of galloping hooves faded away.

"Damn." Cole sank against the counter.

Rachel allowed herself a little smile. "She took off toward the landing strip?"

"Yeah." Cole sounded weak. "Has she been doing that the whole time I've been back?"

"Probably."

"She's been avoiding me. I didn't know what she was doing every afternoon.... I think I'm going to be sick." He hung his head over the sink.

"Welcome to parenthood," Rachel said as the smoldering pancakes finally triggered the smoke alarm.

Cole held his breath as he watched Jenna ride away. His daughter had no common sense. None. She was a danger to herself. He could just imagine her losing control of the black mustang and taking a neck-breaking tumble.

As he watched, they jumped over a pile of fence

posts and then seemed to spin on a dime to race along the airstrip.

"I saw the pony in the pasture, but not that horse." Cole's mouth felt dry as dust. "Are you telling me that he just wanders freely around the place?"

"Yep. Bad things happen when you try to fence Shadow in," Rachel said.

Cole was sure he didn't want to know what those things were. It would only make him more concerned for his daughter's safety. "I thought you were talking about a cat called Shadow the night we arrived. That mustang is as wild as ever."

Matt stumbled into the kitchen, wrinkling his nose at the smell of burnt pancakes.

"After Missy died," Rachel explained, "I brought in a horse therapist who worked with Jenna and Shadow. He really helped her heal. Maybe to you and me Shadow seems wild, but he's tame as a kitten with Jenna." She turned to Matt. "Could you please go outside and call Jenna to breakfast?"

Absently, Cole watched Matt head outside. No horse was that tame. His mom would have a royal fit if she saw Jenna risking her life on a horse. He'd have to swear Jenna to secrecy or get her to stop riding bareback.

Hold on. Was Cole actually considering letting his mom know about Jenna?

The idea of Jenna being a more permanent part of his life was so unexpected that Cole couldn't speak for a moment. Instead, he disconnected the smoke alarm and opened the kitchen window, trying the idea on for size. Was he really considering…

Yes, he was.

Lyle had clearly caused problems for Jenna. What she needed was a positive father figure.

Heaven help him, because the moment Cole walked through his parents' front door with Jenna, it might take his mom another five years to return to something remotely resembling normal. And his dad wouldn't be thanking him, either, not for his mother's tears or her silences. But eventually they'd accept Jenna for who she was, not who she looked like.

Besides, they'd only see her a few times a year, mostly during the off season when Cole would have more of an opportunity to have her visit. The longer he thought about it, the more he believed his mom might actually benefit from knowing Jenna.

"You're gone too much to be raising a little girl, Rachel. Did you see how wild Jenna's hair is? It's a school day. If she takes time to brush out her hair, she'll probably miss the bus." Even to Cole, his voice sounded judgmental. But he couldn't seem to stop himself, because apparently, his daughter needed a keeper.

Rachel straightened in the spindly kitchen chair. Since the swelling around her head had abated, she looked more like the young girl whose picture he carried, ready to spit fire at the slightest sign of attack. "And you came to this conclusion after watching me and Jenna for less than a week? Most of which I spent in bed. How dare you." So much for the attack. Rachel was swaying where she sat.

Despite the way her dark eyes blazed, Cole came to

steady Rachel. "I know the life you lead. But yesterday was the first time I thought you were well enough for me to go out running. And I finally saw just how rundown this place is. Jenna and that horse are an accident waiting to happen."

There was discarded junk everywhere. An old car with broken windows and weeds growing out of the floorboards. A dragster frame with fence posts propped in it. An old wine barrel that had split apart. And he'd run down by the main road. God only knew what was on the other side of the property. It made Cole's stomach churn.

"You think I'm gone too much to raise *kids?*" Rachel emphasized *kids,* plural. "That makes you just as unqualified as I am to parent." Rachel managed to raise her eyebrows at him without wincing too noticeably. "I hope you aren't thinking you'll do a better job than I am. You see how fragile Jenna is. It's been five years since she lived with Lyle and she still bears the scars. Do you want to take her away from everything she loves? From her horse and her brother? From her friends at school?"

"I'm not suggesting I get custody." Far from it. But something hot and a lot like embarrassment crept up his neck. "I'm just saying that things could be better for her, that's all."

"What things?" Rachel studied him with suspicion.

"Her environment could be safer." For starters. Cole returned to the stove and began scraping the charred pancakes off the griddle. "Have you ever wondered if Jenna needed a change? A second chance to gain her confidence?"

"Now you've totally lost me. Are you talking about making over a ten-year-old?" Rachel scoffed, then grew silent. "Maybe if I were in your shoes, I'd think it was that easy." Cole didn't have to turn to see Rachel to know she was fighting tears. He could hear them in her voice. "Missy's gone. You look at Jenna and see a piece of the woman you loved. Of course you're going to want to take her when you leave." Rachel's voice strengthened. "But I won't let you."

"I'm not sure what I want or what the right thing for *my daughter* is." With a frown, Cole scrubbed his hand over his face, then gave up on breakfast and came back to sit at the table with Rachel. "You may have lost Missy years ago, but I've still got to come to terms with it and with Jenna. Of all the scenarios I've played out over the years, this wasn't one of them."

Rachel reached for his hand, some of her fire going out. "If it's any consolation, I still catch myself looking at the front door when I come home, expecting to see her open it, prop her hip against the door frame and welcome me home. I still walk into the kitchen expecting the smell of potatoes—"

"Because that's about all she knew how to cook without burning it." Cole cut Rachel off with a smile that felt heavy with sadness. "And lemon polish in the living room. I never understood why she used so much polish that the furniture was slick with it and you could barely breathe in there."

"Mother didn't like dust," Rachel admitted, her gaze dropping to their joined hands.

"But she was gone by then."

"Things don't stop just because someone's not here." Rachel's voice sounded small and then the words seemed even harder for her to say. "I remember when I came home from Missy's funeral and walked into the living room. Motes were flying through the air and every surface was thick with dust. I wanted to run for the dust cloth. I thought my heart would stop beating until I remembered Mom was gone."

Cole swore and wrapped her hand in both of his.

Slowly Rachel's lips formed a small smile. "I'm okay with the dust, now."

She'd have to be, because the house had been a dusty, cobwebbed mess when they'd arrived. It had taken Cole a few days to bring it up to the standards a bachelor like him thought was livable. And he refused to feed the kids dinner until they'd washed their hands, brushed their hair and put on clean clothes. What a battle that had been, and continued to be.

"But you're not okay with the darkness, are you, Rach?" Cole angled his head toward Rachel's bedroom.

"Someday I'll beat that, too." The way she said it, Cole knew she believed it.

"I bet you will." He tried to lighten the moment. "You always were stubborn."

"And you were reckless."

Although her tone was teasing, Cole's smile faded. "I never meant to disappoint Missy. I loved her. I should never have come back without being prepared to compromise for her."

Now it was Rachel's turn to hold on to his hand tight. "She did love you."

The past tense wasn't lost on Cole. He thought it would make his heart ache, but he was only filled with a regret and sadness.

Rachel continued. "I tried making her go after you, but she wouldn't leave. If I had been the older sister, I would have left Eden a long time ago. I would have..." Rachel's voice trailed off and she stared at their hands and then gently pulled hers back.

"I want to do the right thing now, Rach. I want to tell Jenna that I'm her father. I want to have a relationship with her." Damn, it was a big step for him to admit that out loud.

Rachel opened her mouth, but nothing came out. Her hands gripped the edge of the table. "I don't think telling Jenna is a good idea."

"Why not?" Jenna was his child. Cole had the right to tell his friends about Jenna, and to think of a way to tell his mother without destroying the success of years of therapy.

"She's just a kid. You can't just show up and blurt out that kind of thing. She's thought Lyle was her dad all these years. Telling her the truth will make her resent Missy...and me."

Cole scoffed. "She's very fond of you. Nothing is going to break that bond."

"This isn't *nothing*. This is a heap of trouble. You've only been here a few days. What are you going to want to do after two weeks?" Rachel shivered, sending her body swaying again. "You'll want to sue me for custody, that's what. What she doesn't need right now is a new place and new faces."

How did Rachel know him so well? Cole backed down. "Calm down. Right now, Jenna wants nothing to do with me. She disappears out the door if I so much as try to talk to her."

"Have you forgotten what you were like as a child?" Rachel lifted a hand to her forehead as if it hurt. "Or how hard it is to be a kid with adult heartaches? It must have been tough on Jenna growing up in a house with Lyle."

Instantly, Cole was up retrieving Rachel's pain pills from the bedroom and filling a cup with water. He handed her a pill, then raised the glass of water to her lips. It was a surprise when Rachel said, "Stop."

With his hand suspended in midair, Cole's gaze met hers. "Sorry. I forgot you don't *need* any help."

Rachel wrapped two hands around the glass. "I'm honest enough to say that I still need help. And I'm honest enough to admit that I want my independence back."

"I know, I know. Don't baby you." Everywhere he turned, he was unwelcome in a house that used to embrace him. Only, now he wasn't so sure it had ever embraced him fully.

"Cole, be honest with me about what you want and why. Fatherhood is so new to you that you probably don't even know what to think. Trust me, it's easy to create this fairy-tale family life, but reality is...well, reality." Keeping her eyes steady on Cole, Rachel managed to take a drink without spilling all over herself, swallowing the big white pill. "She's just met you. You said yourself that she's not comfortable with you. You can't tell Jenna something as important as this just yet."

Rachel had grown into a wise woman. Her words were fair when Cole's intentions may not have been. Cole felt very small. He'd always considered himself an honorable man. Now he wasn't so sure.

"I want my daughter." Cole forced the words out of his suddenly dry mouth. "When do you plan on telling Jenna?"

"Do I look as if I've been making plans?" Rachel snapped, then immediately apologized. "I'm cranky. It's hard for me to accept that it's a struggle just for me to sit upright, but to deal with all of this, too..."

But Cole was adamant. "How about in another week?" Surely by then Rachel would have regained much of her strength, balance and patience, and Jenna would be used to him.

"How about no? She's ten. You can't just spring things like this on her. She's got to get used to you first." Rachel dropped her voice to a whisper. "Otherwise, it's the same as telling her Santa isn't real—you leave her with nothing."

"Okay, okay. When we're friends, I'll tell her." Cole made friends easily. He had no doubt he could win his daughter over in the time it took Rachel to heal. After all, he had their evening cooking lessons to look forward to.

But Rachel was onto him. "Do you have some friendship test to measure when that is? You may have contributed your genes, but I'm the closest thing to a parent she's had in five years. You'll wait until she gets used to you, and I'm there to help her understand things."

"Sure, sure." At the sight of Mr. Quinlan in the kitchen doorway, Cole stood, having decided that he and Rachel would never agree. He'd have to do this on instinct, which meant he had to stop letting his daughter run away from him. "I'm going outside to find out what's taking Matt so long."

## *CHAPTER EIGHT*

"I REMEMBER THAT BOY and what he did," Pop said with a put-you-in-your-place tone. He set his coffee cup down before sitting across from Rachel at the scarred, wooden kitchen table. "He raised quite a ruckus around here. I thought he'd changed, but he was just putting one over on me. He should leave, soon." That was the closest Brian Quinlan would come to saying that Cole had broken Missy's heart. Her father handled every upset, from his wife's mental illness to Missy's downward spiral and demise, with pragmatic solutions.

"I know he upset Missy." Rachel didn't want to have the father-daughter discussion her dad so clearly wanted to have. She was too busy wondering what Cole was going to do outside once he found Jenna.

When he'd asked Rachel what she felt was the appropriate time to tell Jenna the truth, all she could think of was never, never, never. If she lost Jenna, there'd be one less reason to come back to Eden at the end of every season, one less reason to remember Missy. Desire for independence or not, Rachel wasn't ready to let her niece go. She was afraid that Cole's news would change their lives forever.

"That boy came from someplace full of trouble—New York or California or somewhere," Pop continued.

"Texas," Rachel supplied before taking a sip of the coffee Cole had made for her. "I didn't think Texas was known for raising troublemakers."

Not sharing Rachel's humor, Pop regarded her over the rim of his coffee cup. "The three of you used to raise hell in this town."

"We weren't so bad. Innocent fun. Kid stuff." But Missy hadn't been a kid when she'd driven off Moe's Curve. Should Rachel ask Pop if he'd suspected Missy had wanted to end her life?

"I'm not so sure about that. There was the *wedding* incident." Her dad tilted his head as if daring her to contradict him.

Questions about Moe's Curve vanished in Rachel's rush to defend Cole. "What happened between Missy and Cole is long past." Rachel suspected that wasn't totally true for Cole. He'd been close to tears this morning when they'd talked through the meaning of Missy's note. "I don't want you to start anything with him, Pop. He could challenge our guardianship of Jenna." Though she wasn't completely sure of that. Cole may have matured, but he still wasn't jumping wholeheartedly on the responsibility bandwagon. He wouldn't want custody.

"He wouldn't dare." Ruffled, the old man sat up straighter. "He may not rank high in my book, but he cares about you…or thinks he does. The way he looks at you…I just don't want him to break your heart, too."

Her father could barely see. "You don't know—"

"I've seen the way you look at him." Pop cut Rachel off with a wave of one hand. "And I've seen how he helps you around. He's hovered over you these past few days and tried to boss us around. It's not Jenna he wants."

Rachel suspected her dad's concerns might have more to do with his pride than his concern for Rachel. What had Cole been doing while she'd been recovering? Rachel looked around and noticed for the first time that there were no dishes stacked in the sink. The countertop and stove looked cleaner than she'd ever seen them on returning from the season.

Pop shook his bony finger at Rachel. "And I don't think it would be above him to try to wheedle his way into your good graces by being nice to Jenna or Matt. So, don't be fooled. There's too much at stake to repeat Missy's mistakes."

"The only reason he's being nice to me is out of respect for the feelings he had for Missy and the feelings he had for me eleven years ago." Rachel lifted her coffee cup, restless and irritable that Cole was making her feel this way and she couldn't do a darn thing about it. She would forever be someone Cole thought of fondly, someone who replaced his younger sister. "The quicker I get back in the air, the sooner he'll be out of here." Rachel paused, realizing the truth in her observation. "And if we hold our tempers and stay rational, I'm sure he'll be happy with visitation."

Pop considered Rachel's words only a moment before shaking his head.

"You think he's just going to walk out of here without upsetting the apple cart?" Pop didn't look pleased. "We'll see, won't we? We'll see."

"HEY, THERE," Cole said, sitting on the porch with Matt when Jenna rode up.

Matt sat very close to Cole, leaning against the big man as if he'd known him forever. Matt was too trusting.

Jenna almost turned to head back out on Shadow, but she was hungry and she had to get ready for school.

"Hi," Jenna answered back, flinging herself off Shadow's back before they'd barely come to a stop in front of the house. Jenna pulled Shadow's head down to her chest for a nuzzle and a kiss, then she gave the dark horse an encouraging shove on the shoulder, and the horse trotted off to the water trough.

"That's a pretty cool trick," Cole said.

Jenna froze, her bare foot resting on the bottom porch step. "Trick?"

"The way you ride that horse." Cole stood up, brushing dirt off the back of his jeans while he stared at her…without the usual weird look on his face, as if he liked her all of a sudden. "Ever try riding him with a saddle and bridle?"

And then he had to ask her a stupid question. She rolled her eyes. "No."

Matt laughed. "Shadow wouldn't put up with that."

Jenna stared at Shadow, who tossed his head as if he'd been listening and wanted to say, "Yeah, right." Shadow stretched his neck toward Taffy, Matt's plump Shetland pony, who had wandered over to the fence to say hello.

"Matt, go inside and eat breakfast," Cole said.

"You burned breakfast," Matt protested.

"Then go have cereal. Go on."

Matt's boots clumped across the porch. The screen door opened and closed.

When Jenna turned back around, Cole was frowning. Jenna looked away, a funny feeling that had nothing to do with hunger in her stomach. She'd made him mad.

But when Cole spoke, he wasn't mad at all. "Don't you ever get scared when you're riding him like that?"

"Nope." Jenna took a deep breath, waiting for his temper to blow. When it didn't, Jenna climbed the three steps to the porch, risking a look at him as she passed. "The Indians used to ride horses that way."

"What does your dad think about you riding like that?"

Jenna swallowed and looked at her dirty toes. "My dad doesn't care."

"I bet that's not true," Cole said. "I bet if you asked him, he'd say he cared."

With a shake of her head, Jenna tried to get rid of the sadness thinking about her dad caused. The only time she saw her dad was in town. He never came to visit. It wasn't like she missed him and his friends yelling at her. Jenna knew dads weren't supposed to be like that. But still…

Cole was smiling again. "You could compete if you put a saddle on him."

"Compete?" Jenna glanced up at Cole.

"Sure." His smile got bigger, friendlier. "Barrel racing. Can't do that without a saddle."

Jenna could see herself on Shadow winning a blue ribbon, then hanging on the fences at the rodeo with friends. She started to smile until she remembered that her dad worked at the rodeo when it came to town. If she messed up… "Why would I want to do something stupid like that?" Jenna stomped across the porch to the mudroom door.

Cole moved with her, shrugging. "They give out prizes for the fastest horse and rider."

"I never win anything." But how Jenna wished she could win something, just once. Maybe then her dad would like her. He'd look at her and smile the way Cole did, instead of looking all mean.

"You might…with a horse like Shadow." The screen door creaked as Cole opened the door for her.

Jenna frowned. "It doesn't matter. Shadow doesn't like saddles."

"Maybe we could change that."

Now it was Jenna's turn to shrug. She wiped her feet on the thick rug and frowned again, this time for a different reason. "What's that smell?"

Cole looked embarrassed, something else her dad had never done, she realized. "I burned breakfast."

"You won't do that to dinner, will you?" Jenna couldn't believe she was teasing the big man and was amazed when he didn't snap at her. It was almost like talking to Pop, except Cole didn't look as if a strong breeze would blow him over.

"I won't if you help me cook. You like learning how to cook, don't you?" Cole smiled but he didn't look at her. He just walked past Jenna into the kitchen. "We'd better move fast or you'll miss the bus."

Jenna lingered in the mudroom, wetting down a paper towel and cleaning the bottoms of her bare feet, thinking about how right the world would be if she could just prove to her dad that she was something other than the nothing he thought she was.

"YOU CAN'T LET JENNA continue to ride her horse like that," Cole said to Rachel after the rest of her family had eaten bacon and cereal for breakfast and then wandered down the hall to get dressed. He hoped Jenna was going to take a quick shower or at least clean up, because she looked like a hillbilly wild child with bare feet, worn overalls and blond hair that stuck out everywhere. At least now he knew why she always showed up looking dirty and windblown.

"Why should I stop her from riding Shadow? He's old. He wouldn't do anything to hurt her. They've had training." Rachel sat against the kitchen wall, gripping her coffee cup as if it alone would help keep her upright.

She might just fly that plane on willpower alone. Cole had always admired how gutsy Rachel was, but he'd also tried to protect her from anything too dangerous. The only way he'd be keeping Rachel on the ground come Saturday was to tie her up in bed—sexy, but not practical, given that the rest of the family seemed to want her to fly. And the only way to keep Jenna safe from harm seemed to be for her to ride that horse with a saddle.

"Rach, I don't care how old that horse is or how trustworthy he's been in the past, Jenna can still get hurt. You have acres and acres of land out here. Shadow could stumble in a prairie-dog hole and throw Jenna off."

Rachel studied Cole for a moment. Her scrutiny awakened something warm and pleasant inside him.

"I'd forgotten that about you," she said.

"What?" He blinked, his mind having drifted to thoughts of Rachel, in bed and in his arms, minus the nightmares, minus the clothes, plus—

"That even though it was okay for you to risk your life, you never wanted me to risk mine. You weren't near as bad as Missy, but…" Rachel shook her head. "You didn't want me to fly—"

"Because it was too dangerous. I think the crash proved me right." Thickheaded woman.

"You don't want Jenna to ride—"

"I want her to be more cautious, is all." Cole could feel his face scrunch into a scowl, all pleasant images of Rachel in bed gone.

"Would it be better if we padded the floor around here? She's learning to make choices on her own. I can't be there for her all the time."

"Why is wanting to protect someone all that bad?"

"Because if it's not broken you don't need to fix it." Rachel sighed. "Look, I don't want to fight about something you know nothing about."

But Cole did know about risks and safety and accidents that happened, leaving you with nothing but heartache. "Damn it, Rachel, she's just a kid who thinks she's invincible. You and I both know that people die from the stupidest mistakes. You're the adult here. Maybe if you acted like it sometimes..." Too late, Cole realized what he'd done.

Rachel's features were set firmly in a you-have-crossed-that-line expression. "I wish I didn't need your help. As soon as I'm recovered enough to take care of *my* family, I want you to leave."

"But Rach—"

She held up a hand and cut him off. And then the phone rang.

"SURE, BRING IT OUT on Saturday." With calm, modulated sentences, Rachel spoke with the airplane broker, though deep inside tremors were building, threatening to shake her until she could no longer hold it together. Her father was excited about the airplane, but that was just his way of making sure Rachel could make a living. Most likely he didn't realize that Rachel hadn't yet come to grips with taking to the air again.

Cole shot her a questioning look, but Rachel ignored him as she turned the cordless phone off. For a few minutes neither one of them spoke.

It had been a week and a half since the accident, and Rachel still wasn't walking on her own. She had three days to pull herself together.

"Could you hand me that bowl on the counter?"

Rachel asked Cole. She wasn't even steady enough to walk over by herself and get it.

Cole did as she requested, then returned to what she was coming to think of as his spot—the vee where the two counters came together. He had a way of leaning into the counter and crossing one booted foot over the other, looking superior and sexy all at the same time.

Rachel kept her gaze carefully averted and dug through the bits of papers and odds and ends until she found what she was looking for—the Privateer's insurance card. She called her agent, who was located on the East Coast, and reported the loss. He was polite about it, but Rachel could tell that she'd be getting notification soon about raised rates or dropped coverage.

"Matt?" she called, once she'd said goodbye to the agent.

Matt came barreling down the hall from the living room where she'd heard him watching cartoons. "What, Mommy?"

"Can you get Pop's cane out of the closet?" Pop didn't like to use the cane. He said it made him look like an old man. "Then brush your teeth and gather your stuff. You don't want to miss the bus."

"You've got to be kidding me?" Cole came to kneel at Rachel's feet, resting one hand on her knee. "You're not going to walk somewhere. You'll fall quicker than a house of cards."

"I need to go out to the hangar."

Matt came pounding across the kitchen floor with the cane and his tennis shoes. He put them on, then thrust his feet toward Cole, who tied them without even blinking.

"I'm going to the bus," Matt called. "Hurry up, Jenna." The front door opened.

"Bye," Jenna yelled a moment later, before slamming the door.

"Please, tell me there's not a plane in that hangar, Rachel, because I will lock you inside the house before I let you fly in your condition."

Rachel ignored the way Cole's words created vivid pictures that would never be. "There's a plane out there—"

Cole swore.

"—but it doesn't have an engine." She was almost done rebuilding the old C119 for a collector in Nevada. She owed the man a telephone call to tell him her work would be delayed. But she couldn't quite remember what still needed to be done on the engine. The doctor had warned her that until she was fully recovered sometimes simple memories or calculations could elude her. But, damn, reaching for something in her memory that she should know was frustrating.

"You don't need to go out there, Rachel," Cole said.

"I do," Rachel insisted. "I won't get paid until the work is done. The insurance won't cover the full replacement cost of my Privateer and since it's highly unlikely that NIFC or the Forest Service will hire another World War II-era plane, I'll need a mint to buy a more modern air tanker. I've been sitting on my duff long enough." She could see a pile of bills on the counter already. "I have responsibilities here that I can't ignore just because I've had a setback."

"A setback?" For a moment Cole didn't speak. He sat in front of her, worry lining his face.

She wanted to comfort him, to reassure Cole that she'd suck it up and get by, like always.

With a sigh, Rachel gave in and cradled his face with one palm. "I've faced worse and kept on going. These kids…my dad…" She wanted Cole to understand that she wasn't a fool, yet she couldn't wait until she was one hundred percent better, not with mouths to feed and a mortgage to pay. It wasn't as if Lyle paid child support. And then there was the way she felt vulnerable relying on others to help her accomplish the most basic of tasks…like walking. Next thing you know, they'd be behind on their mortgage again. She couldn't let Missy down like that. "I need to keep moving forward."

Cole's hand came up to cover hers. Rachel tried to breathe normally. His touch was heavenly. But then Cole's lips compressed into a firm line. With a strong grip, he removed her hand from his cheek, but he didn't let go of her. "For cryin' out loud, Rachel, your head is still a bit swollen and you can barely walk."

"I'm going to change that." Rachel gripped the metal cane with her free hand. She wanted it badly enough to try. "You can either help me or get out of the way."

"And watch you fall like you've done twice already? No, thanks." Cole didn't look happy, but then again, he hadn't looked very happy since he'd been here. He stood, ready to help.

With one of Cole's hands wrapped around her free arm, Rachel pushed herself up using the cane and his help. She wobbled—how predictable—but stood without her entire body plastered against Cole. Which was a good thing, right?

Right.

Rachel blew out a breath and accepted the fact that she'd need a steadying hand to get her over to the hangar. Maybe by tomorrow she'd be able to hobble out there on her own.

"Ready?" she asked Cole, risking her equilibrium to look up at his face.

Cole shook his head ruefully. "Somehow I knew it would come to this."

Though it killed her curiosity, Rachel couldn't look up at him anymore without losing her balance. She took a step to cover her weakness. "Come to what?"

"Me following you around like a whipped puppy dog."

Him following her implied affection and wanting, and a ton of other things that Rachel knew weren't possible. "Have you been around babies much?"

"No. Why?"

"Some babies want to be cuddled and coddled. From the moment Jenna was born, you could tell she only tolerated being held." Rachel started the awkward process of walking across the kitchen. "She'd lean into you, but her eyes were always looking around at what was out there. She just needed you for support. Then, when she was about ten months old, she started trying to walk. It became impossible to carry her. She wanted to grip your fingers and walk all the time."

"You think this is like that?"

Rachel could ignore what he was saying easier than she could the effect of his body touching hers. "When Matt came along, he was the exact opposite. He wanted to cuddle all the time. I don't think he took a first step until he was about fifteen months old. He was comfortable just being with someone." Rachel had always thought Matt needed more tender loving care because of his difficult birth.

They'd reached the mudroom door. Cole held it open wide, and Rachel shuffled out onto the porch, feeling fresh air on her face for the first time since she'd come home. It was enough to keep her going.

"You're saying I should prepare myself for Jenna to be just as stubborn as you?"

"No…I mean, you *should* be prepared, because she will be. But would you let me finish?" Rachel put her feet very carefully on the top porch step. Doing great. She'd be running in no time. "I asked the doctor if I should be concerned with Matt taking to walking slower than Jenna had, and he told me that everybody is different in the way they learn. Some kids buck the so-called rules and walk at ten months. Some kids take longer."

"So you think you have this special power to heal faster than others."

"You didn't let me finish," Rachel chastised as she walked slowly across the hard ground. "The doctor told me that it all depends on a child's will to do something."

"I'm listening."

"You've got to want it bad enough to risk falling. No one's going to be there to pick up the slack if I don't push myself back up."

Cole was silent as they passed the pasture with Taffy in it. The plump pony sidled up along the fence and kept them company on their way to the hangar.

"I suppose," Cole said as they reached the corner of the aluminum building, "I'd be more understanding if you'd tell me why it's so important you do this now instead of tomorrow or the next day. Most people understand that you have to take time to recover your strength. You know, you almost—"

Rachel clapped a hand over Cole's mouth before he became all doom and gloom again. Her ribs protested, but it was worth it since his warm breath tickled her palm, creating mushy sensations throughout her body. "Contrary to what you believe, I do realize the severity of what I've been through." She withdrew her hand, leaning more heavily against Cole as she tried to steady herself. Being near him was a sweet torture. She was close enough to kiss him, yet knew that would never happen because she wasn't Missy. "I've always had to look forward, because looking back just reminds me of all the pain."

"Like with your mom."

An image of Missy on the kitchen floor next to Rachel, scrubbing the linoleum with a toothbrush, snuck past Rachel's defenses. She'd never been able to brush her teeth after that without feeling gross. To erase the memory, Rachel focused on Taffy, watching the way her ears perked up as if to hear their conversation. She was such a gentle pony.

"I suppose," Rachel allowed, handing the cane to Cole when they reached the hangar door so that she could spin the chamber on the combination lock.

She felt Cole's stare like a touch. "I know you don't want to go into details, but was your mother that bad?"

Rachel concentrated on removing the lock and not on her mother. Tried not to picture her short, brassy blond hair, tried not to feel her mother's arms around her when she hugged her good-night. Tried to forget her promises, and failed. "She used to tell me that tomorrow we'd have a better day, but tomorrow never was a better day." In fact, most of the time when her dad wasn't around, tomorrow sucked.

Rachel looked at Cole with those dark, wide eyes that showed no bravado, only fear from something in the past, something Cole had been unable to protect her from.

Cole found himself wrapping his arms around her and pulling her near as if she were made of the finest china. Breakable. "I hadn't realized you were so fragile," he said softly, as if even the words he spoke had to be gentle.

Rachel was turning her face up to his, pressing against him as her lips reached his. And then she was kissing him, offering her warmth, seeking his. All this time he'd tried not to imagine what it would be like to kiss Rachel...and had failed. But her body pressed to his, her lips on his, was better than he imagined.

And then it was Cole who swayed as Rachel pushed him away.

"I am so sorry." Clinging to the hangar door, Rachel inched back. Her cheeks were beet red and her lips still wet from their kiss.

What in the hell did Rachel have to be sorry about? The kiss had been fabulous.

And then Cole remembered Missy and suffered a pang of guilt. He'd loved Missy, hadn't he? Enough to foolishly put his life on hold while he waited for her to come back to him. Could that love fade so quickly?

Using the workbench that lined the wall for balance, Rachel moved deeper into the hangar, away from where Cole stood wrestling with his feelings.

Love could fade because it hadn't really been love and he hadn't truly put his life on hold. He'd charged out into the world without the driving need to find a mate. His fondest memories of Eden, those that he'd shared most with his friends, had been of his time with Rachel. What he'd felt for Missy had been healthy teenage lust.

Cole wandered into the hangar. There was room inside for two planes, but only one rested in the bay. It was another old warplane. Its metal hull was dull with age and, unlike the plane Rachel had lost, this one had two propellers, not four. If the house and Rachel's bedroom lacked Rachel's imprint, the hangar did not. There were posters on the wall of clear blue skies and airplanes rising above clouds. There was also a bulletin board with pictures of Jenna and Matt, articles about wildland fires, and a picture of Missy, her once lustrous hair limp and lifeless, her playmate figure and angular face rounded into housewifely plumpness. There was no sparkle to her eyes. But there was also a picture of Rachel and Missy when they were around Jenna's age, like goofs, their arms looped around each other's shoulders.

Cole plucked that photo from the bulletin board and carried it over to Rachel. "When was this photo taken?"

Rachel sank onto a stool, looking as if she'd seen a ghost. "A lifetime ago."

When Rachel didn't expand on her remark, Cole realized she must be feeling some of the same guilt he'd wrestled with. "It's weird, isn't it? You and I without Missy?"

Rachel drew a hand over her eyes.

"Maybe *weird* isn't the right word," Cole said, peering at Rachel, trying to read her reaction. "Maybe something like...*surprising*." Was that why he'd let Missy marry Lyle all those years ago? Because deep inside he'd known what he felt for Missy was superficial and physical?

"Surprising?" Rachel finally spoke.

Cole nodded as memories tumbled fast and furiously through his mind. Like the time Rachel had dared Cole to jump off the high-dive platform at the school pool and then followed him. They'd gone again and again, laughing so hard they'd been unable to jump anymore, while Missy looked on from a bench, unwilling to get her hair wet. Or the time Cole and Rachel had raced on horseback down by the gully while Missy followed at a more sedate pace with the rest of their friends. Or the many times they'd spent entire week-ends taking apart Cole's truck engine and putting it back together, their coveralls splattered with grease while Missy shopped with friends in town.

Missy may have satisfied his hormones, but almost any high-school girl could have done that. It was her spitfire of a sister who had set Missy apart from the other girls. He felt alive when Rachel was around.

"I am such a fool," Cole muttered.

Rachel blushed crimson.

"Oh. No, not about that...about you." He couldn't tell Rachel he'd just got over her sister, or that he'd realized he'd always had stronger feelings for Rachel. Go figure. He was falling for the most independent, frustrating, beautiful woman on the planet.

Meanwhile, Rachel stood, using the cane for support. "I need to uncover that engine over there."

Still reeling from his revelation, Cole dutifully took Rachel's arm and helped her cross the hangar. He was totally unprepared for the burning need to wrap his arms around her and kiss her again. Only the rigid set of her spine kept him from doing so.

After about twenty feet, Rachel paused and looked down at an old oil stain on the concrete. "I remember fixing that leaky gasket." Then Rachel looked up, as if at a wing that should have been there. She swayed into him, then tensed and inched away. "Something isn't right."

He hoped she was remembering the foolish risks she'd taken in the air, not their kiss.

No such luck. "I think we need to pretend that didn't happen," she said.

"No. Not in a million years, sweetheart." Just remembering the feel of her lips on his heated Cole's blood.

"I don't know how many more times you want me to apologize. If I offended you by kissing you and you won't accept my apology, I'll understand," she said, moving again.

"I don't want your apology."

"You loved Missy. I was just your surrogate little sister." Rachel's voice seemed strained. "You've been taking the news about Missy really hard. I kissed you in a weak moment. I'll understand if you can't stay here anymore."

"You want me to leave?" Just when Cole was starting to see clearly?

"No… Yes… I mean, you can go if I've totally overstepped the bounds of our friendship."

Cole turned Rachel to face him. "You have leapfrogged over the friendship line, Rach. And I don't much care."

Unaccountably, tears spilled over her cheeks. "You're not making this easy."

"I'm not saying you've offended me, damn it. I'm saying that maybe I wanted that kiss as much as you did." Gently he wiped away her tears. "This is new territory for me, but maybe it's where we're meant to go."

"Meant to go?" Rachel couldn't think straight for a moment because Cole Hudson thought they might be destined for more than friendship.

Her lips tingled from the memory of kissing Cole. He kissed hot enough to melt her bra straps off. It was both better and worse than she'd imagined, because Rachel was doomed to either succumb to temptation or carry the memory of that one kiss to her grave.

When Rachel had come to her senses, staggering back from their kiss, Cole had looked at her as if those straps *had* melted away, giving him full access to Rachel. Then he'd started babbling about how foolish he'd been, and Rachel had wanted the floor to swallow her up.

And then he'd said the words she'd dreamed of...well, almost. He hadn't said he loved her, but that maybe they were meant to be.

Now, as they stood in the hangar, his arms wrapped around her supportively, Rachel could just imagine Cole pulling her closer, urgent with need. She had no trouble at all visualizing him pressing her against the hangar wall, exploring her flesh with hands whose touch sent dizzying spirals of desire through her until she could no longer resist the hunger between them.

If Rachel turned slightly, she could kiss Cole again, perhaps pursue her fantasy. Rachel's pulse quickened. She risked a half glance at Cole, and he reached up to brush her cheek with the back of his hand.

Something in his hand caught her eye—the picture of Missy and Rachel.

*Missy gripped Rachel's hand in the hospital room after Matt was born. "When Cole comes back, don't let him sweet-talk you into anything. You know he doesn't always think things through, and you two are so alike it scares me."*

Rachel's pulse slowed. Even if Rachel and Cole

made love in the one place on the Quinlan ranch that wasn't haunted by the painful ghosts of Rachel's past, Rachel knew with gut-wrenching certainty that the heat in Cole's eyes would fade. He'd remember Missy after their physical needs had been quenched, and he'd have regrets. Rachel's regrets could fill this hangar. She didn't need any more.

They may be struggling to retool their friendship, but Rachel doubted their friendship could survive the betrayal of making love.

And that's what love between Rachel and Cole was—a betrayal to Missy.

"I need… We can't…" But Rachel couldn't finish either sentence. With deliberate movements Rachel leaned on the cane and walked away from Cole.

He didn't break the silence with his usual battery of questions. Rachel should have felt grateful that she'd made Cole realize "they" could never be. And yet she couldn't ignore the wave of disappointment.

## *CHAPTER NINE*

JENNA FELT SICK. She sat in front of the computer after school while Aunt Rachel lay down on the couch. Aunt Rachel had been waiting for Jenna to get home to show Jenna the pictures she'd been hoping she'd never have to see.

"Just keep clicking Next until the pictures are loaded," Aunt Rachel said.

"'And Princess Penelope was locked away in a tower by the evil queen who was jealous of Penelope's beauty.'" Aunt Rachel was reading *The Sky Tower* story to Matt again.

"Penelope was sad," Matt said, "because she didn't know she was going to be rescued."

"That's right," Rachel said, then turned the page. "Are all the pictures on the computer yet, Jenna?"

"No." Jenna didn't want to look at the pictures, but she knew she only had to look this one time, just like she did every year. It seemed to make Aunt Rachel happy. But it scared Jenna to death.

The first picture came up. It was a photo of a beautiful forest and tree-covered mountains. It would have looked like the forest in *The Sky Tower* book, except—

"Look at how high that fire went," Aunt Rachel said, pointing out the flames that climbed twice as high as the trees that were burning. "It sent up a draft of air that bumped the Privateer at least ten feet vertically."

"Ten feet, huh?" Pop sat in his comfy chair near the fireplace, his head tilted back against the pillows. He couldn't see the pictures that well, but he always liked when Aunt Rachel told her stories.

Unlike Jenna.

"'The tower rose up in the bright blue sky until it almost touched the clouds. It was so lovely that Princess Penelope would have been happy, except she missed her family.'" Rachel read on. "'And one day, a knight in shining armor climbed the tower and showed Princess Penelope the way out.'"

"The princess couldn't fall in love until she was rescued," Matt said, turning the page. "And by a prince, too."

As if everybody in the room hadn't read the story a thousand times. Jenna rolled her eyes.

Cole moved closer to the computer, leaning over Jenna's shoulder. "Where is that?"

"Michigan," Rachel said, putting the book on the coffee table. "Go to the next one, Jenna."

The next picture showed a plane dumping slurry on the flames.

"I took that one as we flew over their plane," Aunt Rachel explained. "We were setting up for our run."

"Did they..." Jenna struggled to ask. "Did they crash, too?"

"No, sweetie. That was back in June," Aunt Rachel said softly. "Besides, planes hardly ever crash."

Cole made a snorting noise. Jenna took that to mean he didn't believe Aunt Rachel was safe in the air, either. She suddenly felt she should like Cole, because they were the only two in the house who feared for Aunt Rachel's safety. Jenna turned her head to look at the big man and smiled.

He smiled back and put a large hand on her shoulder, giving it a squeeze. It felt good, like when Pop did that.

They went through more pictures of fire and planes flying at impossible angles that turned Jenna's stomach. She didn't want to think about her aunt in one of those planes, but she couldn't stop. It was almost good the Privateer had been smashed, because that meant Aunt Rachel might not have the money to buy another plane. Jenna had heard Pop and Aunt Rachel talk about the plane coming Saturday. She'd heard the worry in Aunt Rachel's voice and been glad. She wouldn't fly if she was afraid.

"The sky looks orange." Matt came to stand on the other side of Jenna, looking at a picture of a tanker flying in the smoky sky.

"I've seen skies that color," Cole said, looking at Jenna. "Have you ever seen a pink sunset? The sun must have been setting and it made the brown smoke look orange."

Then came a picture of Aunt Rachel's copilot, Danny, standing next to the silver wing of the Privateer.

"I'd forgotten about that one. He looks really happy, doesn't he?" Aunt Rachel sniffed, as if holding back tears.

"He reads stories really good," Matt said. "When is he coming back?"

"He's dead," Jenna said, nearly crying herself. She stared at Aunt Rachel. "You could be dead, too, if you fly again." Jenna couldn't think of much else other than the fact that Aunt Rachel's plane had crashed and that if Aunt Rachel flew again, she might die.

Matt launched himself at Aunt Rachel and started to cry.

Aunt Rachel flinched. "Nothing's going to happen to me."

"I hate looking at these pictures. How can you show them to me and then promise you won't die?" Jenna stood, stepping past Cole and then hopping around the coffee table until she had a clear path to the door.

Maybe this time she'd hop on Shadow and never return. Maybe then Aunt Rachel would be sorry that she wanted to fly again.

"THAT WENT WELL," Cole observed with an arch of his brows. "I can see why you were afraid to lose those pictures."

Rachel wanted to deck Cole. Instead she held Matt close and wished she hadn't kissed Cole that morning. Coward that she was, she'd been pretending to sleep all day so she wouldn't have to talk to Cole about why she couldn't have what she wanted, thus appearing foolish. She'd been the one to kiss him, after all. And

Rachel hated being a coward. Which was why she'd suggested they all look at her flying pictures. That way she could remind herself how strong and capable she was. Only, now she rediscovered what an idiot she actually was.

"Any fool can see that Jenna is scared of losing you. Do you feel good knowing that she's upset and out there riding that wild mustang without any gear to protect her?" Cole paced the room.

Rachel glared at him. He was right. How had she not seen Jenna's fear before? He'd thought Jenna had been afraid for Rachel back at the hospital, too.

"I don't see what the problem is," Pop said. "Jenna's always enjoyed looking at pictures with Rachel at the end of the season."

Cole pointed at the computer. "Those pictures are scaring her. I don't know if it's just because of this crash or if she's always been afraid. This might be the first time she's had the nerve to tell you."

Unaware that Rachel agreed with him, Cole rolled brutally on. "What are you trying to prove with these things? What a daredevil you are? Hell, I'm an adult who works on fires and some of these shots worry me."

Matt turned his head in Cole's direction. "You're scaring me, mister."

"That's okay, Matt. I think Cole's scared, too." Rachel rubbed Matt's back. "Why don't you go get a snack?"

When Matt had gone, Rachel announced, "I may have scared Jenna, but she's fine now. On that horse she's as confident and strong as I am in the air." Or at least as confident as Rachel had been.

"You wear a safety harness when you fly, don't you?" Cole pressed on. "Sure, you can fly without it, but that one precaution saved your life."

Rachel's stomach felt queasy at the mention of her close call. She pushed any thought of flying aside. Was Cole right? He was so overprotective that it was hard to tell. Or was Rachel a poor guardian if she didn't try to protect Jenna better?

"Maybe you could try to saddle break him," Rachel allowed. "Although," she added when Cole started to look superior. "Shadow won't be easy to convert from bareback to saddle and bridle." More likely it would be Shadow who taught Cole a lesson, because Cole was sure to be gone long before a horse could be saddle broke. It was a good compromise.

"He's worn a saddle before, and carried people a whole lot heavier than Jenna on his back." Cole was quick to reassure Rachel, so conservative and unlike the boy of her teenage fantasies. "I broke him the first time."

"The operative word being *broke,*" Pop pointed out.

Cole frowned.

Rachel wasn't sure this was the answer, but the activity would keep Cole busy and away from Rachel.

"I know what I'm doing. We've had horses all my life," Cole said. "I'll have Jenna riding in a saddle in no time."

"Is Jenna going to put the saddle on Shadow?" Matt asked, returning from the kitchen with an oatmeal and raison cookie. "Can I ride Taffy with her when she does?"

"Cole thinks he can saddle break Shadow, but he's not going to start until tomorrow." Rachel emphasized the word. "For now, he can help you with Taffy. Why don't you go and get your boots on? You can ride around the pasture until Jenna comes back." Cole leaned over to help Rachel up. He really needed to stop touching her. When he did, the memory of their kiss returned and with it thoughts of what might have happened if she hadn't come to her senses.

"Just go slow with Shadow, okay?" Rachel said, praying for a speedy recovery.

"I know what I'm doing," Cole repeated. "I don't know why I have to wait until tomorrow."

"I do." Rachel struggled for balance. "We've had enough drama for one day."

"Is Mommy paying you to babysit her?" Matt asked as he tried to put a bridle on his little pony. "'Cause you don't live around here."

"Your mom...both your moms and I used to be good friends when we were in high school," Cole said, testing the old bridle he'd found to make sure the leather was still strong. He scanned the horizon for Jenna and Shadow, but they were nowhere to be seen. "Friends help each other." Cole had thought he and Rachel were friends. Then she'd kissed him and everything had changed, including how Rachel interacted with him—or rather didn't interact with him. She'd avoided all conversation by pretending to sleep the day away.

Yeah, he'd known Rachel was faking. If the whole

concept of Cole and Rachel hadn't been so overwhelmingly new, Cole might have called her on it. As it was, he could use a little time to sort things out on his own. He wanted to make sure he wasn't letting his lengthy abstinence lead him into a relationship where his heart wasn't fully committed.

Meanwhile the pony kept tossing its head every time Matt's little arm came near its nose. Matt seemed unconcerned. He just doggedly kept trying. "I have a friend at school. His name is Bob. He can stick a pencil in his ear and not even cry."

"That's quite a talent," Cole said, smiling despite himself. The little boy was growing on him.

Warming to the topic, Matt kept talking and moving his arm up and down in response to the pony's head toss. "There's a girl in my class named Arlee. She can't wear shoes because her toes are 'fected all the time. She says when it snows she's gonna wear her flip-flops 'cause she has a doctor's note."

"Is she your friend, too?" Cole couldn't stand it anymore. He took the small bridle from Matt's plump fingers and slipped it behind the pony's ears before she had a chance to toss her head. He looped the reins around the fence railing and looked around for Jenna.

"No, Bob is my only friend." Matt sounded sad to admit it. "Most of the kids don't like me."

"Why not?" Cole took stock of the little boy. He could guess the kids were cruel because Matt wasn't as slim as he might have been, or the lightest on his feet. Kids of any age could be so cruel, but Matt was such a nice kid it was surprising.

"Do you promise you won't tell Jenna?" Matt asked, looking around with big, worried eyes.

The boy was so earnest that Cole found himself promising with the three-fingered Boy Scout salute. "Wild horses couldn't drag it out of me."

Matt pressed his lips together, then looked around some more. "I sometimes wet my pants in class," he admitted in a soft voice, his plump cheeks turning bright red.

Ouch. That would scare off a roomful of five-year-olds really quick. Rachel hadn't warned him about that. "You only do that in class? Not at home or at night?"

"Just in class," Matt whispered.

Before he realized what he was doing, Cole was saddling the golden pony. "You know, I don't see a lot of adults walking around with wet pants, so I don't think your condition is permanent."

"What does that mean?" Matt squinted up at Cole, looking so much like Rachel with dark slanted eyes and that intense look, that Cole couldn't imagine Matt belonging to anyone else. Missy may have been this kid's biological mother, but Matt was imprinting Rachel's morals and character.

"It means that very soon, maybe by Halloween, maybe by Thanksgiving, you won't be doing that at school anymore."

"Really?" Matt's smile was so wide, it practically split his pudgy cheeks.

"Really."

"Cool." Matt came around to stand in front of Cole,

raising his arms up as if asking to be lifted into the saddle.

Cole hesitated. “Uh, did you go to the bathroom before you came out here?”

“Uh-uh.” Matt’s arms were still up.

“Why don’t you go do that first?”

The little guy ran awkwardly to the house in his boots, stumbling but gamely picking himself back up. The poor kid might just as well paint a bull’s-eye on his back when he went to school.

Cole shook his head. There had to be some way he could help Matt fit in.

When Matt returned, Cole asked, “What does the faucet in the bathroom look like?”

Matt frowned. “I dunno. Why do you want to know?”

“Did you know there are thousands of different faucets out there? All kinds of shapes and colors? When I was little, my dad and I used to play a game where we told each other what the faucets were like at the places we visited.” Later, Cole had realized the game was his dad’s way of getting him in the vicinity of a bathroom so he’d empty his bladder, instead of forgetting to take care of business until the last minute.

Matt crowed with laughter. “That’s cool.”

“Yep,” Cole agreed, wondering what other errand he could send Matt on that involved the school bathroom.

“AUNT RACHEL AND I decided you should try riding Shadow with a saddle.” Cole put a saddle and bridle on the fence railing. He must have found the dusty old stuff in the small shed in Taffy's pasture. "Do you want me to show you how to saddle him?"

"I know how to saddle a horse." Jenna had ridden most of the afternoon on the far side of the Quinlan property trying to outrun the fear of losing Aunt Rachel and chase away her anger at Aunt Rachel for having such a scary job. She'd only just come back and was brushing Shadow while he ate his oats. "Besides, Shadow doesn't like saddles. Aunt Rachel knows that." Aunt Rachel would never agree to something so stupid. In an instant, the anger she'd felt toward her aunt switched over to Cole.

"But it's safer to ride with one."

Jenna didn't answer. Biting her lip, she just kept brushing. She was still scared for Aunt Rachel and embarrassed that she'd yelled at everybody. If she didn't say anything, maybe Cole would go away and forget this saddle business.

Cole didn't leave. Instead he fiddled with the straps of the bridle.

"What you did today was very brave," Cole said. "With the pictures."

Cole thought Jenna was brave? She didn't feel very brave.

Jenna snuck a peek at Cole to see if he was joking or not. Shadow did the same thing, then sniffed and started to eat his alfalfa.

"Did you know I used to own Shadow?"

Jenna stopped brushing and turned to look at Cole. "Shadow doesn't like men. You couldn't have owned him before."

"I was only seventeen, not much older than you," Cole said. "He was a high school graduation present from my dad. He found Shadow at a government auction with a bunch of other wild mustangs."

"Like Hidalgo," Jenna said. She'd already known that.

"Just like that." Cole smiled. "Anyway, I was too busy getting a job after graduation and I didn't spend as much time with him as I should have. So he never really finished his training."

Jenna liked that Shadow was wild. And she liked that she was the only one able to ride him. "Then my mom bought him."

"I think someone else had him next. Your aunt said Missy…your mom…bought him about five years ago." Cole looked a little sad, like maybe he'd cried when he'd sold Shadow.

Jenna was never selling Shadow. They were going to grow old together. She wrapped an arm around Shadow's neck.

"Anyway, I think you and Shadow are a talented team. I'd hate to see anything happen to the two of you because you weren't using the right equipment."

Jenna frowned. "I don't want to use any of that stuff. We like riding our way."

"If Shadow took the bridle and saddle, you could ride him in places other than the ranch. Would you like that?"

Jenna had thought about that before, but she remained quietly loyal to Shadow.

"What if I can train him to take the bridle and saddle?" Cole asked.

Jenna looked at Cole's worn boots, which were the only thing about him that hinted that he might be a cowboy. He didn't even tuck his shirt in or wear a belt with a big, shiny buckle. "Are you sure it wouldn't hurt him?"

Cole shook his head. "Other horses have no problem. Matt rides the pony with a bridle and saddle doesn't he?"

And Taffy was a cream-puff pony. She'd been Jenna's before Shadow had come along.

Jenna would like to be able to take Shadow other places. "As long as you don't hurt him…."

CARRYING THE SADDLE and a saddle blanket, Cole approached the dark gelding. He remembered the last time he'd tried to saddle break this horse. He still had a scar in his hairline from the fence post he'd hit. It was a good thing Matt and Jenna stood at the fence railing. Things could get dangerous out here.

Undaunted, Cole actually had to work at not smiling. It had been a long time since anything other than a fire had sent adrenaline pumping through his veins. It must have been the combination of the challenge ahead and the chance to do something for his daughter.

Jenna hopped off the fence. "I changed my mind."

"This is like a rodeo," Matt said enthusiastically. "Without the clown."

"This is nothing like a rodeo," Cole said evenly, trying not to startle the horse and calm Jenna at the same time. "It's more like television—boring, predictable. Get back on the fence, Jenna."

Shadow had accepted the bridle easily and now chewed it, tossing his head in occasional irritation, but otherwise he seemed fine. Cole walked slowly to the horse, talking nonsense and trying to show Shadow that he meant him no harm.

Not buying it, Shadow whinnied nervously and swung his hindquarters away from Cole, who just kept talking and coming closer. This was definitely an improvement over the ass-kicking horse Shadow had been when Cole had tried to break him eleven years ago. Perhaps Shadow had mellowed.

"He doesn't like this," Jenna said, climbing up on the fence with Matt.

"How can you tell?" Matt asked. "Do we need Mommy?"

"He'll be fine," Cole reassured her in that voice tempered to soothe both horse and girl. Rachel had wanted Cole to wait, but why waste a day?

Shadow was just being cautious. He watched Cole's approach with suspicion, but Cole hadn't seen the whites of his eyes or excessive foaming at the mouth that might indicate stress. This was all posturing—a test of wills. The gelding hoped Cole would back off. Shadow was no dummy. This kind of behavior probably kept Rachel and Jenna in line. What the gelding didn't know was that Cole wasn't going to back off.

Cole carefully placed the saddle on Shadow. The hide on Shadow's back shuddered reflexively and Cole got swatted by the thick black tail, as if the gelding was shooing away an irritating fly that had landed on him rather than a saddle. Cole just kept talking.

It had been years since Cole had saddled a horse, but he'd been quite the cowboy growing up on the rolling planes of South Texas, and later, here in Eden. He made short work of the task, easier since Shadow stood stock-still, his reins looped over the fence railing.

"Atta, boy." Cole ran a hand down Shadow's neck a few times. "That wasn't so bad." Cole had been expecting bucking and biting, but Shadow seemed to be the big pussycat that Rachel made him out to be.

With a flick of his wrist, Cole loosened the reins and led Shadow away from the fence, getting him used to the feel of the saddle on his back and the cinch around his girth.

"You got the saddle on him." Jenna sounded amazed as she stepped down from the fence and came in through the gate.

"Yep, he's good, like a real bronc rider," Matt said, the pride in his voice unexpectedly as pleasing to Cole as Jenna's amazement.

"I told you." Cole stopped and rubbed Shadow some more, on his neck, underneath the bridle where it lay behind Shadow's ears, underneath his forelock.

Big baby that Shadow seemed to be, he leaned into Cole's hand, silently asking for more attention.

"Get back on the fence, Jenna. I'm going to mount up." Cole's voice was still low and light, as if he was talking endearments to Shadow, which only reminded him how he'd like to try talking endearments to Rachel. After he straightened out Shadow, he was going to corner Rachel for a talk.

Out of the corner of his eye, Cole saw Jenna take a few steps back. "You won't hurt him, right?"

"Me?" Hurt fifteen hundred pounds of compactly muscled horse flesh? "No. I'm not going to hurt him." He had planned to get Shadow used to the saddle over the next couple of days, but Shadow didn't seem fazed by it at all. Maybe Shadow was saddle broke and Rachel didn't even know it.

Jenna climbed back on the fence rail with Matt.

Gripping the reins tight, Cole swung up into the saddle and slid his right boot into the stirrup. Shadow turned his head and looked at Cole, blew out a breath, and…

Just stood still.

That was it? Disappointment weighed on Cole's shoulders. He'd expected the gelding to fight for his independence just as he had when Cole was eighteen and Shadow had been too wild to tame.

He half turned toward Jenna and Matt. "See? There's nothing—"

A rocket exploded beneath him, lifting Cole a belly-dropping foot or two into the air.

Plunging. Twisting. Rocking forward then back.

The reins were of no use. Shadow would have made some rodeo company good money as a bucking bronco.

Jenna came rushing toward them, waving her hands in the air and shouting. Right into their path. What was that girl thinking?

Cole kicked his feet out of the stirrups and rode the momentum of a strong buck right over Shadow's head.

With a tooth-jarring thud, Cole hit the ground and rolled to a skin-flaying halt. Miraculously he didn't get trampled, but the good news was that neither did Jenna.

"I'm okay," he gasped, holding up his hand as Jenna ran toward him.

She ran right on past. "Shadow! Shadow! Are you okay?"

Cole spit bits of dirt and grass out of his mouth, then rolled onto all fours, taking stock of his aches and pains. Nothing seemed broken, except maybe his pride. He'd been beaten by a horse, a creature that supposedly had half the brainpower of a human.

"That was funny," Matt crouched next to him. "Just like the clowns. Can you do it again?"

"No." Cole stood, carefully stretching the kinks out of his back, testing muscles and bones for something worse than a simple deeply humiliating bruising.

"I'm okay," he repeated, glancing over at Jenna, who had tossed Shadow's saddle to the ground and was removing his bridle. "In case you were concerned."

Shadow stood with his tail in Cole's direction, his ears cocked as if listening to Cole. Most likely Cole would see a pair of horse shoes if he tried to come any closer.

Jenna ran her hands up and down Shadow's legs, stroked her palms over his neck and back, soothing the beast that had almost killed her and Cole. "It's all right, Shadow. That mean old man won't hurt you anymore."

"Mean?" Jenna thought *he* was mean?

Jenna picked up the bridle, sending the bit jingling and Shadow off at a hurried trot. "I told you he doesn't like this." She stomped over to the shed and threw the bridle in, then slammed the door and spun to face Cole. "Don't you ever do that again."

The first inklings of anger teased over Cole's bruised body, dumping too much adrenaline back into his veins. "Hey, he almost killed both of us. What you did was totally irresponsible." Cole picked the saddle up out of the dirt.

"What I did? What I did?" Her voice was dangerously close to hysterical. "He's not even your horse, and you hurt him."

Cole hung the saddle back on its wooden platform and the bridle back on its peg. He wiped at something trickling down his face, not surprised to find his forearm streaked with blood. "I think the only one hurt here is me, trying to save your butt from getting trampled. Or maybe you think I should have let him grind you into the dirt."

"Shadow would never hurt me."

"You are not to ride him anymore, not until I can train him to the saddle." Cole was adamant. If his mother ever heard about this, she'd have Cole's hide.

"You can't boss me around. I'm going to tell Aunt Rachel." Jenna spun on her heel and ran toward the house.

"Wait a minute," Cole said, limping along after her, but Jenna didn't wait.

"I HATE HIM!" Jenna barreled into the kitchen with her boots on. Her face was red and her ponytail was askew. She stood in Rachel's bedroom doorway, gripping the frame as if she could squeeze splinters out of it. "He almost killed Shadow."

"What?" Moving quicker than she should have, Rachel pushed herself upright in bed. The nausea was still there, but not as sharp as it had been in the hospital or even yesterday. "Who almost killed Shadow?" But Rachel knew.

"Cole." Jenna stomped her feet. "He put a saddle on him and then he tried to ride him."

Uh-oh.

"Shadow wheeled around like a bucking bronc. He could have banged into the pasture fence and hurt himself."

"Is he okay?" Was Cole?

"Yes, no thanks to Cole." Jenna blinked back tears.

The screen door creaked open.

"Send him away." Jenna spun around and ran through the kitchen to the other end of the house. "You're better. We don't need him."

Heavy footsteps approached. Cole appeared, looking as if he'd been dragged facefirst through the dirt. His T-shirt was torn, and scrapes marred his arms and one cheek.

"Are you all right?" But she didn't wait for him to answer. "I told you that horse doesn't like to be fenced in, saddled up or dictated to." Rachel was simultaneously concerned that Cole was hurt and pleased that Shadow had stood up to Cole. "And yet you tried to ride him even when I asked you to go slow with him."

"Yeah, you told me." He wiped a hand over his face, wincing as he touched his scrapes. "I think he's too wild for Jenna."

"He's not too wild for Jenna. He's too much horse for you."

"I don't want her riding a horse that an adult can't handle."

"You know horses are not one size fits all. They have different preferences, just like people." Cole looked really beat up. With effort, Rachel softened her words. "Face it, Cole, you are no horse whisperer."

He pulled off his boots and tossed them into the mudroom, then came back to sit on her bed with a weary sigh. "He's an old horse. He's not that big. He should be trainable."

"He's mature, not old. He's all muscle and between Jenna and an *experienced* horse trainer, we were able to train him for our purposes just fine. Why do you have to come in here and rock the boat?" Rachel was incredibly worn-out, because she knew the truth. "I'm at fault just as much as you are for agreeing with you. I change my mind from what I said earlier. We don't like saddles. Not ever."

Cole stared at his hands. "I feel as if I'm letting Missy down if I don't make an impact here."

"This has nothing to do with Missy or Jenna and everything to do with you. You charge in without thinking things through in the name of safety and protection." When Cole scowled, Rachel took a deep breath and tried to calm down. "You can make an impact. With Jenna. But not like this. Not coming in and changing things just for the sake of change. Things are the way they are around here because they work for us."

"I want Jenna to be safe."

"So do I. So does Shadow." Rachel sighed. "Why is it so hard for you to see that we are doing all we can to keep each other safe?"

"We? Do you think Jenna believes you're keeping yourself safe every time you fly?" He shook his head and stood. "I'm going to clean off this grime."

"You do that." Because they both needed some time to cool off.

## *CHAPTER TEN*

"TELL HIM TO GO HOME," Jenna said when Rachel entered her bedroom.

It had taken Rachel ten minutes to walk with slow, unsteady steps down the hallway, one shoulder on the wall and the cane in her other hand. She hoped that Cole took a long, cold shower. He wasn't going to be happy to find out she was trying to walk on her own, but to heck with him. Jenna needed her. Rachel knew she'd made the right decision when she'd opened Jenna's bedroom door and seen her niece's distraught face.

In four shaky steps, Rachel made it from the door to the four-poster bed, grabbing onto the bedpost to keep herself from falling to the floor. Ignoring the stab of pain in her rib cage using her upper body muscles caused, Rachel swung herself around, using the momentum to carry her to Jenna's mattress. The way her eyes wouldn't focus had Rachel squeezing them shut and holding her breath.

She was weak, but she'd made it.

Jenna's tear-streaked face was pinched, as if she didn't want to cry anymore. Rachel dropped the cane and held out her arms.

With a sob Jenna crawled across the bed and into Rachel's embrace, tucking her head into the crook of Rachel's neck. "He's stupid. You don't need him anymore, do you?"

Rachel stroked Jenna's hair, not wanting to admit that she wanted Cole, that some part of her craved his supportive touch. In all fairness, she couldn't send Cole away without letting Jenna know the truth. Yet she knew now wasn't the time to tell Jenna, not when her niece was hell-bent on protecting her horse. "I can't make him go away just yet," Rachel admitted.

Jenna hiccupped and then wound herself up for what promised to be a glorious rant fest. "Why not? You should have seen him out there with Shadow. He was a bully. You should have seen the—"

"Wait." Rachel cut Jenna off. She knew Cole wouldn't abuse a horse. "When Cole was a kid, he was a great rider. Are you sure you aren't exaggerating?"

"No." Jenna shook her head against Rachel's neck. Her fingers were twisting the edge of Rachel's shirt. "He was awful. You should have seen him. Why did he do that?"

"It's not all his fault," Rachel felt compelled to admit. "I agreed that he could start training Shadow." Although, she'd also told him to wait until tomorrow and to go slow.

"No. You wouldn't have let him be so mean," Jenna's voice trembled.

"I should have come out to watch him. I'm sorry." Rachel gently brushed Jenna's hair off her forehead. Jenna loved Shadow so much, she'd probably never understand why Cole would want to break him. "Was he that mean? Did he use a whip?"

"No." Jenna wiped at her nose.

"Did he have on spurs?" This was certainly sounding like a young girl's exaggeration.

"No, but—"

"Did he wrestle Shadow to the ground and hog-tie him?"

With an angry elbow to Rachel's rib cage, Jenna pushed herself to the other side of the narrow bed. Robbed of air, Rachel doubled over, sending stars shooting across her vision. Cussing right now would not be appropriate, but would have made Rachel feel a whole lot better about the pain.

"You're on his side," Jenna accused, then repeated louder, "You're on *his* side!"

"Jenna, I'm just trying to understand what happened." Rachel straightened.

"No, you're not. You're defending him," Jenna shouted, drawing herself up against the headboard in a tight ball.

Rachel scooted closer. "Jenna—"

And then all hell broke loose.

"Get out! Get out! Get out!" Jenna cried.

It took Rachel a moment to realize that Jenna wasn't yelling at her, but at someone behind her. Rachel swung her legs around with care so that she could see who stood in the doorway. Not that it mattered. She already knew who it was, knew how devastatingly hurtful Jenna could be when she wound herself up like this.

Cole stood in the doorway, a wounded expression on his face. "I'm sorry," he began.

"*Get out!*"

Although Rachel felt sorry for him, she had to remember that it was nothing more than he deserved. Cole was always jumping in without thinking about the consequences, always butting in when he hadn't been asked.

Jenna would have a hard time getting over this.

"I AM *NOT* SLEEPING in the same room as you," Rachel said after Cole had helped her back to her room. She sat stiffly, without moving, as if any movement made her dizzy, or perhaps she was so mad at him that she really didn't want him to touch her.

He hoped it wasn't the latter. "I don't think you're ready—"

"And I don't think I care. I asked you to wait. I asked you to go slow. Why on earth were you trying to saddle break Shadow in one day? You talk about me frightening Jenna, but you scared that little girl half to death. She loves that horse." Rachel leaned back against the headboard. "It's going to take an act of Congress to get her to forgive you, and even then—"

"You mean I'll have to wait even longer to tell her?" The idea of waiting longer for the truth to be known overshadowed the fact she wanted nothing to do with him.

"Well, you sure as hell can't tell her now, can you?" Rachel didn't seem particularly upset about that part. "Why don't you think things through?"

"I did think it through," Cole protested, more than a bit frustrated now. "I noticed this ranch is a hazard for a horse, much less a girl riding a horse without a bridle or saddle who can't see a thing because she's crying." His voice hardened. "I saw something wrong and I did something about it."

"You hopped into the saddle in front of Jenna when Shadow hasn't even had a saddle pad strapped to him in over five years. And you accused me of having the patience of a five-year-old." She blew out a frustrated breath. They were both so mad that the conversation was going around in circles. "Let's not argue about it *or* the sleeping situation."

"Wait a minute. Back up. I admit I jumped the gun with Shadow." Cole gritted his teeth. The admission cost him a chunk of his pride. "But that has nothing to do with me sleeping in this room or not. You need care, yet you're willing to risk falling because you just don't want to talk about that kiss earlier today."

Rachel passed a hand over her face. "Look, it's bad enough that you escort me into the bathroom and stand on the other side of the door while I pee—"

"If you lose your balance—"

"—but I draw the line on sharing a bed with you."

"—you'll be right back in the hospital."

Rachel closed her eyes, swaying slightly until she opened them. "You may remember that I have problems with authority."

"And rules and advice and anything that logically makes sense." She'd never listened to anything Cole had said when they were younger.

"You're one to talk. If anything, I learned all my daredevil ways from you."

"You've got to be kidding me. I was an upstanding young citizen." That was far from the truth. Back then he'd been hell on wheels. "As I recall, the local sheriff kept bringing *you* home in his cruiser." And despite it all, Mr. Quinlan had continued to encourage Rachel in her reckless pursuit of flying.

Rachel's pallor faded, and Cole was afraid she'd faint. He was about to apologize when she spoke. "Maybe I should refresh your memory. You're the one who raced down a gulley on his motorcycle during a flash flood just ahead of the raging water...on a dare."

"If I hadn't, I wouldn't have found you." By the time he'd seen Rachel, she'd been clinging to a tree mere feet above the turbulent water line. "I was your hero." Back then he'd felt he could do no wrong in Rachel's eyes, so unlike what he faced at home. And now that he realized he wanted her, wanted to be with her, he'd done nothing right.

But Rachel wasn't giving up. "You were pushing your drowned motorcycle back to the ranch in the pouring rain."

"Things turned out all right in the end." He'd crawled across a snag to get to her and brought her safely back to shore. After that she'd worked her mechanical magic on his water-flooded carburetor and introduced him to her sister, who'd never chastised him for his crazy deeds, unlike his dad.

"And what about the time you jumped across the

second-story ledge at the high school when you were late for finals and they locked the doors?"

"Childhood pranks. No harm, no foul." He was a totally different person now. "I could bring up the time you hid in Marney's store after closing so that you could set up the nativity display."

She waved him off. "I only did that because you dared me to. Besides, Marney had asked you to do it, and it was almost Christmas. I was covering your ass. Anyway, just because your shenanigans never sent you to the hospital doesn't mean they weren't dangerous."

Cole looked at the one person in the room who had been in the hospital recently, and didn't have to say a word.

"I took a calculated risk on that last run," Rachel allowed. "But I bet those Hot Shots I saved are thankful I did. You can't say the same with the risks you used to take."

"I was young and stupid. Those days are gone, barely a memory for anyone but you and me." Without Missy, Rachel was probably the only one left in Eden who remembered his time there.

Rachel pinched the bridge of her nose for a few seconds before blinking at him. "Everyone knows about you. You set quite a standard in Eden. You've become an urban legend and left humongous shoes that teens attempt to fill every year. Sheriff Tucker wishes you'd never been born."

"I…I…" He'd never thought anything he did in Eden was any more than self-destructive behavior, a reaction to his parents' grief.

Rachel sighed. "Missy thought you were Evil Knievel, some kind of immortal daredevil she wasn't brave enough to hold on to. Why do you think she chose Lyle? He seemed safe compared to you."

Cole swallowed the hurt Rachel's words inflicted. He'd been anything but cautious back then. "I never gave Missy a reason to doubt what we had."

Rachel's smile was sad. "She watched us from the sidelines. It was her perception of herself and you as a couple that mattered, not yours."

That got him. "If that's true, she never said a word," he said, suddenly finding himself without much patience. "If anything, I loved her enough that she shouldn't have doubted me." Right or wrong, he'd waited for Missy, hadn't he?

"Loved her? You loved her enough to walk out the door and never look back." Rachel sucked in a heavy breath. "Look, this has been an emotional day for all of us. Why don't we take a time out for a little while?"

Cole wanted to drive too fast, to punch his fist in something. Anything to blow off some steam. "Sure, I'll just go to my corner of the kitchen and make dinner for a family that doesn't want me here."

"RACHEL...RACH...wake up. You're dreaming." Cole sat on top of the covers and pulled Rachel close. He'd tried sleeping out on the couch, but he'd been restless around midnight, which was when Rachel usually started dreaming.

Rachel turned her face into his chest, her breath

passing through his thin T-shirt and warming the skin beneath. Her breathing slowed, became more even.

"God, baby, I wish I could chase those nightmares away permanently." Cole pressed a light kiss to her forehead.

He told himself it had been less than a day since they'd kissed and he'd realized Rachel was the woman he wanted now, not Missy, despite his defense of his love for Missy. However, things didn't look so optimistic. Rachel didn't want him. Jenna hated him. And over Cole's green bean casserole, Mr. Quinlan had spoken the words every man hates to hear—"I told you so"—about Cole's attempt to civilize "that horse."

Okay, so Cole did tend to go off half-cocked sometimes, but he had good intentions. Couldn't anyone see that?

Cole tucked Rachel closer. She may avoid him when she was awake, and Cole may have disappointed her, but when he held Rachel like this, he could dream, couldn't he? Of holding hands, candlelight dinners and laughing over a shared bucket of popcorn at the movie theater. Of things that could be.

Dreams. That seemed to be all Cole had left.

"YOU'RE IN MY bed again."

Cole awoke with a start to find Rachel's face mere kissable inches from his. "It does appear to be that way."

As Cole watched Rachel, her face illuminated by the bathroom light, her gentle smile turned to wariness, as if she was waiting to see what he'd do next. This close, with her complexion so pale, he could see that she still had freckles, although they'd faded considerably since childhood. He wanted to kiss her, but he didn't want her to start apologizing if they kissed again.

"You can let go of me now. I'm awake."

"I can see that." He could also see how kissable her lips were, slightly parted and inviting. "I'm just enjoying holding you."

Rachel sat up, pulling away from Cole. She hooked her elbows around her knees. "You can't do that."

"Why not?"

She shoved the hair out of her eyes. "Because of Missy and what you meant to her."

"I think I already told you that I'm over—"

"Please. You're making this harder than it already is."

Cole chewed on her words for a bit. "I think you're making this harder than it has to be. What's holding you back?"

Rachel dropped her head onto her knees. "I made her a promise."

"What kind of promise, Rachel?"

Looking at him with tear-filled eyes, Rachel admitted, "I promised I wouldn't let you talk me into anything if you came back."

Rachel wanted to crawl under the bed. She didn't know what held her back. She seemed to have gotten very good at crawling over the past few days.

Cole stared at Rachel with raised eyebrows and lips drawn tight with disapproval. "And you agreed?"

"Yes." Rachel had never really believed Missy when she'd predicted Cole would come back. Or that Cole would express any interest in her whatsoever. Sure, she'd had her fantasies, but she'd never believed...

"With Missy gone, your promise... I don't understand why Missy dragged that promise out of you or why you agreed to such a thing, but—"

"She loved you. She wanted to be with you. It was in the hospital after Matt was born and she seemed so upset."

"Eleven years ago she wanted to marry someone else." There was anger in Cole's voice. "And then Missy drove off a cliff, depriving two kids of their mom."

"Missy was a good person." Rachel defended her sister staunchly because no one else would.

"Missy was all about control," Cole scoffed. "The more we talk, the more I realize she was wrong for me. She enjoyed telling you and me what to do and when to do it. She didn't want to do anything that messed up her hair and makeup."

"Don't say things like that. She sacrificed a lot for me and Pop. You loved her." Missy's behavior wasn't her fault.

"But I wouldn't have stayed in love with her," Cole said calmly. "Over time I would have realized we had nothing in common. I would have realized that I needed someone more like you. Maybe Missy figured it out sooner than I did. Maybe you misunderstood what she said to you, maybe you read more into it, just like the note she left."

Rachel didn't dare believe him, even as her heart begged her to. He was just being Cole and not thinking things through.

It took a moment for Rachel to find the courage to speak. Even then, she couldn't bring herself to smile to ease the impact of her words, because she was giving up on a long-held dream. "Even if I could be with you without any guilt toward Missy, it would upset Jenna after what happened today."

"I'll make peace with her," Cole said in a gruff voice, getting off the bed to lie on the floor. "Jenna can't stay mad at me forever, and you can't always deny there's something between us, either. Until then, you and I will be friends." He made sure that Rachel looked at him before adding, "And someday we'll be more."

"WHAT KIND OF GIRL was Sally?" Rachel had been moving around under that sheet for too long, her movements making Cole crazy after she'd banned him to the floor.

Cole didn't want to talk about his sister. Of course, the alternative was talking about how he'd screwed up his best chance with Jenna, which in turn had screwed up his best chance with Rachel.

"Never mind." Rachel pulled the covers up over her head when Cole didn't answer.

Cole hesitated. He'd never told Missy about Sally. Hell, he didn't even talk about Sally to his Hot Shot buddies, and he'd known some of them for nearly ten years. Still, this was Rachel, who already knew something of his sister.

"Sally was ten, three years younger than me when it happened." As he spoke, Rachel flipped the covers back and looked at him over the edge of the bed, her dark eyes wide in her pale face. He pulled his gaze back to the ceiling. "She was all about ribbons, dresses and bows. But she was a good little sister, I guess." God, it was painful thinking about Sally. No wonder Rachel didn't want to talk about Missy. "She, um, used to follow me around when I was younger, but then I went on to junior high school and figured I was too good to have a little kid trailing after me."

He checked to see if Rachel even cared about what he was saying. If not, he was off the hook.

No such luck.

She had her head resting on the edge of the mattress, looking interested in what he was saying and beautiful, despite the mussed-up hair.

"I played a lot of sports. Mom didn't encourage that in Sally, although Sally was a pretty good little athlete, even at ten. Did she ever tell you how Sally died?"

"She said there was a fire."

Cole's words slowed as he recalled that fateful afternoon, considering what he should say. "One day I was playing in this football game, you know, youth football where they teach you how to be a dumb jock at an early age?" Cole tried to smile, but his heart wasn't in it. He cleared his throat instead. "Anyway, Sally had some Girl Scout meeting to go to and somebody else's mom was going to take her so that my mom could come to my game." Cole sucked in a breath, dreading the next part. "The plan was that Sally would get home before us and turn on the Crock-Pot so that we'd come home to supper. Back then, Mom was into nutrition." Some of the bitterness crept into his voice. Cole swallowed it back. "Only, the Crock-Pot started a fire while Sally was napping."

"Oh, my God." Rachel tried to sit up and then her eyes rolled in her head and she lay back down again with a hand on her injured ribs, repeating, "Oh, my God."

"They say she never woke up, that the smoke got to her before the fire did." Cole could just see Sally's stupid smile, could almost—even after all these years—hear her high-pitched squeal when he tickled her.

"I'm so sorry."

Cole blinked his eyes. Wimp that he was, he still wanted to cry about it all these years later. "My mom never quite recovered. No one blamed her. She just couldn't stop blaming herself. And then she was left with me. A dumb jock." She'd stopped coming to his games, and soon Cole had stopped wanting to play.

"So you moved to a place where no one knew you."

He nodded. "And Dad and I pretended there'd never been a Sally, because that's what we thought Mom wanted."

"Such a sad situation. It couldn't have been easy on your mom to hide her grief from you and your dad all these years."

Cole clenched his jaw as he spared Rachel a glance. "Do you think I wanted it easy on my mother?"

When she gasped, Cole wiped at his nose with the back of his hand. Embarrassed to be falling apart like a little kid, Cole kept his mouth shut.

Rachel's hand was on his arm again. "I'm sure she was grateful that she still had you."

"No. No, she wasn't."

"SO ALL THAT TIME I thought you were so brave, living on the edge, taking any dare, you were just trying to get your mother's attention?" This new perspective on Cole's childhood explained a lot to Rachel, especially about the way Cole was now, and why he was always on everyone about being safe.

Cole frowned. "It wasn't like that."

"Oh, yes, it was. Come here." Rachel lifted the covers and held out her arms. She wanted to hug him for the way he'd handled the hardships of his childhood, to help him forgive his mother.

Cole climbed back into bed with her. "If I'd known that telling you about Sally was the way to get an invitation into your bed, I would have done it a whole lot sooner."

"Don't try to make light of it." Rachel wrapped her arms around him. "You should have told me about Sally when you lived here before."

"That would have been highly inappropriate." Cole tucked her head beneath his chin, careful of her wound. "Sheriff Tucker would have hauled me in for seducing a minor for sure."

"Not to mention it would have broken Missy's heart."

"Rachel." Cole clasped her hand. "You can't let Missy stand between us. Whatever it is that we've found here, it's more than what Missy and I shared all those years ago."

"You don't know that, and that's what scares me," Rachel admitted, staring at their joined hands, wanting to be as certain as he was. "What is it that we have? How long will it last?" Rachel held her breath, unable to believe she'd asked the question.

"No one can answer that until we trust each other enough to let these feelings grow."

Rachel blew air out of her lungs. She'd been hoping Cole would profess his undying love. "That's not good enough." When Cole stared at her, Rachel couldn't help but add, "That's so typical of a man. You want a woman to put out before you commit."

"Shhh. This isn't about sex."

"Oh." Rachel couldn't hide her disappointment.

Cole grinned. "Honey, don't get me wrong. That's an important part of the relationship we're going to explore." His right hand trailed down her neck to her breastbone.

Again, Rachel couldn't draw a breath. If Cole slid his hand lower…

His hand crossed to her shoulder. "I enjoy being with you, even when you're a pain in the ass." Cole shook his head. "You know, we'll never be bored with each other." He studied Rachel. "What's wrong?"

"I want this to be real. I want wine and roses with you. I just can't help but think of what—" Rachel nearly choked on the words "—what Missy would say." Rachel doubted she'd hear her sister's blessing.

"I know how much a rough home life can bring you nothing but sorrow, and how that makes you want the good that comes your way all that much more. But sometimes you choose what's the most convenient, not what's best. And that could be what happened with Missy and me." Cole leaned forward and pressed a kiss to Rachel's forehead. "I told you about Sally. Don't you think it's time we talked about your mom?"

Maybe Cole was right. "I haven't told anyone about my mom," she said. Maybe he could help her heal the scars of her past. "Missy made me promise right before Mom went away."

"Rach, you were a kid. You're mom can't hurt you now." He clasped her hand.

Rachel hesitated a moment before trying to make him understand. "My mom was fine when she took her medication, which she did when Pop was home. We were happy then. Things were normal. It was when Pop left that things fell apart." Rachel paused, then blurted out with childlike indignation, "She didn't think we gave her the respect she deserved."

"What were you doing?"

"Just breathing." Rachel shrugged, trying to make light of the painful memories. "Missy never talked back because she knew bad things happened when you talked back. I was more of a slow learner."

"Stubborn even then." Cole ran a hand over her hair. "Did she…hurt you?"

"She didn't beat me, if that's what you mean," Rachel said hastily. "Her punishments had a more lasting impression." She hesitated once more, not wanting to admit her past. Somehow, when it was unspoken, it seemed less real.

Cole waited her out, until Rachel could no longer stand the silence.

"Sometimes we'd clean things over and over again." When Rachel cleaned now she did the chore as quickly as possible. "Mostly, she'd make me stand somewhere, like in a closet, or in my room, or outside. For hours, and if I moved, or talked, she'd turn off the lights or leave me there after dark, sometimes all night. The few times we tried to tell Pop he didn't seem to believe us. Sometimes he got really mad, which made things with Mom worse. So we stopped telling him."

Gathering her close, Cole murmured compassionate sounds, but Rachel wasn't done.

"She locked me outside one night in October." A shiver went through Rachel as she recalled the way each sound had made her heart race as she'd huddled in a tight ball beneath the blanket on the porch. "I think that was the worst. Missy snuck out with a blanket and, of course, Mom found out. So, she locked Missy up in a closet and left me out all night. When Pop came home the next morning, he saw me on the porch and thought I was camping out. Then he found Missy in the closet with deep scratches on her arms." Rachel clenched a fist. "Missy had scratched herself, hoping the blood would make Pop do something. And Missy told him everything, except she told it as if all those bad things had happened to her, not me."

"To deflect your Mom's anger?"

"She said it was because she was older, almost twelve, and I was only eight. But it was because she was braver than I was. She knew what to say in front of our parents when I wanted to say nothing. I didn't correct Pop when he found me outside that morning. I would have suffered for years if not for Missy."

"You see, she was protecting you even then."

"Pop sent Mom away to a care facility, and he was never quite the same." A tiny sob escaped Rachel's throat. "I think we broke his heart by making him choose between his kids and his wife."

"Aw, honey." Cole gathered her close. "Talk to me."

"Missy always put me first. Why would she give up and leave me like that?" Rachel sniffed against his shoulder.

"We'll never know. She might have thought she'd survive the crash and you'd take care of her. After all, you were keeping the family together by then, not her." His caress was gentle. "You are a capable, sexy woman."

Rachel felt odd, as if she were balanced on a fence rail, not sure which side to climb down on. It would be so easy to tilt her head and kiss him again. Her loyalty was to Missy, but her heart yearned for Cole.

"I'd like to think that Missy would approve, but—"

"You keep remembering the adult, hurt Missy. What about the Missy of your childhood? The little girl whose picture you keep in the hangar? Wouldn't she have wanted you to be happy?"

Rachel's head swam as the enormity of his suggestion sank in. "She used to braid my hair. We played dolls and she always helped me dress my Barbies." That Missy would have been happy that Rachel found a man who cared for her. "We were best friends."

Rachel pulled back to look at Cole. "I loved her. Unlike the post-marriage Missy, who..."

Cole's gaze was accepting. "I don't think I would have liked the person Missy became. I think she loved you, but I also think she was jealous of the freedom you had. But that doesn't mean I can't hold a soft spot in my heart for her and wish that things had turned out differently."

A burden seemed to slide off Rachel's shoulders and she cried harder. She cried for her lost sister and for herself. When the tears dried and the sobs receded, Rachel said, "What a fine pair we make. Ruined mothers and broken childhoods."

Cole stroked her back, considering—and rejecting—her observation. "My mother wasn't ruined. She just tuned out of life."

"She had a responsibility to the child she had left. Even if she was grieving." Rachel sniffed and sat up, grabbing for a tissue. "I wish I could have helped her."

"You were just a kid." Cole shook his head. Rachel was always so forgiving. "As her son I had a responsibility to her, to keep her from hurting anymore."

"Right. And you did that by crashing your dirt bike, racing your truck so fast you blew a gasket and spun out or by staying out all night." Rachel blew her nose. "That didn't hurt her at all, did it?"

"Back then, I didn't understand. I was selfish. I wanted to know that my mom cared for me as much as she had for Sally." Now he was more concerned with protecting his mother than winning back her love.

Rachel latched on to his hand. "I'm sure she did. She just didn't seem to know what to say or how to say it."

Cole shrugged, as if coming second in his mom's heart was no big deal. "I think it was my first season as a Hot Shot when I realized my behavior was pushing her away." He stared down at their hands. "I was clearing a line through the trees, knocking down these huge pines in a race with some veteran chainsaw swamper." Cole smiled at the memory. "And then I miscalculated, and the tree I was felling almost crushed me."

Rachel's eyes widened.

"Yeah, there I was, trapped beneath a tree trunk and wondering how my mom would go on if she lost me, too." Cole blew out a breath. "She'd probably been preparing for that to happen since we'd arrived in Eden, because I kept on cheating death." Sending a silent apology to his mom, Cole closed his eyes. "Sobering thought."

Rachel's hands caressed his face—soft, warm and forgiving against his skin. Cole could have ended his confession there, but this was Rachel and she deserved the entire truth. "I thought I could tell my mom. Jenna looks just like Sally, but she seems to have inherited my reckless streak. And that's why I won't tell my mom about her. Heaven forbid, but if Jenna kills herself on that horse, I don't think my mom could take it."

"Jenna feels confident when she's riding Shadow. You should be proud of the skill she has and encourage it." Rachel leaned gingerly against the headboard and considered him quite a while before adding, "I'm not sure keeping her existence a secret is fair to either Jenna or your mom."

"Would you rather have my mom show up and fence Jenna in? Hang on," Cole said when Rachel opened her mouth to answer. "Do you realize that not only did Jenna speak to me after the saddle debacle—in full volume, I might add—but she told me off, too? In the few days I've known Jenna, she's done nothing more than mumble or avoid me."

"I..." Rachel started to say something and then stopped. "You're right."

"Yeah, pretty amazing. I don't want Jenna to get beaten down by my mom, do you?"

"You can't keep Jenna a secret from your mother." He could tell by the flint in her eye that Rachel wasn't going to bend on this one.

"Why not? You kept her a secret from me for ten years."

"Cole—"

"Rach, in the end, it's my decision. To protect them both, I'm not going to tell my mother about Jenna."

To Cole's disappointment, Rachel didn't seem to agree.

## *CHAPTER ELEVEN*

JENNA'S PLAN HAD BEEN to never see Cole again. She figured she'd get up early and spend all her time outside until Aunt Rachel was better and Cole left.

Trouble was, it wasn't even daylight and Cole was cooking breakfast. Which smelled delicious. Even if she hated him, food would be good. She hadn't eaten dinner.

No. No food. If she ate now, she'd have to talk to him. She should just go.

Jenna stood frozen at the end of the kitchen counter and started backing away. She'd go out the front door.

"Good morning, Jenna," Cole said with his back to her. "I'm making waffles. Come in and get some before you go out riding."

Aunt Rachel sometimes told Jenna to close her mouth before flies got in. Good thing there weren't any flies in here this morning.

"Pour yourself some milk and sit down." Cole hadn't turned around. He hadn't looked at her. There was still a chance. She could still run away. Jenna lifted one foot.

Then Cole did turn around and smiled at her as if he hadn't lied to her about how Shadow would like a saddle, as if he hadn't tried to kill her horse. "Riding takes a lot of energy. And these waffles are almost done."

She stood like the cranes she'd seen while out riding by the creek, standing with one foot in the air. Those waffles did smell good. And they weren't the frozen ones. And she was hungry. And riding did take a lot of energy.

Jenna put her foot down. And walked to the refrigerator to pour a glass of milk.

She'd eat, but she wouldn't say anything. She'd give Cole the silent treatment.

Soon, Jenna was sitting at the kitchen table, and Cole set a plate of waffles in front of her. She started buttering her waffle, pouring syrup and cutting bites. When she was done she looked up to see Cole standing across from her. "What?" So much for the silent treatment.

One word didn't mean she was talking to him. Jenna took a bite of waffle so she wouldn't say anything else.

"I made a mistake yesterday. I went too fast with Shadow and everybody got upset." Cole touched one of the bandages on his arms. "I'm sorry." He *did* look sorry.

Jenna chewed and chewed because her throat didn't seem to want her to swallow. Aunt Rachel always said if someone said they were sorry and meant it, that you had to accept it.

Then Cole had to go and ruin it. "Anyway, I just wanted you to know that I'm sorry, and that if you decide to try again, we'll go slow."

Try again? She swallowed and poked another piece with her fork. Jenna knew what that meant. It meant Cole was going to saddle Shadow again whether Jenna wanted him to or not. Adults were always like that. Always doing stuff they thought was good for you and telling you it was your choice.

Cole definitely deserved the silent treatment.

Jenna started eating faster, then drank half her milk, carried her dishes to the sink and went out to ride Shadow.

All the while keeping her mouth closed tight.

"YOU SHOULD BE HOME in bed," Cole grumbled Friday night as he pulled into the parking lot at Marney's grocery store. "You could have just given me a list."

"A list is so predictable. I like to look around and see what interests me." Besides, Cole had offered to rent the kids a movie and Rachel didn't want them going into town alone with Cole. The kids needed her to smooth things over with him. She'd overheard him talking to Jenna this morning, trying to make peace, but Jenna had wanted none of it.

"I'm glad you're here, Mommy," Matt piped up from the back seat of Cole's truck. "You helped me pick a good movie."

Rachel had to smile. Matt was such a cute bundle of joy, oblivious to the woes of his family, which made him that much more important to their peace of mind.

"Are you sure you should be walking around?" Jenna, always the worrier, asked. She'd hardly spoken to anyone since the incident with Shadow and had only suspicious looks for Cole.

"I'm fine, Jenna," Rachel hastened to reassure her niece. "I'm sure I'd go crazy if I was lying in bed doing nothing while you were all in town."

"I could watch my movie with you when we get home, Mommy," Matt said. He'd chosen a movie where three elementary school boys kick bad-guy butt with their incredible karate moves.

"I'd like that." With any luck, she'd fall asleep ten minutes into it…all three times Matt watched it. Still, she liked to have the little guy cuddle up next to her.

They all got out of the truck. Cole brought her a shopping cart to lean on, which Rachel clutched, focusing so much on keeping her balance that it took her a minute or two to realize that although Cole walked on her left, his right arm was around her back.

"Slow down, kids," Cole called as the two skipped into the store ahead of them.

"Slow down, yourself," Rachel said. "They're going to check out the latest toys in the vending machine. They'll be fine." She, on the other hand, felt as if she was on the verge of getting personal with the asphalt.

Thankfully, Cole took her words to heart and slowed down. "Marney's is just the same."

"I don't care how many super grocery stores open in Eden. I'll still shop here." They reached the ramp that crossed the sidewalk to the main doors. The slight incline felt like Mt. Everest to Rachel. While Cole pushed the cart, Rachel held on, letting the cart's momentum practically drag her into the store.

"This is a mistake," Cole said.

"I'm in now," Rachel argued, still moving forward.

Cole cast his gaze about, looking for the kids, apparently finding them, because he waved at someone.

Rachel didn't feel confident enough to check.

"I suppose I could put you in the cart."

"You wouldn't dare." Rachel gripped the cart handle tighter. Cole was just the type to do it.

"Don't do anything stupid and I won't have to," Cole said as the kids ran up and took their places on either side of the cart.

"Hello, Rachel."

A shiver ran down Rachel's spine as she looked up into Lyle's cool features. He probably wouldn't have said a word to her except Rachel had almost pushed the cart into him as he stood loading a case of beer into his own cart. A quick glance found Jenna fidgeting and Matt sneaking looks at Lyle.

Cole stiffened his hold on Rachel. "Whitehall."

"Hudson." Lyle flicked Cole a dismissive glance. He didn't acknowledge either one of the kids. "You look like hell, Rachel, and so do the kids. But, hey, what's new?"

Matt finally gave a shy wave. "Hi, Dad," Jenna said dutifully.

Lyle's expression turned cold. "So, Rachel, you and your old man finally found someone to cough up child support for Missy's bastards." He laughed and turned his attention back to his cart full of beer. "I bet that big S on your forehead looks mighty fine in the mirror." Lyle mouthed the word *sucker* at Cole.

"Nice seeing you, Lyle." Rachel pushed the cart past him, although she wanted to run him over with it.

They turned toward the produce section while Lyle went on to the checkout. The kids dragged their feet next to the cart.

"Well, will it be red or green grapes this time?" Rachel asked in a voice that sounded suspiciously like a fifties sitcom mom. Heaven only knew what Cole was thinking or feeling at this point. He was probably wondering if Lyle was Matt's father—she was sure he was—and assuming Lyle treated them this way every time they bumped into him. Much as Rachel tried to avoid Lyle, whenever they did meet, it tended to be ugly.

"Nobody eats grapes," Jenna mumbled.

Matt just kicked the front wheel of the cart, which reverberated up Rachel's arms, threatening her balance.

"Does he always talk to them like that?" Cole demanded. Rachel didn't have to look up to know how angry Cole was. She could hear the indignation in his voice.

"Can we talk about this later?" Rachel was very much aware of the two pairs of ears with their radars fully tuned to the adults behind them, even if Cole wasn't.

"I think we need to talk about it now."

"Cole, please."

"I need some air." The hard way Cole's words came across, Rachel knew he was going to look for Lyle.

"Where are you going? Cole?" But he wasn't listening, damn it. "Cole, don't do anything…" that Rachel had been dying to do for years, like slug the daylights out of Lyle. "Just don't do something that brings Sheriff Tucker over here." The chill air of the produce section hit Rachel full blast as the heat of Cole's body left her.

"Where's he going?" Jenna asked, falling behind as Rachel tottered forward with the cart.

"Nowhere."

Jenna was persistent. "But—"

"Matt, Jenna, stay with me. We've got shopping to do." Rachel knew from experience that confronting Lyle was a lost cause. "Now, what about some potatoes with dinner?"

No one answered her. Rachel turned as much as she could, practically hugging the cart now, but she couldn't see the kids.

"WHITEHALL." Cole caught up to him as he was finishing loading his truck.

Lyle tossed his keys into the cab and faced Cole, not quite taking on a come-get-me, WWF stance but still ready for anything.

Cole held up his hands. "I'm not looking for trouble." At least, not right now. He just wanted Whitehall to understand that there would be hell to pay if Lyle didn't start showing Rachel and those kids some respect.

Lyle seemed disappointed that Cole hadn't followed him out for a fight.

"But if I ever hear you talk to those kids that way—" Cole hesitated, then amended forcefully "—to Matt and *my daughter* that way again, I'll remind you why you stayed away from me in high school."

There was a small gasp behind Cole. He didn't have to turn around to realize Jenna had followed him outside. So much for Rachel's let's-go-slow-and-get-to-know-each-other plan. Or his desire to smooth things over with Jenna.

Lyle sized up Cole as if he were a piece of beef he was considering buying. Then he looked Cole dead in the eye. "You know something? I've been waiting eleven years to pound the crap out of you. You left without giving me the satisfaction. You ruined everything for me. You ruined *her!*" His face contorted in rage, Lyle started coming at Cole. "Because of you, she didn't think she was good enough to live!"

With a backward glance, Cole made sure Jenna was far enough behind him that she wouldn't get hurt. He was surprised to see her standing a few feet away with her arm around Matt. And then Cole's attention was one hundred percent back on Lyle.

A noisy streak of silver metal careened into Lyle. The cart took the tall man by surprise, stopping his charge. And then the kids were screaming and running out into the path of an oncoming car, toward a woman crumpled on the pavement.

Rachel.

Lyle was forgotten, and Cole's heart sank to his toes as he headed in the direction of Rachel and the kids, lifted his arms frantically and waved off the on-coming car.

Whitehall's words barely registered above the chaos around him. "You ruined her!"

"THIS IS BECOMING a bad habit." Cole's voice cut through the fog that had closed around Rachel's vision when she'd shoved that cart at Lyle.

"I'm all right," Rachel insisted. "My vision just tunneled down into nothing when I fell, kind of like a head rush you get when you get out of bed too quickly." Two warm, familiar hands were clasping Rachel's. She heard someone sobbing. Matt? She couldn't see well enough to tell. "I'm okay, guys. Let's just get a new cart and get this shopping trip done with."

The heavy sigh must have been Cole's.

Her vision was spreading from a fuzzy tunnel into a panorama of the parking lot. They'd drawn quite a crowd. Two old ladies Rachel didn't recognize and a woman with two kids in tow, who barely paused as she passed with her full cart on the way to her car.

"Look at me," Cole commanded. "How many fingers am I holding up?" He held up two fingers.

Ignoring Cole's test now that she could see, Rachel reached out and high-fived him, although it lacked much energy. "Team spirit. That's what I like to see."

Matt was crying, but so was Jenna. Cole's face was red with apparent anger. Or maybe standing on the asphalt during a humid Indian summer had heated him to boiling.

"We're going home," Cole announced, studying Rachel closely.

"No, we're not. My hands sting and my elbows are throbbing, but we still need food. Give me a hand." Rachel lifted her aching arms, surprised when Cole did help her up. "There's no need to fuss."

"Yes, there is," Cole said. "As you're so fond of saying, we've had enough drama for one day."

"I DON'T WANT HIM to be my dad," Jenna whined when Aunt Rachel had been tucked into bed. Jenna stood by her aunt's dresser, rubbing the smooth wood with the palm of her hand.

Cole—her dad—and Matt were out feeding Taffy and Shadow.

"Oh, baby, come here." Rachel opened up her bandaged arms. Man, she looked horrible. If Jenna hadn't felt so numb from learning that Cole was her dad, she'd be scared for her aunt Rachel all over again.

Jenna climbed onto the bed and into Aunt Rachel's lap. She had the best hugs. She hugged tight, as if she cared so much she wouldn't let you go, no matter what.

"Do you remember how many times you told me you didn't want Lyle Whitehall to be your daddy?" Rachel asked.

Sniffing, Jenna nodded. "Hundreds."

"Thousands," Rachel corrected. Jenna could feel Aunt Rachel's smile.

"But why him? He doesn't even like me."

"That's not true. Cole may have just met you, but he—"

"He's always telling me how to do something better or different. You always told me that you'd love me any way I was, clean or dirty."

"Well, most of the time you are dirty. You've got to admit that, Jenna. After all, you live on a ranch."

"He almost killed Shadow trying to saddle him," Jenna protested. "Why are you on *his* side?" To her horror, these last words came out in a high, baby voice, but Jenna was unable to keep the hurt inside any longer.

Aunt Rachel hugged Jenna tighter. "I'm on your side, Jenna. Yours and Matt's."

"Is he Matt's daddy, too?"

"No."

Jenna felt sorry for Matt. "Who is his daddy?" she asked quietly.

Rachel hugged Jenna tighter. "Those aren't questions for today or even for you."

Wiping tears from her eyes, Jenna hiccupped. "You and Mommy always kept secrets."

Aunt Rachel's voice got really sad. "Your mom and I talked about adult things, stuff that didn't concern you."

"That's a lie. You must have talked about who my daddy was and you never told." It was hard to breathe, almost like when she had bad hiccups. "You never told," she repeated, although Jenna didn't want to say anything.

"But you know now, and when you're ready, you'll give Cole a chance to be a good daddy. And someday, I bet—" Rachel touched Jenna's nose "—you'll see that Cole Hudson is ten times the daddy that Lyle Whitehall was to you."

Jenna thought about that for a minute. It was hard to imagine that, when Cole had made her so unhappy, but at least he'd never yelled as much or scared her like the man she used to think was her dad.

"Do you really believe that?" Jenna whispered, almost afraid to trust that it might be true and that someday she'd actually have a dad who cared about her.

"Yes, I do, Jenna."

"I want a daddy to love me, too," Matt cried from the doorway before running on his chubby legs over to the bed and climbing up.

Jenna was mad that Matt had been listening to her cry. "Go away, Matt."

"I need a hug," Matt said, barely crying as he buried his face in Aunt Rachel's shoulder.

Aunt Rachel made it worse for Jenna by giving Matt a one-armed hug. If Jenna had been Aunt Rachel, she'd have pushed her little brother off the bed. She did not want to share Aunt Rachel right now.

"That feels better," Matt said, tears spilling over his cheeks. "Can I share Jenna's daddy?"

"You can't share a daddy," Jenna said. "You are so dumb."

"Don't talk to your brother like that," Aunt Rachel scolded Jenna. "Everybody had their feelings hurt today. Friends come and go, but family is something you hang on to. You wouldn't talk to your friends that way, so don't talk to Matt like that."

Jenna rolled her eyes. She'd heard that speech before.

Matt sat up with a goofy grin. "But I want him to be my daddy. My dad said he had an S on his forehead like a superhero. And Cole has such big muscles it has to be true." Matt smiled at Jenna. "Is it cool to have a superhero for your dad, Jenna? Have you found out where he's hiding his costume? I didn't find it in his bag."

"Matt, tell me you did not go through Cole's bag." Aunt Rachel used her teacher voice.

Matt, dummy that he was, admitted it with a nod. "I was just trying to find his superhero costume in case he needed it. That's why he didn't catch you today when you fell because he left his costume at home."

Jenna didn't care what Aunt Rachel said about family. "You are so dumb, Matt."

"DO YOU THINK I ruined Missy?"

Rachel woke up with a start. She'd been dozing in bed. It was dark outside.

Instead of answering Cole's question, Rachel asked one of her own. "Where've you been?"

"Outside. Thinking." Cole looked sad. He didn't come inside. He didn't invade her space or pace in anger. There was a quiet determination about him that nearly brought Rachel to tears.

"And?" Rachel pushed herself up to a sitting position.

Cole swore as he slid down the wall to the floor. After a moment of heartbreaking silence, he asked, "Do you think Missy drove off Moe's Curve because of me?"

"I can't answer that. Missy hadn't been happy in a long time."

"You said she blamed you for her unhappiness. Lyle accused me of pushing her over the edge. Did Missy blame me?" He sounded tortured.

"She never mentioned you until that note." Rachel suspected that was because Missy was afraid of what Lyle might do if he heard Cole's name in any context. "You can't take what Lyle says as gospel. In the end, Lyle didn't know Missy any better than you or I did." Rachel had never suspected Missy could be so self-destructive, perhaps because her sister had always been so caring of others.

Cole didn't look convinced. They sat with a heavy silence between them.

Cole's voice dropped to a whisper. "The other night when I read the note, I thought it was tragic, but I didn't think I was to blame. I may have contributed, but I never thought—"

"Cole, don't do this to yourself," Rachel warned. "It's hard enough knowing that you couldn't save her." Rachel would carry that burden along with Cole and Pop. "But to think it was all you—"

"Did you see Lyle's face in the parking lot? He believed it." Cole hung his head between his knees.

And so had Rachel, to some extent, until Cole had come back to Eden. Still, she had to deny it. "You said yourself, she carried far too much. Letting you go on to live your life while she had your baby was just one."

"Shove over," Cole said gruffly, having come over to the bed. He nudged her away from the edge. "Being with you makes me feel better."

Although she felt the same way, she didn't know how to respond.

When Rachel moved over, he climbed in next to her, under the covers with only his blue jeans and her T-shirt and boxers between them. Then he wrapped his arms around Rachel and pulled her close, careful of her ribs. "If you weren't so good at being independent, you might swallow that pride of yours and ask for help every once in a while. I wouldn't mind giving it."

"Nine months out of the year we wouldn't know where the other one was." That would only be true if Rachel returned to flying.

Cole sighed against her cheek. "Let me tell you about this new invention. It's called the cell phone. Now, reception can sometimes be crappy, but it does allow you to stay in touch even when you don't know where someone is."

"How clever of you to have discovered such a newfangled thing." As he chuckled, Rachel snuggled more comfortably against him. Missy would have called her shameless, but Rachel wasn't about to pass up the opportunity to create a memory with Cole when she had years of loneliness ahead of her.

He pressed a light kiss to her temple.

"I really want to kiss you properly," Cole said, his breath warm on her skin.

It was all Rachel could do to keep from begging. Instead, she tilted her chin and drew Cole to her. She'd wanted more since their kiss in the hangar, but there had been Missy's promise to keep. Now, though, it seemed that Cole was just as broken inside as Rachel was. He needed the loving, nurturing touch of someone close to him. What harm would another kiss do?

And then she was losing herself in the heat of his touch and her world tilted crazily. She couldn't tell if it was still the result of her concussion or something else. When Cole pulled her on top of him and his hands slid down to the small of her back, she decided she didn't care.

*You could have him. Just this one time.*

Rachel clung to the thought, reluctant to deny it.

Cole's fingers tugged at her boxers. "Honey, these will have to go."

Every cell in Rachel's body seemed to vibrate with enthusiasm. It was only her brain that held her back. Cole was perfect, everything she'd dreamed of. And yet, he wasn't the same person she'd fantasized about all these years. He could be controlling and protective, sometimes to the point where she felt suffocated. Cole had claimed they'd never be bored, but Rachel suspected their days would be filled with energy-draining fights because she wasn't as cautious as he'd like her to be. But the nights…

Rachel knew they'd go up in flames in bed. There would be no promises of love or plans for the future. Still, she knew this was a memory she'd treasure forever, just as she knew they'd probably never have a future beyond these few weeks. She was in the process of shedding all the lies from her life, so she couldn't lie about that.

But when he touched her, her heart demanded this one time, this one memory, before the spell was broken and reality separated them. Slowly, deliberately, she gave in to her heart's demands.

"AT THE RISK of ruining this tender moment, I don't want you to fly tomorrow," Cole whispered in Rachel's ear as they spooned together later that night, his hand caressing the bare skin of her hip. "You know it's too soon. You're not strong enough."

There it was. The spell was broken. Rachel had hoped it would last beyond the brief afterglow they'd experienced.

But that, too, was a lie. Deep down, she'd hoped something magical would happen when they were together, something that would melt all their differences away and leave them head over heels in love. Which just went to show what a foolish dreamer she was.

Rachel rolled away from Cole and sat up, clutching the sheet to her bare chest, giving herself a little head rush and some much-needed breathing room. "And you know why I have to try."

"You don't have to fly it yourself. Let the salesman fly it for you." Cole's disappointment bled through his words.

She rubbed her arms, trying to hide the fact that she was scared of flying behind anger with herself at such gullible vulnerability. When would she learn? "You wouldn't buy a car you hadn't driven."

"Something else will come up later when you've had time to fully recover. Some plane that's just as good." Cole got out of bed and pulled on his jeans. "Don't do this, Rach. I don't want anything to happen to you."

Staring at the hard planes of his chest, she wanted to acquiesce, she longed to reach for him, yet she couldn't. "Since Missy got married, I've had to be strong for my family, even when I didn't want to be."

How Rachel wanted Cole to lend her his confidence, his strength. "I have to do this. We can't afford to pass this opportunity up." Not until her knight in shining armor came riding up on a horse and told her she didn't have to fly anymore, that he'd help shoulder her responsibilities. Was Cole that man?

"Then don't expect me to help around here after that." He walked away.

No, Cole wasn't that man. Rachel crawled back beneath the covers, reminding herself that her future was in her own hands.

"WOULD YOU READ TO ME?" Matt asked on Saturday morning, pushing a kitchen chair next to Cole's seat and climbing carefully into it. He thrust a dog-eared book in Cole's direction.

Cole resisted taking it. He and Rachel had made foundation-moving love last night and then ended up fighting about her flying today. Rachel was hell-bent on killing herself, regardless of what Cole said. Helpless, all he could do was sit back and wait, because he couldn't bring himself to watch.

Across the table, Jenna rolled her eyes. "Oh, my gosh, I got over that book when I was four, Matt."

Holding the book in his plump fingers, Matt thrust out his bottom lip. "I like it. It's Aunt Rachel's favorite book. She knows it by heart and so do I."

Cole peeked at the title—*The Sky Tower.* There was a castle on the front, set against a bright blue background.

With wide puppy-dog eyes, Matt shoved it at Cole again. “Please.”

Who could resist that look? Not Cole. With a sigh, Cole took the book, opening the frayed, worn cover to the title page, where someone had scribbled a name in crayon. Cole expected to see Jenna’s or Matt’s name. But the messy scrawl started with a big pink R.

Curious, Cole flipped to the first page and began reading aloud. “‘Once upon a time, there was a beautiful princess…’”

# CHAPTER TWELVE

THERE WASN'T A CLOUD in the sky on Saturday morning. Visibility went on for miles and miles. It was a beautiful day for flying.

And Rachel couldn't bring herself to eat a thing.

She dressed and managed to walk across her bedroom without the stumbling she'd suffered just a few days ago. It had been close to two weeks since the accident, and her head no longer looked swollen. The tiny cuts on her cheek had healed, as well.

She stared at herself in the bathroom mirror and thought, *You're ready to fly.* But she didn't believe it, and neither did her reflection.

*Pitiful.*

Someone knocked on her bedroom door.

"Hop to it, Rachel. He'll be here soon," Pop called.

*Piece of cake. Are you up to it?* Cole's young voice sounded a challenge in her head.

But that Cole didn't exist anymore. The Cole Hudson of today had made it perfectly clear that Rachel was in no shape to fly. But Cole didn't have a mortgage to pay and mouths to feed. He wasn't looking at making a two-hundred-thousand-dollar investment to get back in business. Hell, all he needed was a shovel and a chainsaw and he could work any fire.

*Pull yourself together.*

She worked her hair into a quick braid that was crooked in places and loose in others.

*You're a pilot, damn it. Act like one.*

Walking with her hand against the wall for support, Rachel made it to the dresser and put on the cheap mirrored sunglasses she'd purchased at Marney's. Immediately she felt better, more capable.

More like *it.*

But then she opened her bedroom door a little too quickly and had to grab the door frame for support.

More like *idiot.*

Jenna didn't look up as she buttered her toast, and Cole glowered from the kitchen table. But he didn't speak. Thankfully, he must have figured he'd said enough last night. Rachel wished they'd made love a second time before Cole had tried to put her back in a protective bubble.

Matt ran over to Rachel and hugged her. "We're getting a new plane, Aunt Rachel. Aren't you happy?"

An engine rumbled in the distance. Rachel had trouble filling her lungs with air. The last time she'd flown—

*Don't go there.*

"Don't dawdle. Let's get out to the hangar," Pop said, already walking toward the mudroom and the back door. "I can't wait to see what this beauty can do."

Hesitating, Rachel finally understood—she'd been

pokey in the hopes she wouldn't have to fly, but no one was going to stop her. Certainly not Cole. That was the price of independence—people just let you do scary shit.

Her palms began to sweat.

By the time Rachel got out to the hangar, the S2 had done a flyby and was lining up for a final approach on the runway. It looked smaller and more agile than the Privateer. With its bright red color and angular belly, it seemed flashier, too. It was just what they were looking for to keep the Fire Angels in business.

Rachel immediately disliked it.

The pilot taxied up to the hangar and powered down the engines. Then the pilot salesman climbed out of the cockpit and introduced himself. He was just like any other salesman Rachel had ever met—middle-aged with a sagging middle. Even the gaudy, large gold rings on his fingers were predictable.

"Mark Tuttle, Flying Machines." He shook Pop's hand then Rachel's as they introduced themselves. In true salesman form, his eyes dropped to her chest. "Well, what do you think?"

"It's a beaut." Pop fairly crowed with enthusiasm.

Rachel wanted to tell her dad to slow down. "I'd like to see the engines." She could tell a lot about a plane from the look of the engines.

Eager to please, Mark had the engine bays open in a flash. Holding on to Pop's shoulder for balance, Rachel stared into the underbelly of one engine. It seemed almost unbelievably clean, except for a thin trickle of oil coming out of one piston.

"Looks great." Pop praised the engine, even though Rachel was pretty sure he couldn't see a thing.

"Let's see the other side," Rachel said, casting a glance back at the house. She couldn't tell if anyone was looking out the windows, but it was clear that Jenna and Cole were boycotting the event.

After checking the other engine and seeing nothing but clean equipment, Rachel frowned. "Could you start them up?"

Once again, Mark jumped to the task while Rachel and Pop stepped back. Rachel held on to Pop's shoulder, closing her eyes and listening to the engine as the propellers began to move.

And she heard exactly what she didn't want to hear—a healthy rhythm.

"What do you think?" Pop yelled over the engines.

Rachel scrunched her eyes closed tighter. It was too good to be true. It had to be. There was that bit of oil. It *could* just be lubrication overflow after the engine had been cleaned…

Only, the engine pinged.

Rachel cocked her head to one side. "Did you hear that?" Rachel opened her eyes and yelled in Pop's ear.

"Eh?"

"Did you hear that pinging noise?" Rachel clarified, louder this time.

"What noise?" Pop listened hard. "Can't hear a thing but the sweet sound of pistons humming."

Waving at Mark until she got his attention, Rachel made a cutting noise with her hand across her neck. Immediately, the engines quieted.

"There's something wrong with the number-one engine, Pop," Rachel said, pointing to the engine with the oil leak.

"You're crazy. I didn't hear a thing." But Pop leaned closer to Rachel and lowered his voice as Mark got out of the plane. "It don't matter if the engine needs some work. You know how to fix it. You can make this beauty really fly."

But she didn't want to fly the S2. Hell, she didn't want to fly anything.

"We need a plane to make a living, Rachel," Pop said, warning in his voice.

Rachel swallowed. It was true. Once upon a time she'd loved to fly, longed for the freedom of the air, but no more.

"Who's going to take her up?" Mark asked, smiling a trust-me smile that had probably sold any number of items, from nuts to Xerox machines.

"Rachel's our number-one pilot." Pop practically swelled with pride. "She's a crack mechanic, too."

"I've heard that about her," Mark said, his smile as genuine as Pop's.

Not trusting Mark, Rachel looked back at the house. Still no sign of Jenna or Cole. She did not want to get into that plane, which was ridiculous, because Mark had flown it here, so it must be safe. Still…

"It has a ping in the number-one engine," Rachel blurted, feeling foolish. She wanted Mark to tell her the plane was unsafe to fly.

"Really?" Dutifully, Mark glanced at the engine in

question. "It ran like a dream coming out from Boise. Why don't we take it up and see how you like it from the pilot's seat?"

Although Rachel didn't move, she dug in her imaginary heels. Every instinct screamed at her not to get on that plane, to return to the house and hug those kids tight, reassuring them that she wasn't going anywhere.

"Rachel," Pop peered into her face. "This is no time for daydreaming. Give us a minute, Mark." Pop led Rachel away from the plane and lowered his voice. "There are two kinds of pilots in this world—those who fly and those who've flown. You get right back in the saddle after something like that happens or you give it up, savvy?"

Rachel blinked back tears and sniffed her suddenly stinging nose. She was going to have to fly.

Pop looked away. "You've never been a coward and I've never had to force you to do anything, Rachel. You've always known what to do, what was right and what needed to be done." He scratched the back of his neck. "I can't help you with the business anymore, I know that. But I can give you advice." Pop met her tear-filled gaze. "You've always loved to fly. You've always loved the freedom of it. If you give it up, what will you give up next?"

A door banged behind them.

Rachel turned and saw that Cole and Jenna had come outside. They leaned against opposite sides of the porch. Matt came out to join them. But no one came out to rescue her, to try to talk her out of this madness. If Rachel was looking for a sign, none was forthcoming.

Even though she'd wanted to see Cole and the kids before, Rachel didn't want to see them now. Pop was right. She'd loved that untethered feeling flying gave her, but flying wasn't about her feelings anymore. Flying was about mortgages, and debt, and braces, and college. It was about obligation and sacrifice—everything Missy had died to escape.

"Will you turn to waitressing? Working at Marney's?" Pop drew Rachel's attention back to him. "The drab kind of life ain't for fliers like you and me." Pop shook his head. "We live life large, Rachel. We take our lumps and we don't complain. That's what it means to be a Quinlan."

Rachel stared at her father's tanned face, stared at the lines he'd earned through loving a wife who was mentally ill, and the faded brown eyes that had seen too much sadness. Yet, he smiled at her now, encouraging her to follow his lead, Missy's lead.

Breathing was once more a struggle. Was this how trapped Missy had felt? Missy had known paradise in Cole's arms, had had a glimpse of a different life, only to give it up for Pop and Rachel, just as Pop had done before her.

"You don't have to pretend the crash didn't scare you," he continued. "It would have scared anybody. But you're stronger than the fear, and I'm proud of you for it." And then he slapped Rachel on the back just hard enough to make her head wobble and the world swivel. "Let's take that ride."

"SHE'S GONNA DO IT," Jenna said, watching Aunt Rachel walk slowly to the plane. "This is it." Aunt Rachel was going to die for sure.

"It's a cool plane," Matt said, swinging his legs over the edge of the porch.

*Bite me.* Jenna held back the words because her father was sitting with them. She stared at Cole for the first time since she'd learned the truth. "Aren't you going to do something?"

Cole shrugged. "I told her not to do it."

"Don't you want Aunt Rachel to get a new plane?" Matt asked. "We've got to have a plane. Quinlans are fliers."

"Shut up, Matt." Jenna spun to face the only adult on the porch. "She's scared to fly. Did you know that? She hasn't talked about flying again, even when we looked at her pictures. She used to talk about flying so much I didn't want to hear about it anymore. Do you want Aunt Rachel to die? If she...you know...I'll have to live with *you.*" Jenna gestured to Cole. It was so weird to think of him as her dad. "Matt, you'll have to go live with Lyle."

"He doesn't even like me." Matt's voice got all whiny.

"Jenna, don't talk like that," Cole said.

"Why not? She crashed before, didn't she?" Jenna jumped when the engines started.

"Your aunt Rachel knows how to fly a plane."

"Yeah." Matt wiped at his nose. "She's a great pilot. The best in the whole world."

"Anything could go wrong." Jenna spoke louder to

be heard above the engines. "Did you know that if a bird flies into the engine it could stall? Do you know what that means?" Jenna leaned over Matt. "She could be killed by a stupid bird!"

Matt started to cry and Jenna didn't even feel sorry for him because she wanted to cry herself. But what good would that do?

The plane turned around and taxied toward the runway just as Shadow stuck his head around the corner of the house to see what all the commotion was about.

THE CONTROLS on the S2 were very similar to the Privateer's, but the view from the cockpit was different because the S2 had hardly any nose. And instead of Danny beside Rachel making jokes about fate and death, Mark the salesman sat in the copilot seat.

"What's it feel like?" Pop demanded over the hum of the engines.

"Like a smaller plane." Like a plane Rachel didn't want to fly. She wiped her palms on her jeans.

Mark droned on about how efficient the S2 was.

As the end of the runway came closer, Rachel realized her head hurt. There was pressure behind her eyes, tunneling her vision. She wanted to assume it was panic rather than something worse, like a death-inducing brain aneurysm. She'd certainly put enough pressure on her head these past two weeks for it to give out. But if that did happen, would Cole be sorry they'd parted on such crappy terms? Or would he just say, "I told her so"?

Mark continued to point out the S2's features, and

Rachel powered up the plane's engines. She couldn't see the house, standing as it was behind the hangar, so she couldn't see Jenna or Matt, couldn't wave goodbye and pretend her heart wasn't breaking as she left them.

*Ping.*

"Do you hear that?" Rachel asked. "That pinging noise."

"No," her father said too quickly.

Mark paused in his sales pitch long enough to listen to the engine.

Rachel varied the throttle to see where the out-of-place sound was most likely to happen. The high end, she decided. Where the most stress was placed on an engine. Lovely.

A hand squeezed her shoulder. Pop's. "Come on, girl. Let's see what she can do."

Rachel moved the S2 forward, gaining speed. It was only a small sound, after all. Many engines had them.

Her stomach clenched and her palms were clammy. They were nearing the midpoint of the runway now. The plane was starting to strain upward, as if it wanted to launch itself into all that blue sky.

Rachel started to pull back on the throttle and the nose responded, lifting skyward.

*Ping-ping.*

"Did you hear that?" Rachel leaned toward Mark.

"No," he yelled.

"JENNA, DON'T!" Cole shouted at his daughter as she mounted Shadow and galloped toward the runway.

Matt stumbled up next to him. "No one can run as fast as Shadow. Not even Taffy."

The plane was gaining speed. Shadow and Jenna were just a blur losing ground as they raced after the plane.

"They'll be fine, won't they?" Matt asked, slipping his hand into Cole's.

"Yeah." Unless the engine suddenly fell off or the plane stopped, or some other catastrophe occurred. As the plane, horse and rider disappeared from view behind the hangar, Cole couldn't stand it. "Come on." He tugged Matt into a jog across the ranch yard.

It only took a few steps for Matt to trip. "I can't run that fast in my boots."

Unwilling to slow down or leave the boy, Cole swung Matt up into his arms.

FEAR OR ADRENALINE, or both, pressed in on Rachel, making it hard to see, hard to breathe. All she could hear was the pinging in the engine.

Three-quarters down the runway. Go or no-go. Her fingers flexed on the controls as her brain reminded her that she was running out of room.

*Indecision kills.*

*I don't want to die.*

The kids needed her. Pop needed her. Maybe even Cole needed her.

Rachel powered down, the momentum throwing her upper body against the safety harness, sending shards of pain through her ribs. She struggled to fill her lungs with enough air to bark at Mark, "There's something wrong with the number-one engine."

A dark blur raced past to her left. Jenna on Shadow. The pair slowed and turned in a graceful arc back to the plane. Even from this distance Rachel could see the tears streaking down Jenna's face.

If she'd been looking for a sign, one had just been delivered.

A bitter taste similar to fear rose at the back of Rachel's throat, followed by an exhausting rush of relief.

"YOU WON'T EVER FLY AGAIN?" Jenna was saying as they walked toward Cole. Rachel had her arm around Jenna for support, although she was too short to provide Rachel with much of that.

Rachel hadn't flown. Had she been too afraid? Or had something been wrong with the plane? Either way, Cole had never felt so relieved. Rachel's face looked white as she watched the plane take off down the runway without her.

"There was no ping," her father insisted, not for the first time. "And even if there was a ping, you could have fixed it."

Having no idea what the old man was referring to, Cole kept quiet, though concerned she might collapse under the stress, he slipped next to her and held on to her arm. She didn't even acknowledge his touch.

"Did Shadow really catch up to Aunt Rachel's plane?" Matt asked. "He's fast. Can I ride him someday?"

"What are we going to do now?" Mr. Quinlan demanded. "I should have told Mark that I could fly the plane. He'll come back if I call him."

"You'll do no such thing," Rachel snapped. "Look

at me. Do I look like I can fly anything bigger than a single-engine Cessna?"

Everybody froze.

Cole nearly smiled. She'd finally realized her physical limitations.

"You," Rachel poked a finger into Cole's chest. "Come with me." Without waiting for him to respond, Rachel marched as best she could over to the hangar. To her credit, she hardly wavered. Cole wanted to wrap his arms around her as soon as they were alone and tell her how proud he was of her decision.

As soon as Cole stepped inside, he closed the gap between them. "Rachel, I—"

She waved Cole aside as she sat on the stool, leaving him with a sinking sensation in his stomach.

"I'm tired, Cole. And I just screwed up." There were tears in her eyes, which she blinked rapidly to control. "There are things I have to do whether they scare me or not because of the responsibilities I have to my family. I let my family down today. I let fear get the better of me."

Jenna was right. Rachel was scared to fly. "Rach—"

"Please." She drew a deep breath. "When I get serious with someone, he's got to be brave enough to help me face my fears. I'm not blaming you, I'm blaming me. You used to encourage me to do anything. And when you did, I felt as if I could do everything." She glanced up at the ceiling. "I felt alone in that plane today. And when I'm alone, I lose my nerve. I can't do this." She pointed from herself to Cole.

What was she saying? They'd just spent an incredible night together, and she was ending it? "But—"

"You have to know that we'll never work this out. It's not just the flying. It's the security blanket you want to keep me in. That, and the fact I won't live a lie again. What am I supposed to say to your mother when I see her? That I have two great kids, one of whom she'll never meet?"

Cole felt as if he'd been riding an elevator that had unexpectedly dropped a floor or so. "Aren't you jumping the gun? We've only just—"

Rachel jabbed her finger in his direction again, only this time he wasn't close enough for her to connect. "Do you know what your problem is?"

"No, but I think you're going to tell me." The sinking sensation intensified.

She scowled at him. "You never think anything through. You just react and then you disappear without thinking about the consequences."

Cole snapped. "Like when I pulled your ass out of that airplane and then came back to drive you home?"

"Like when you heard Missy was getting married and you raced back here to put your mark on her, then left her behind." Rachel scowled.

Cole's entire body tensed. It always came back to this. "I asked Missy to go with me. It was her choice to stay."

"Or how you tried to ride Shadow too soon. Or how you followed Lyle out to the parking lot to pick a fight when I asked you not to. But, no-o-o, you just had to bulldoze right through. Why not? You don't care how

Lyle will treat those kids afterward. It's not as if you'll be hanging around."

Cole had been thinking about staying, but a man could only take so much. "Cut the crap, Rachel. You know I did all that because I care. You do know I care." Cole leaned his face close to hers. "I don't want to fight with you."

"This isn't a fight." Rachel pushed him away, even though it made her teeter on the stool. "This is about how you butt into everyone's life as if you know better. But you don't know what people need. What Jenna needs. What I need." She paused. "You run from trouble the same way you run from straightening out your relationship with your mom. You aren't even going to give her a choice when it comes to Jenna. It's easier to try to fix other people's problems your way, but that doesn't mean you're right."

"Do you really believe that, Rachel?" *Say no.*

Her mouth was set in a grim line. "I do."

"Then I'll leave."

Rachel blinked, as if just realizing what had happened, how she'd boxed him in. Then her expression grew determined. "I think that's for the best."

Cole didn't want to go. "No," Cole said, choking back his pride, holding his broken heart in place. "I promised Matt I'd watch him ride Taffy. And I promised Jenna we'd make a cake from scratch this afternoon. And I promised…I promised…" He searched Rachel's face for some sign of regret. "I promised myself I'd do this."

Cole closed the distance between them, pressed his

lips to hers and kissed her the way he'd been wanting to since they'd fought last night—as if she were his.

Rachel clung to Cole and let him kiss her, let him react the way he always did—with no regard for the consequences. She had to. Otherwise, Rachel wouldn't be able to prove to herself that she was right to let him go.

In his kiss Rachel tasted the passion she'd been longing for, a need that only she could fulfill for Cole…for now. Who knew how long Cole would stay? And even if he didn't leave, Rachel was done with deceptions, finished with covering up the truth to protect the feelings of others. Being with Cole would just bring lies back into her life. If he didn't understand what she needed from a relationship, they had no future together.

So Rachel let him kiss her, drifting on the edge of a bliss that she'd never have, because she loved Cole and wanted him to be happy. She was more like Missy than she'd imagined. She, too, was willing to let Cole go.

Cole pulled back and scowled at her. "I didn't take you for a coward, Rach. You and I have always gone after what we wanted when we wanted it." He tugged her close, his breath warm on her face.

"You keep telling me that you've matured."

"I have. In wanting you…"

"Maybe I've matured, too." Rachel interrupted Cole because he was talking about desire, not love, then she struggled to swallow. *You could have what you've always wanted.* Rachel rubbed one hand across her thigh.

*But it wouldn't be real.* Because she needed him to support her and be honest.

"You've matured? In two weeks?" Cole leaned close. "Uh-huh. Not a chance. Kiss me." He pressed his lips to hers, brushing them with his tongue. "Thank you for not flying today."

Despite her best intentions, Rachel sighed. "I'm not going to kiss you, Cole." Barely breathing, she pulled away from him. "I'm getting my life back in order. I've got you to thank for giving me back the good memories of my sister, for forcing me to face the truth about the way she died."

"Thanks to me." Cole's words were hollow.

"Thanks to you," Rachel acknowledged again. Thanks to Cole, Rachel would be changed forever. She just hoped she could live with herself for not letting Cole's desire for her be enough.

SOMETIMES LIFE just leaned over and booted you in the ass. Sometimes you deserved it. Sometimes you didn't. Unfortunately, Cole was pretty sure he deserved the blow he'd just been dealt by Rachel.

Cole shoved his deodorant, razor and toothbrush into his shaving kit, when what he really wanted to be doing was groveling at Rachel's feet for a second chance.

"What are you doing?" Matt asked, poking his head in Rachel's bedroom door.

Jenna stepped around her brother. "He's leaving." She crossed her arms over her chest and gave Cole a disgusted look.

"You know—" Cole met Matt's gaze and ignored Jenna's "—your aunt Rachel is better. She almost flew a plane today. You guys don't need me around here." Besides, Rachel didn't want him anymore.

"Yes, we do," Matt said, putting on his brightest smile.

Jenna made a huffing noise that would serve her well in about three years when some teenage boy tried to put one over on her, or later, when she dated some guy who wouldn't stop and ask for directions.

"Nobody will cook for us if you're not here," Matt insisted, his eyes now welling with those crocodile tears that had no impact on Cole whatsoever. Well, almost no impact.

Cole cleared his throat. "Uh, buddy…you see…" Cole floundered around for something appropriate to say to a five-year-old. Somehow, admitting that Rachel had kicked him out didn't fit.

"He didn't help Aunt Rachel today," Jenna said. "She was scared and needed everyone to be brave for her. She's always trying to be brave for us, but she didn't want to, today."

"Huh?" Both males looked at Jenna in confusion.

Jenna made that indignant noise again. "Aunt Rachel didn't want to fly that plane. She was scared."

"I asked her not to!" Cole raised his voice, and then noticed Jenna wincing. "Sorry, but I did tell her I didn't want her to fly."

"You're too bossy. I bet you didn't ask her how she felt about flying." Jenna sounded disappointed with him. "Or wish her good luck. Or tell her to be careful," Jenna pointed out, then admitted, "I didn't, either. That can make you feel lonely, and more scared. Sometimes it's better to be alone than have no one care what you're feeling."

Holy crap. Cole stopped stowing his gear. Rachel had given up so much for her family that she'd lost the one thing she'd truly loved—the courage to fly. He truly was an unthinking SOB. "When did you get so smart?" He demanded of Jenna.

"Every family has a genius." Jenna spread her arms as if she were unquestionably this family's.

"What's a genius?" Matt asked.

"Not you," Jenna said in the way only an older sister could.

"Not me, either," Cole mumbled. He was in-the-corner-dunce-cap-on stupid.

THE HANGAR DOOR creaked open.

Pretending to clean the grease off an old piston she'd picked up at a swap meet last January, Rachel's shoulders tensed. The tears were done, thank heavens. Now, if she could just keep it together until Cole left....

"Cole's gone," Jenna said, coming up behind her.

Rachel slumped on her stool. "He left?" Without saying goodbye? Without trying to convince Rachel to let him into her life—just a little bit—before he went? She must have meant close to nothing to Cole.

"Yep." Jenna sounded almost happy.

"I bet you didn't make that cake," Rachel said, getting mad at Cole all over again.

"He gave me a rain check." Jenna waved a piece of

paper. "And said he'd bring me a cookbook next time he sees me."

"Oh." That seemed awfully adult of him.

"He told me to tell you..." Jenna sneezed, and Rachel held her breath. Tell her? Tell her what?

"...that Matt needs to read more."

Rachel slouched over so far under the weight of her heart breaking that she almost fell off the stool. "So, he's gone."

"Are you sad?"

"Why would I be sad?" Other than the fact that she half believed she'd made the biggest mistakes of her life today? What would she do without flying or Cole, now that she'd lost both?

Jenna shrugged. "I don't know. He said he'd call."

"He said he'd call *you,*" Rachel bet. She wasn't answering the phone ever again in case it was Cole. Mature? You bet.

Shrugging again, Jenna smiled. "I'm gonna miss him."

This was not the conversation that Rachel wanted to have. "Give me a hand back to the house, will you?"

"Sure, you can lean on me, Aunt Rachel."

"Why are you so chipper?"

"Because I just figured out that I'm your knight in shining armor. Kids aren't supposed to save adults, you know, but sometimes they do."

Rachel recalled the image of Shadow and Jenna streaking past the airplane. "So, you're feeling pretty special."

"Yep."

"Well, you are special. And you always have been." Pride in her niece nudged heartbreak a little to one side.

Jenna hugged Rachel. "It used to be that you were the only one who made me feel that way."

Rachel kept her breath shallow so her ribs wouldn't hurt any more than they did—not that she wanted Jenna to stop hugging her. "And now?"

Pulling back, Jenna grinned at Rachel. "And now I have a dad who likes me."

## *CHAPTER THIRTEEN*

THERE WAS SOMETHING cathartic about driving when you were alone and the stereo wasn't on. The only thing making noise was your brain.

Cole set the cruise control and sank farther into the seat of his truck and prepared to face the harsh realities of his life as seen through the eyes of Rachel.

What had he been thinking when he'd come back to Eden on Missy's wedding night? He'd thought he'd been charging in to her rescue. Lyle Whitehall? Total asshole. Everyone knew that. *Not the point. Think.* He'd been sharing an apartment with Spider at the time, learning the ropes of the firefighting world and, other than stopping the wedding, as far as Cole could recall he'd lacked any other plan.

Years later that sounded a little…selfish.

And there was the most recent incident with Lyle.

Yeah. That was a bit selfish, too. He'd wanted to pound Lyle, only Rachel had intervened.

Oh, hell. What had Cole done in the past fifteen years since his sister had died that wouldn't be considered butting in and then dropping out? There had to be something.

He'd taken care of Rachel, hadn't he?

And Jenna. He planned to stay in touch with Jenna.

But what about Matt? The little guy wasn't his. Cole frowned. It didn't really matter. Matt had won a place in Cole's heart.

Cole loved them all. Even the old coot had carved out a corner in his heart. But that wasn't enough. Rachel had pushed Cole away for good reason. He hadn't been supportive of her when she'd needed him most. And it wasn't fair to ask her to keep part of her life a secret from Cole's family, either. Cole hadn't wanted to cause his mother any more pain, but that was selfish, too. Rachel was right. It wasn't his decision to make.

So Cole had some groundwork to lay and some fences to mend before he saw the Quinlans again.

Cole flipped open his cell phone and dialed his parents' house. It wasn't Christmas or Easter or his mother's birthday, but his unexpected visit wouldn't be shocking for that reason.

Cole was going to tell his mother about Jenna.

---

"RACHEL, CAN I COME IN?" Pop stood in the doorway to Rachel's bedroom.

"Sure." Rachel tugged down her T-shirt over her ratty old sweats, the latter of which she'd dug out of the back of a drawer because they reminded her of the sweats Cole had worn at night. She glanced at the digital clock on her nightstand. "Kind of late for you, isn't it, Pop?"

"Might say the same for you. You're usually asleep by now."

It was a sad state of affairs when a grown woman was up past her bedtime at nine-thirty. Truth was, Rachel couldn't sleep because she was scared of the bogeyman and was second-guessing her decision to send Cole away. Had she blown her one shot at happiness? With no appetite, no desire to fly and little interest in much of anything, she felt as if her life was ruined.

Pop sat down on the corner of her bed. "Kind of quiet back here since Cole left," he observed.

Too quiet for Rachel's peace of mind.

How had she slept in this room before the accident, before Cole began sleeping with her and wrapping her in his arms at night? Rachel rubbed her arms against the sudden chill, but she could do nothing to bring the warmth back to her heart. Sending away someone you'd loved from afar and in your fantasies for fifteen years was more difficult than she'd imagined. In her mind the young, daring Cole had accompanied Rachel everywhere, encouraging her to soar to new heights, to ride the edge of risk in order to save someone. That Cole had been replaced with a Cole who saw danger in every step Rachel took.

Rachel missed being able to take steps that weren't safe.

It took Rachel a few moments to realize that her dad was still perched on her bed as if he was waiting for something. "Are you feeling okay?"

"Me? I'm fine," Pop was quick to reassure her, and then he rocked back a bit and stared at the corner of her room.

*He's going to apologize for today.*

"Pop? What's wrong?" Rachel would graciously accept his apology, even though Pop had pushed her too soon and no one in their right mind would buy snake oil from that slimy salesman. But then again, maybe something more serious had happened. "Did the S2 crash on the way back to Boise?"

"No, no. Nothing like that."

Rachel relaxed against the headboard, relieved.

"It's just…I wonder if you—" Pop looked pained and Rachel hoped he'd just spit out his apology so that she could get on with mourning her lost relationship with Cole "—know how proud I am of you."

Rachel blinked and couldn't answer. She and her dad never talked mushy. She nearly choked saying his name. "Oh, Pop."

His eyes seemed more watery than usual. "To me, you're invincible. I mean, look at you. You survived that crash. You walked away."

"I did *not* walk away." Far from it. Rachel didn't even have to close her eyes to relive those last blurry moments skimming the treetops.

"You're walking now." There was no mistaking the pride in Pop's voice. Then the emotion behind his words shifted, became more…humble. "But that wasn't the only thing you survived, is it?"

Rachel didn't say anything. Pop plucked at threads on the comforter.

"Missy told me stories about her…about the way she was treated by Darla." Pop's voice cracked. "She swore that nothing happened to you. Even though you tried to tell me about Darla before, I hadn't wanted to believe it."

"Missy told me that we'd get in trouble if we both told you what happened. She told me not to say a word." Rachel's voice had lowered to a whisper. "We made a pact. She was my older sister. She protected me. Later on, I realized you had enough sorrows without knowing about mine."

"I always thought you were the lucky one, the one that Darla didn't touch. Why wouldn't you tell me what she did to you?"

"Pop, we don't need to go into this. It's all in the past." Something bitter rose at the back of Rachel's throat.

"It's not in the past," Pop insisted. "Not if you're still having nightmares because of it. Not if it affects your ability to fly again."

"I don't want—"

"For God's sake, Rachel, that was nearly twenty years ago. Don't you think it's time you shed those memories?" Pop was standing now, shaking with anger. "I sent Darla away so you girls would be safe. I thought it was over. I thought we'd gotten past the rough part and moved on."

Rachel tried hard not to cry. "Missy never moved on. You know that."

"I take full responsibility for the way Missy turned out. But you… I thought you'd been untouched by most of Darla's…episodes. You were bolder than Missy, more confident and outspoken."

"Because of that, I was the one who talked back."

Rachel couldn't stop the words from spilling out. "That's why Mom was harsher on me than with Missy, because I was stupid and I wouldn't shut up. I wouldn't take whatever demented punishment Mom dished out without asking her why, without begging her to stop, without opening my mouth and making it worse." Air shuddered through her lungs. "Missy just took it all without a word of complaint or protest. She was smart. She knew that it only got more horrible if you said something, probably because Mom had been abusing Missy a lot longer than she'd been abusing me."

They stared at each other, and the air seemed sour with regret.

"I couldn't save Missy, Pop, not when I was eight and not when I was twenty-one. And as time went by, it became easier to pretend that nothing had happened to me."

Pop hung his head. "I didn't believe Missy at first. I probably was mad. I don't remember. It was all such a shock."

"Missy took care of me. She wanted me to be happy." And Rachel had ignored Missy's wishes that she stay away from Cole, and look what had happened. Rachel's heart was in pieces. How had Missy known Cole was all wrong for her? Missy hadn't extracted the promise from Rachel out of selfish reasons as Rachel had originally thought. Somehow Missy had known Cole's weakness and that it would be too much for Rachel to bear.

Tears spilled over Rachel's cheeks. Her father came over and embraced her awkwardly.

"Rachel, you've always been so determined to go your own way. I wish you'd set that pride of yours aside once in a while, and ask for help, even if you think it'll hurt me. I may be old, but I can take it."

Rachel hugged her dad tighter. "Am I really like that?" Cole seemed to think so.

Releasing her, Pop sat on the edge of the bed next to Rachel. "Like what?"

"Too proud to ask for help?" She reached for a tissue. It was her last. "I thought people you loved were supposed to know when you need help."

"Nobody is a mind reader, Rachel. You can't always give what you haven't been asked for."

Pop's assessment didn't make Rachel any happier. Had she made a mistake by not asking Cole to help her be strong?

"MOM? DAD?" Eight hours after leaving Eden, Cole walked into his parents' home in Boise. He knew what he had to do to get Rachel back. He only hoped it wasn't too late.

"Cole? Is that you?" Tom Hudson climbed out of his plaid recliner with a series of joint-popping movements. Being a bronc rider in his twenties had left its mark on the older man.

Cole embraced his father with a hearty hug and a manly back slap. Then he noticed his mother standing in the kitchen doorway. She dried her hands with a dish towel, but said nothing. He walked over to her and, much to her surprise, hugged her for the first time in years.

She gasped.

"I think I owe you an apology," Cole said, still holding her. "You know what? I miss talking about Sally. I should have said that years ago."

His mom started to shake. Pretty soon, his dad had his arms around both of them, and they were all crying.

Later, when a box of tissues had been passed around and Cole's mom had gone to retrieve some old photos, Cole's dad said, "That's one hell of a way to come home."

"I never was one to do anything half-assed," Cole replied. He swallowed thickly. "After we reminisce about Sally, I have something I want to tell you two."

"Bad news?" Cole's dad frowned.

"No. It just might shock Mom, though."

"Better tell me first, then." Tom clasped and unclasped his hands, not looking at Cole.

"Dad, I'm not keeping this from her."

"You tell me first, and I'll decide what Nan should know." There was steel in the elder Hudson's gaze.

"Stop it, Tom. Quit trying to protect me." Cole's mother had returned. She frowned at them.

Cole caught his mother's eye and smiled gently, hoping the news wouldn't break her. "You're grandparents of a beautiful ten-year-old girl. It's up to you whether or not you want to see her."

The photo albums clattered to the floor.

"WHO WAS ON THE PHONE?" Jenna asked. She'd become very interested in Rachel's telephone conversations.

And Rachel knew why. "It wasn't Cole," she said

with as much cheer in her voice as she could muster, considering she hadn't heard from Cole in nearly two weeks.

During that time, he'd never been far from Rachel's thoughts. She missed his steadying presence and helping hand. She missed the way they could talk about their past and joke with each other. And even though the nights were easier since Rachel and Pop had started talking about the source of Rachel's nightmares, she missed being held in Cole's arms.

And, of course, the family was stuck with Rachel's cooking.

"So? Who was on the phone?" Jenna persisted.

"It was the collector from Nevada. His plane is ready to go. We get paid on Saturday." Rachel had called in a couple of local mechanics to do the heavy engine install, and spent several hours making sure the C119 ran like a dream. But she had yet to take it to the air.

"Oh." There was no mistaking the disappointment in Jenna's voice.

Now that Rachel had regained her equilibrium, she could bend over and hug Jenna without sending them both to the linoleum. "He'll call soon." At least, Rachel hoped so, for Jenna's sake.

Matt stumbled into the kitchen in his cowboy boots. "Can you read to me?" He thrust *The Sky Tower* at Rachel.

"Give me a minute." Rachel had to put a tray of frozen lasagna into the oven first. "If you can't wait, maybe Jenna could read it to you."

"Jenna said only you can read *The Sky Tower* to me now." Matt plunked himself down into a kitchen chair and started flipping pages.

Rachel shot Jenna a questioning look.

"Babies," Jenna whispered with a shrug, then hurried outside.

"Be careful," Rachel called after her niece, knowing Jenna was going out riding. She lined up a can of green beans and a can of peaches on the kitchen counter.

"You sound like Cole," Matt said. "Has he called yet?"

"No." Rachel wished they'd all stop talking about Cole calling. Despite what she'd said, she wasn't so sure he would call. It was easier for him to forget that he had a daughter and that he'd ever felt something "surprising" with Rachel, than risk hurting his mother.

Immediately, Rachel felt guilty for wishing Cole was capable of giving his mother a shocking dose of reality. Who was she to assess how much pain another person could take? She was having a hard enough time moving on without Cole.

TWO WEEKS TO THE DAY since he'd seen Rachel, Cole pulled up in front of the Quinlan home to the sound of airplane engines. A quick glance in the direction of the hangar revealed a plane pulling out toward the runway. It was the old warplane Rachel had been working on before the accident.

"She can't be flying." Cole jammed the truck into Park and leaped out into the brisk October air. Hadn't she said she needed him there by her side so she wouldn't be scared?

Cole raced to the hangar, determined to get on the plane with Rachel before she took off.

The plane paused at the beginning of the runway. Its engines revved and then quieted, then revved again as it prepared for takeoff.

Cole's booted feet pounded across the pavement as he came up behind the plane. The propellers were spinning and the roar of the engines was deafening. Knowing Rachel wouldn't be able to hear him yell at her, Cole launched himself at the wing of the plane several feet away from the propellers and scrambled on, sending the entire plane rocking.

Someone looked out the window of the cockpit.

Someone who wasn't Rachel.

The engines powered down and Cole slid off the wing to the pavement.

"What are you doing?" Rachel's voice. From behind him.

Cole turned, feeling like an idiot. "Stopping you from flying without me." He attempted a peacemaking smile.

"Just like in *The Sky Tower.*" Matt came to stand at Cole's feet, tilting his head back so that he could see Cole. "Finally, you came to her rescue."

Rachel crossed her arms over her chest. "Only, I didn't need rescuing."

"But he thought you did." Jenna flashed Cole a thumbs-up.

Cole attempted another weak grin. Nothing like putting your best foot forward…and tripping over it. He'd wanted to return to Rachel and reassure her that he wasn't as impulsive as she'd thought. So much for the best-laid plans. "I thought you were flying the plane, Rach."

She didn't even crack a smile. "And jumping on the wing?"

"Was my way of getting you to stop and let me go with you."

"I'm not flying the plane. Mr. Warner drove a rental car here so he could fly his plane home," Rachel explained. Her dark hair was pulled back into a long braid. Boots, blue jeans and attitude. Looking none the worse for wear, given what she'd been through a month ago. Just the way Cole liked her.

"What in the hell is going on here?" The side door of the plane opened and a man stuck his head out.

"Mistaken identity," Mr. Quinlan said, catching up with the rest of the family. "Who's that?" Rachel's dad pointed back to Cole's truck.

Everybody turned to look, even the pilot of the plane.

Rachel's arms dropped to her sides. "It's Cole's parents."

"I have more grandparents?" Jenna asked.

"Lucky," Matt said.

"You brought them here?" Rachel turned to look at Cole.

Cole shrugged. "I gave them a choice." But he wasn't giving Rachel much of one. He was here to convince her he loved her and wanted to marry her.

"And they took it." Rachel shielded her eyes and studied Cole's approaching parents. She glanced back at Cole and opened her mouth to say something.

"Can I go now?" the pilot interrupted, clearly irritated. "There's nothing wrong with the plane, is there?"

"Not even a scratch. I'm sorry, Mr. Warner." Rachel started herding her family back off the runway. "We'll get out of your way."

They headed toward the hangar where their paths intersected with Cole's parents. Cole made the introductions, and to his mother's credit, she didn't fall to the ground and shatter into a million pieces, although Cole and his dad stood on either side of her, just in case.

"You look an awful lot like your Aunt Sally," Cole's mother said, wiping at her eyes with a handkerchief. "But you got your mother's beautiful eyes, too."

"I think I'm more like my dad." The look Jenna sent Cole had his heart swelling.

"Can she be my grandma, too?" Matt asked, tripping over the toe of his boot and stumbling into Cole's father.

"I feel a bit left out," Tom Hudson said, holding the boy steady. "Grandpas are special, too."

"I know," Matt said solemnly. "I have one of those."

Cole's dad gave Matt a lollipop and exchanged a glance with Rachel's dad. "Maybe we can work out a deal. I don't have any grandsons. How about honorary grandfather?"

Matt's mouth gaped open. "No grandsons? But you're so old."

They all laughed at that.

Rachel stood apart from them, watching the proceedings with tears in her eyes.

Cole worked his way to her side. "I think the conversation is rolling here. Come with me." He didn't risk taking her hand, but he wanted to.

While the old warplane took off down the runway, Cole escorted Rachel into the hangar and sat her down on the stool.

"I have some things to say."

"Do you?" Rachel appeared a bit shell-shocked. "We weren't expecting you back."

"*You* might not have expected me, but Jenna and Matt were."

"You told them you were coming back." Rachel's gaze turned suspicious. "That's why they kept running for the phone."

"Smart kids, those two." Cole didn't look back at them. He was too busy drinking in the sight of a vibrant and healthy Rachel. "I told them I'd come for Jenna—"

Rachel gasped.

"—and Matt and your dad and you."

"Me?" Rachel squeaked, so surprised that Cole had to smile.

"You and I need to come to terms." Cole walked around Rachel to the bulletin board filled with pictures of the limitless blue sky Rachel craved so much and the planes that took her there. He wanted to give it back to her.

"You got in that plane two weeks ago for a reason, and it wasn't just because you needed the money and couldn't pass up on a deal. You got in that plane because you love to fly. Someday you'll fly again."

"You just tried to stop me," Rachel pointed out.

Unable to keep his distance, Cole came back to her side and leaned close. "Only because I thought you might need me to tell you to be careful or to go along with you."

"Oh." The way Rachel stared at Cole's lips was entirely too distracting.

He straightened and put some distance between them, because he still had a lot to say. "I apologized to my mom about being such an ass when I was younger."

Rachel raised her thin eyebrows. "Really?"

"And I told Mom about Jenna, and about how I almost didn't tell her she had a granddaughter because I didn't want her to have another breakdown." Cole sighed, risking a small grin. "She was furious, of course. Apparently, depriving a grandmother of her grandchild is akin to a felony."

"Agreed." Rachel crossed her arms, but her expression was open.

"Save the 'I told you so' for later, like when I tell you, yes, Rachel, you were right about Shadow."

She smiled briefly. Sitting there with the sun's rays illuminating her face, Rachel looked radiant. A stranger wouldn't know she'd almost lost her life four weeks ago. It was all Cole could do not to sweep Rachel into his arms and kiss her senseless. But her smile faded and the opportunity was lost.

"And my dad." Cole rolled his eyes at the image of his dad's face mottled with indignation. "My dad called me to the carpet for treating them as if they were already in the old-folks' home and barely capable of making a decision on their own."

"Good man."

Big breath. "So, I came back here today, Rachel, with a couple of things to work out."

"You were successful in ruining my client's takeoff, but the introductions went well." Her mouth crooked up in a polite half smile, as if she was afraid to show much emotion, as if he'd hurt her before.

He never wanted to hurt Rachel again. "I figured you'd earned the right to hear me say I've been an overbearing idiot where you and your family are concerned. I shouldered my way into your life, dragging all my baggage along with me. I almost killed myself trying to tame a horse that was already tame, and I nearly drove you crazy with all my questions."

"The truth had to come out. I'm glad of that." She gazed past him out the hangar door.

He stuffed his hands in his pockets so that he wouldn't reach for her too soon and have her reject him like the last time they'd been in this hangar. "And I was selfish that night we made love, because I wanted you and yet I hadn't accepted the whole you, warts and all."

"Warts?" He had her complete attention now, and it made him sweat.

Cole hurried on. "I wanted you, and even Jenna, to be as docile as a well-trained horse, but that's not the way it should be. You and Jenna need space and challenges and freedom. You can't love somebody and want them to change. You have to love somebody the way they are."

He sighed in apparent relief. "So, you need my signature on custody papers."

"Custody? No. Adoption, yes." Cole wanted to adopt Jenna and Matt.

"I see," she murmured, blood draining from her face.

Hell's bells. He'd done this all backward. Panicked, Cole blurted, "Rachel, I know I took forever in figuring out that it's you I want. And if you don't want me, Rachel, me—just a slow cowboy Hot Shot who appreciates the fact that you're a beautiful woman who's in her ele-ment when she's flying free and not standing on the ground being held back—well, damn me to hell, and I won't mention how much I love you again."

"You love me?" She looked genuinely surprised.

"That's what I've been trying to say. What did you think I was spilling my guts for?"

"I thought you might have come back because you wanted to 'explore' these feelings between us. I hadn't realized…you never said…"

"Oh, come on, Rachel. I know you love me."

Rachel stared at Cole too long. A tear spilled onto her cheek, then another. "I think I can set aside my stupid pride long enough to admit that I do need help. I'm lonely at night without you holding me. I miss the way you watch out for everybody."

"And…" Cole prompted.

"And I love you. I always have." Rachel wiped away her tears. "And I think I've learned that a person has to ask for what she needs, and there are times when I need your strength. But you've given me the most precious gift. You gave me back my sister by reminding me of who she was before she made some wrong turns. She was my friend, my surrogate mother, my confidante, and she only wanted the best for me. I'd lost that under the weight of responsibility I had to take on to keep this family going. I guess you could say I'm so thickheaded it took a really big bump to get me back on track."

Cole dropped to one knee at Rachel's feet and then glanced back at their family with a mumbled curse. "I forgot the flowers and champagne in the truck."

Rachel reached for him. "Flowers don't matter, and we can toast later."

Cole hesitated. "I wanted to do this right."

She smoothed away his frown. "You did. You scaled the Sky Tower and saved the princess. It just took me a little longer to believe it, because no one's ever done that for me before. No one, except you...."

And then Rachel kissed him, making him believe he had, in fact, saved her.

# *EPILOGUE*

"SPIDER, I'D LIKE TO MAKE IT home in one piece." Logan unleashed the worry the three passengers in Spider's truck were feeling. They'd been tossed about on the twisting road for most of the past hour as they returned from the first fire of the spring season.

Spider offered Logan a snappy comeback that Cole ignored, because they were approaching a corner on the winding mountain road too fast.

"Spider!" Logan, Jackson and Cole all yelled at once.

"Sheesh, all right. We're at the city limits, anyway." Spider eased up on the gas pedal as they climbed the last hill into Silver Bend. He'd been in a hurry because he and his wife were having a special ceremony at the Painted Pony and they'd invited plenty of friends and family to it.

The life-size plastic horse that sat in front of the Painted Pony Bar and Grill was visible on the right. The Painted Pony was the traditional meeting place of the Silver Bend Hot Shots. They went there before they left to fight fires and when they returned.

There was a crowd milling about outside on the

wooden porch, and a couple of SUVs were pulling into the gravel parking lot. Cole glanced at his watch. School had let out about fifteen minutes ago. Spotting Rachel and the kids, he didn't wait for Spider to put the truck in Park before he got out of the vehicle. He paused only to pull his red bag out of the back of Spider's truck. Logan and Jackson were doing the same.

"Dad! Dad!"

Cole turned with his gear just as a freight train barreled into him. Cole had officially adopted Matt this past winter. Cole never tired of hearing his two kids call him Dad. Sometimes he did wonder if Rachel would prefer Jenna call her Mom.

"Matt, be careful," Rachel said, following close behind their little guy. Her smile made him wish they were dropping thc kids off somewhere to spend the night alone.

"I'm always careful," Matt said, smiling up at Cole. "Right, Dad?"

"Right." Cole rubbed his thigh. He'd have a bruise there later. Matt was going to make a great linebacker someday. He'd started out fresh at Silver Bend with no accidents at school, and with a lot of new friends, although none of them could stick pencils in their ears.

"Did you feed the horses while I was gone? And read to Pop?" The Hudson family had a small ranch outside of Silver Bend large enough for a family of five and a black mustang with an aversion to fences.

"Yes, Dad." Matt's grin was wide.

Jenna ran up and hugged Cole with less gusto than Matt but just as much love. "Can I go over to the McCalls' house after this? Hannah and Tess invited me. I'm going to show them how to make peach cobbler."

Cole couldn't help but be perplexed. "Peaches aren't in season."

"But Mrs. McCall canned some last fall." Jenna had become quite the cook, even helping out on Saturdays when Cole worked the grill at the Painted Pony.

"All right. Maybe you can spend the night?" Cole suggested hopefully.

Jenna laughed. "Mrs. McCall already asked if Tess and Hannah could spend the night at our house."

"Why are you guys trying to get rid of us?" Matt tilted his head back to look at Cole. "Didn't you miss us?"

"Of course I did." Cole ruffled Matt's thick dark hair. "You can each have someone spend the night as long as it's lights-out at ten o'clock."

Both kids whooped and ran into the Painted Pony with an enthusiastic chorus of "Thanks, Dad."

Cole turned to a waiting Rachel. Marriage suited her, and for a moment he was satisfied to drink in her appearance, including those light freckles, barely visible in the spring sunshine. "Does it bother you that Jenna doesn't call you Mom?"

"No. That's one thing I'll leave Missy." Rachel flipped the truck keys in her hand. Her smile was peaceful, accepting of her life as it was.

She was just as beautiful as always and, clearly, just as patently stubborn. "You don't always have to be last. Come here, woman." Cole dropped his gear so that he could fit Rachel's curves snugly against his body.

Rachel practically leaped into Cole's arms and with very little encouragement, snuggled close when he was done spinning her around. "I don't mind."

"Well, I do." She gave so much and deserved so much more. Cole lowered his head to give Rachel a kiss that was far too brief, interrupted by Logan tapping his shoulder and reminding him that Spider expected them inside.

Rachel wrapped her arms around his neck. "They'll grow up way too fast, Cole, and then they won't want us around."

"By that time we'll be ready to let them go." Cole couldn't resist kissing her again.

But Rachel had a point to make. "Everybody deserves a love like you've given me. I never thought it could happen, but you, Cole Hudson, love me, and I still have my freedom." She'd rented space at a hangar in Boise and had started rebuilding planes for collectors. She'd also regained her courage to fly again and was even teaching Jenna how to pilot a plane.

"About that freedom," Cole whispered in her ear. "I traded that bottle of whiskey you packed me off with for a pair of handcuffs."

"You didn't." Rachel's eyes opened wide, dark and dangerous.

"Well, no," Cole admitted. "I picked up a pair of plastic ones in the airport for Matt. If you can get those kids to bed by ten, I'll have you locked up by ten-thirty."

"Now that much freedom, I can give up." Rachel tugged his mouth down to hers again.

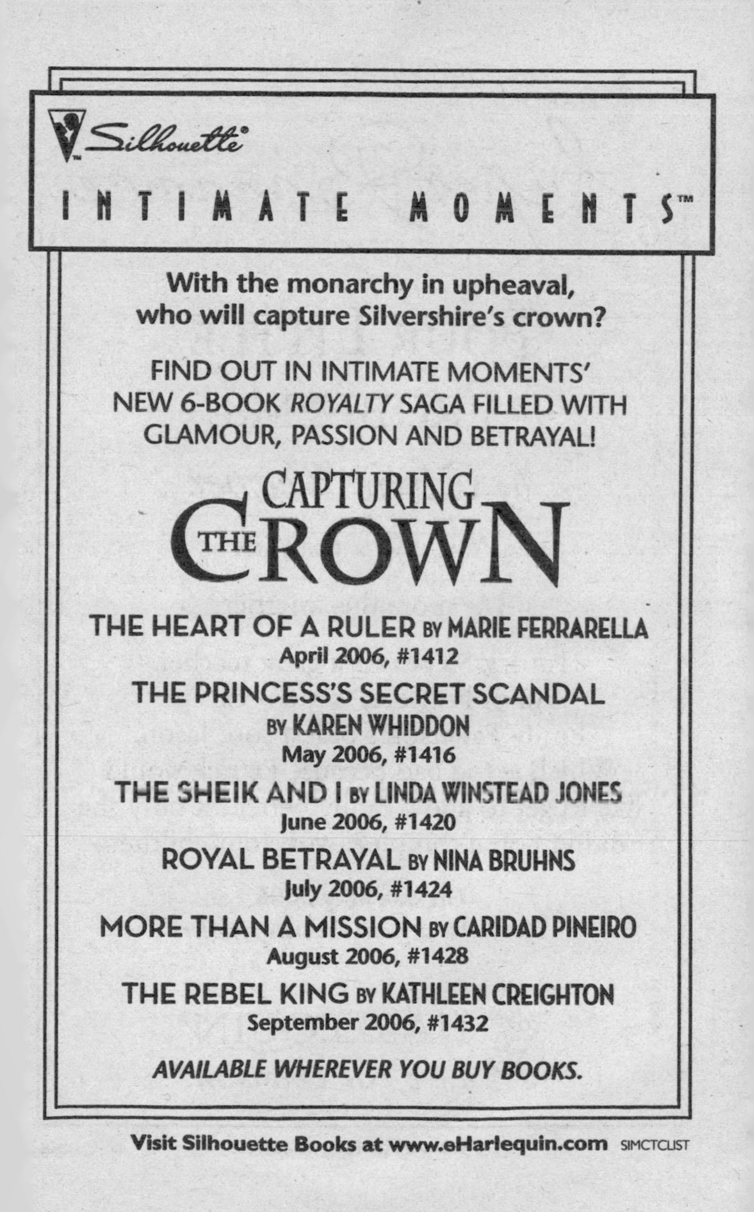
Silhouette®
INTIMATE MOMENTS™
With the monarchy in upheaval,
who will capture Silvershire's crown?
FIND OUT IN INTIMATE MOMENTS'
NEW 6-BOOK ROYALTY SAGA FILLED WITH
GLAMOUR, PASSION AND BETRAYAL!
CAPTURING THE CROWN
THE HEART OF A RULER BY MARIE FERRARELLA
April 2006, #1412
THE PRINCESS'S SECRET SCANDAL
BY KAREN WHIDDON
May 2006, #1416
THE SHEIK AND I BY LINDA WINSTEAD JONES
June 2006, #1420
ROYAL BETRAYAL BY NINA BRUHNS
July 2006, #1424
MORE THAN A MISSION BY CARIDAD PINEIRO
August 2006, #1428
THE REBEL KING BY KATHLEEN CREIGHTON
September 2006, #1432
AVAILABLE WHEREVER YOU BUY BOOKS.
Visit Silhouette Books at www.eHarlequin.com
SIMCTCLIST